Ghost Ranger

The Seven Stars Universe Book One
Written by Dayne Edmondson

This is a work of fiction. Similarities to real people, places, or events are entirely coincidental.

GHOST RANGER

First edition. March 20, 2019.

ISBN: 978-0998426358

Written by Dayne Edmondson.

Also by Dayne Edmondson

The Dark Tide Trilogy
Emergence
Eclipse
Ruin

The Mageborn Saga
Mageborn
The Cursed Tower
Halls of Light

The Seven Stars Universe
Ghost Ranger
Space Commando

The Shadow Trilogy
Blood and Shadows
Time of Shadows
Shadows Fall

Standalone
The Complete Dark Tide Trilogy
The Complete Shadow Trilogy

Watch for more at https://www.darkstarpublishing.com.

Table of Contents

A special thanks to the typo hunters of my ARC team:

Kathy Brown

Brian Busby

Judith Dickinson

Dick Kellerman

Ketan Mehta

Rob Naylor

Allen Randall

Part One

Chapter 1

My name is Rachel, and I am a ghost. Not the spooky kind spoken of in children's tales. But I fit the definition. I am dead, technically, and I am among the living. My story began when I was seventeen years old. It's the story of how I died, and rose again, and how I became one of the deadliest beings in the known galaxy.

It started one day in high school. There I was, sitting in history class with my communicator out, doctoring up photos of myself to post to social media. You see, I was self-absorbed back then. My life revolved around sleep, school, social media and sports. The four S's, I joked. Oh, to joke again.

I pulled myself away from typing my status update to look over at my friend, Isabelle. She was one of my best friends in the universe. Which wasn't saying much, since Galatia IV was in the armpit of the Federation and had a relatively piss-poor population to match. Anyway, I leaned over and whispered, "hey, where's Kimberly?"

Isabelle shrugged, not looking up from where her hand was splayed. She continued stabbing her pen knife down into the wood between her fingers faster than I could track with my eyes. I remember thinking what kind of person did that for fun? It should have been a clue. "She said out sick when I messaged her."

I frowned. That wasn't like Kimberly, at all. Being out sick would ruin her perfect attendance record. For as long as I'd known her, she'd had perfect attendance *every* year. She had even refused to participate in senior skip day a month earlier.

Turning my attention back to my communicator I began typing a message to Kim. *Hey, where are...*

Our teacher, Mrs. Vanderwell, chose that moment to step into the classroom. "Electronic devices away, children," she said in her annoyingly deep voice. I swear she'd been a man. She sniffled and wiped her nose with a tissue. Her face was pale. Paler than usual. "And weapons," she said, staring at Isabelle amid groaning from half the class as they put away their devices.

Isabelle finally looked up, after an awkward pause, rolled her eyes and tucked the pen knife up her sleeve. She always looked so bored in history class, which was surprising since she aced the class. In fact, she aced every class with ease. I would be lying if I said I wasn't jealous of her.

"I am not feeling well today," our teacher continued. "So, I will brook no sass from any of you. It'll be straight to detention. Understood?"

"Yes ma'am," came a ragged chorus from the first hour crowd. Only the teacher's pet at the front of the class sounded cheerful.

"Good." She broke into a coughing fit.

A boy behind Rachel started coughing as well. Was *everyone* getting sick? No, two people coughing was not an epidemic, but it was unusual for spring.

Mrs. Vanderwell's communicator buzzed on her desk. She picked it up and read something on it, her lips moving silently and her eyes widening as she went. She said nothing but turned on the video display in the corner and switched it to a news station.

A news reporter stood outside Beverly Hospital. "I am live outside Beverly Hospital where police are responding to reports of mass hysteria and violence. I'm told that half an hour ago a distress call came from the hospital and police arrived on the scene and entered. We have not yet heard any..." A loud bang sounded behind her and she ducked and turned. "There's been an explosion." The camera rose and panned out to where flames blossomed from one of the top floors. "Additional police forces have arrived." The camera turned to where multiple SWAT vehicles, police and even FIA vehicles trundled up. Skycopters hovered overhead.

"There are people coming out," the reporter said, coughing and wiping her brow. The camera focused on the entrance. A mass of figures emerged. They did not run but appeared to be shuffling forward.

Police and other security forces lined up and started shouting for them to put their hands up. The figures continued walking forward.

"What the hell is going on," I wondered aloud. I looked toward Isabelle to gauge her reaction.

Isabelle had a distant look on her face. It reminded me of the look my father adopted when he was communicating with work. But I didn't think Isabelle had a communication implant. "Isabelle? Are you watching this?"

Isabelle shook her head before meeting my eyes. I shivered at the intensity in them. Something had changed. "Yes, I'm seeing it. I was just communicating with my parents."

"Oh." The mysterious parents who were never home yet found time to sign permission slips for field trips. In the two years I'd known Isabelle I had never seen the inside of her home. I pointed at the display. "Well, that's some crazy shit. Right?"

"That's one word for it." She eyes Mrs. Vanderwell and the boy who had coughed earlier. Another student coughed on the other side of the room by the window. "We need to get out of here. Now."

"What do you mean?" I asked, frowning. "We can't just skip school. I did it last month and my dad grounded me for a week."

She ignored me. "Come to the cafeteria with me." She stood up and walked toward the door, leaving her backpack behind.

Mrs. Vanderwell noticed the movement, turned and snapped her fingers. "Where do you think you're going, Miss. Perigren?"

Isabelle paid her no mind. She opened the door and left.

I groaned. She was going to get a week of detention for her stunt. And I would have to bring her backpack along too. I took one last glance toward the display where... "Holy shit," I said.

The police were *firing* on the people. The camera showed several lasers striking one man in the chest. He stumbled but continued toward the line of police. *Okay, that's weird*, I thought. That many laser blasts to the chest should have brought him to his knees, whether they were stun blasts or not. The man's face looked strange, contorted not in pain but in a sort of...vacantness. "Ah, what the hell? Shit has gotten crazy today anyway." I stood up, slung my backpack over one shoulder and Isabelle's over the other and walked toward the door.

"And just where do you think *you're* going, Miss Chaskey?" Mrs. Vanderwell demanded. Sweat covered her face and she looked paler than before. She struggled to rise but fell back in her chair with an oomph.

I hesitated, just for a second. I was soft back then. "I...uh, I'm sorry, I'm not feeling well." I exited into the hallway, trying not to think about my teacher threatening not one but two weeks of detention if I didn't return that instant. *I hope this is worth it,* I thought.

"Isabelle," I called. "Where are you?" There was no one in the hallway. Just me, the deviant one. My dad was going to kill me. I walked toward the cafeteria. I passed Mr. Kold's class but didn't look inside. A scream erupted from within. I froze, backed up and peered through the window of the door.

A student lay on the ground, arms flailing. Someone, I wasn't sure if it was a student from that angle, straddled them. Blood pooled on the ground around them. The one on top was...ripping at their throat with their teeth! The poor soul on the ground gave a final scream before falling silent, blood spurting from their throat.

Two students tried to pull the assailant off the dying student. They succeeded but the attacker, who looked like Mr. Kold now that I got a good look, grabbed the arm of one and gnawed at it. That student screamed and stumbled backward. Mr. Kold then grabbed the second student, bit into their shoulder and forced them to the ground.

Shock had given way to panic and the rest of the class ran toward the door. I stepped aside as the door whipped open.

"Help!" several students shouted. "Someone help!" They paid me no mind as they fled in either direction down the hall.

It was as if the flood gates had been opened in Panic-ville. Students and teachers poured from classrooms. Shouting from every direction melded into a stew of confusion. The students and faculty stampeded toward the exits. Screams of pain and roars of anger erupted in the distance. Were more people acting like Mr. Kold?

I muscled my way through the crowd toward the cafeteria, running as best I could without tripping over people. Was Isabelle okay or had she been attacked? I stumbled back when a blood-soaked student stepped out of a classroom in front of me and I got a close-up look at what was causing the hysteria.

The bloodied student looked at me with eyes devoid of emotion. There were empty pits of nothingness in place of eyes. Dead eyes. Eyes people say I have now. He moaned and started toward me.

Shit, I thought. I darted to the right, hoping to skirt around the guy, corpse, whatever he was. But he reached out with surprising speed and grabbed at me. He caught my shirt and scratched me in the process. My momentum caused the shirt to rip and I felt a burning sensation run down my arm. I stumbled but didn't fall and raced the last few meters to the cafeteria doors, which were wide open ahead of me, but conspicuously no one ran in or out. The area around me had emptied. Not looking back to see whether I was being pursued, I stepped inside.

Bodies littered the floor. Victims with their throats chewed open, staring at the ceiling with empty eyes. Others with limbs missing or wounds to the head. I even saw one person decapitated. I found the nearest trash can and threw up. Boy was I weak back then. One victim I could handle, but this? This was carnage on a scale I'd never seen outside of television shows.

Movement at the far end of the cafeteria pulled my gaze away from the corpses, for which I was thankful.

A figure, a woman I thought, based upon her stature, fought several of the infected. That's what I was calling them now. The infected. Clearly their coughs hadn't been harmless coughs. The stories I'd read for fun were right - we were amid a zombie apocalypse.

The woman wore black armor and wielded a pair of black swords. Where had she come from? That shit was a throwback to the early days of Tar Ebon. She kicked one of the infected, sending them stumbling back, stabbed his eye, and all the way through his skull, before spinning and decapitating another.

A part of my mind told me to run, to go back through the door the way I'd come and hope the first zombie I'd encountered wasn't smart enough to follow me. I turned to do just that when a moan warned me I was wrong.

The guy stood in the doorway, gazing at me with vacant eyes. He started shuffling toward me.

I didn't think I'd make it past him a second time, and the scratch on my arm burned with greater intensity at the thought of falling into his clutches. *I'll take my chances with the sword-wielding badass*, I thought, before running toward the maelstrom of steel occupying the far end of the cafeteria.

As I approached, I gasped, stumbling to a halt. "Isabelle?"

My friend must have heard me, for she met my eyes before ducking a swipe from an infected person and stabbing up into their jaw and through their head. Then the impossible - more impossible than Isabelle fighting off uncounted zombies with archaic weapons in an outfit I'd never seen her wear - happened. Isabelle turned to smoke. Not gray smoke, no, pure black smoke, like ink turned to vapor and thrown into the air. Where had she gone?

I got my answer an instant later when a shadow cloud formed in front of me and materialized into the size and shape of Isabelle. I admit it, I screamed. "What...what?" was all I could stammer.

"Listen," Isabelle began, "there isn't much time and things have progressed further than I originally thought. I am going to take you home. Take my arm."

What? Why? How had Isabelle, the girl I'd known for two years, done that? Those questions and more filled my mind, percolating around. But instead I found myself putting a hand numbly on Isabelle's arm and staying silent.

Behind Isabelle, the remaining zombies were regrouping and shuffling toward us. For moving so slow they managed to cause a lot of havoc.

Isabelle glanced down at my right arm. "Were you scratched?" She sounded neither afraid or overly concerned. Like a doctor asking if I'd broken a bone. Not that I'd ever broken a bone before, but if I had that was how I'd imagined a doctor would ask.

I followed her gaze and winced. The scratch had festered into an angry red sore with blood and dark green fluid oozing out of it. "Yeah. It looks worse than it is." It throbbed with pain, but in the moment it didn't hurt *that* much. "One of the...infected...zombies, whatever, grabbed my shirt when I tried to run past."

Isabelle averted her gaze and said nothing. Behind her, the zombies continued their inexorable advance, while the first dude who had scratched me was still a couple meters away. "Hang on tight. And whatever you do, don't let go."

Before I could open my mouth to reassure her that I would hold on for dear life, the world around me shifted into a grayscale version of itself. Complete with infected people, food and even the sky outside the window colored gray. A moment later the scene shifted, and I found myself standing in front of a gray version of my house. Before I'd had a chance to look around, color returned to the world. I stared wide-eyed and slack-jawed at Isabelle. Had they? Had she? I took a moment to gather my thoughts and then asked, "You can shift?" I'd heard it described but never witnessed it or felt it first-hand.

I half-expected Isabelle to smirk and triumphantly reveal a secret about herself or explain what happened. Had she been injected with a special serum, struck by lightning or something else to give her this unexplained power? But she offered nothing. Instead, she again met my eyes and said, "Rachel, Go inside. I will explain more later. Right now I must go." She turned, suiting action to words.

"Go where?" I asked.

My friend looked over her shoulder, then gave me the smirk I knew so well, removing any doubt that *somewhere* inside the body of a killer was my friend. "To help save the world, of course." She disappeared in a cloud of shadowy smoke.

Chapter 2

No sooner had the shadowy mist disappeared than I was racing up the stairs of our porch and rushing inside. "Dad!" I shouted. Not waiting for a reply, I dropped our backpacks on the floor, grabbed the remote control and clicked the TV on.

A well-known news reporter from KLYC Rapid Falls was reporting live from outside my school. The running caption read "Viral Outbreak rapidly spreads."

The camera zoomed in on lines of police firing beams of light toward lines of infected, lumbering, ragged looking people who shrugged off bolts of energy as if they didn't even feel them. Judging by the faces I'd seen, they probably didn't.

Another camera in the lower corner showed aerial footage of Beverly Hospital. It was fully engulfed in flame and bodies littered the ground. There was no sign of the poor reporter who had been on the ground.

My father came out of the kitchen. He wore body armor, suspiciously like what Isabelle had worn in school. Where was everyone getting body armor from and where could I get some? A pair of hilts peeked over his shoulders and two holsters holding pistols hung from his belt. He took one look at me and asked, "Were you scratched, at all, anywhere? Did any bodily fluid from any of the infected touch you?"

The ferocity of his questions caught me off-guard. He could be intense sometimes, but normally he was pretty chill. I nodded, holding up my arm so he could see it. "Yes, one of them scratched me while I was escaping."

"Damn it," my father said, running a hand through his black hair.

"It was just a normal day," I protested. "The teacher had a cold and so did a couple students, but I didn't think anything of it." Talking helped me calm down, to rationalize what just happened. "Then some kids collapsed and...it all went to hell. Isabelle shifted, which I still can't believe, and brought me here. Oh, and before that she was decapitating zombies like it was her job or something!" I was rambling and I knew it, but I couldn't help myself. "Then she disappeared again, talking about helping to save the world." I lifted a hand to my forehead where sweat was beading and dripping down my face. "Kimberly stayed home today too. I don't know what's going on, Dad." Terror gripped me in that moment, as all the events crashed down on me at once. My world, literally, was falling apart.

"Isabelle can take care of herself," my father said. He sounded completely unconcerned, and unsurprised, by the revelation my best friend could shift. Perhaps he was in shock too? "As for Kimberly, we don't have time to worry about her right now." His eyes took on the familiar distant look of him using his communication implant. He forbade me from having my own implants until I turned eighteen, which was still three months away, yet used his own all the time. He claimed it was for his job at the security giant Omnion, but I had my doubts. Why was he communicating with his work during a viral outbreak? Was he really calling in sick at a time like this? Shouldn't they be evacuating?

"Dad, what are you wearing?" I thought asking something mundane might snap him out of the funk he appeared to be in.

It worked. He focused on me but ignored the question. "Show me your arms, now."

My eyes widened in surprise. "My arm? Why?"

"Do it." The command in his voice was unmistakable. His eyes bored into me.

I felt compelled to do as he ordered. I rolled my sleeve up. Red marks with black in the center covered my arm. "Am I infected?"

My father didn't answer - not at once. He studied the floor and averted his eyes. "You can roll your sleeve back down."

I hurried to obey, hand shaking. "Dad, what's going on? Tell me!" The last word came out as a shout and served to pull his eyes up to meet mine.

"You're going to die, Rachel," he said, point blank.

The way he said it made me shiver more than being shirtless or the content of the words. He was so matter-of-fact. No ifs or buts, just a statement. He may as well have been saying it was going to rain. I could only hope his prediction of my death would be as inaccurate as the meteorologists. "How do you know that?"

"Because that's how the virus starts. First marks appear below the elbow. Fatigue, high fever and sweats follow. Then, a brief time after initial infection, the host dies."

He wasn't doing a wonderful job of reassuring me in that moment. I wouldn't be nominating him for father-of-the-year. "But...isn't there anything we can do?" Tears brimmed in my eyes. I wanted my mom in that moment, though I didn't remember her. Anything would be better than the clinical way he told me of my impending death.

"Yes, there is," my father said. His face softened as he saw the emotions warring on my face. "Oh, Rachel." He embraced me and held me as tears flowed down my face in a torrent. I shook with sobs. "I'm sorry for scaring you. You will die, but I'm going to ensure you don't stay dead."

Not caring about the contradictions in his statement, or the fact that raising people from the dead was impossible, I sobbed even harder.

We separated after several seconds. My father pointed at the couch. "Lay down and rest - it will slow the spread of the virus a little. You're sweating already." He put a hand on my forehead. "And your fever has spiked. Any other symptoms?"

"Chills," I said as I stumbled to the couch and laid down. My legs felt weak - like I'd run a marathon. "But I thought that was just from everything that's been happening. But that's the virus, isn't it?"

My father nodded. "I'll get you something to drink." He strode to the kitchen, returning a minute later with a cup filled with cloudy water. "Here, drink this. It won't stop the spread, but it will make you more comfortable."

"How do you know so much about this?" I asked after emptying the glass in three gulps.

"I'm in the business of protecting people. It's what I do."

"Oh," I said. "What about..." I stopped, feeling light-headed. My vision blurred and I felt drowsy. "What did you...," my words ceased as darkness overtook me.

Chapter 3

I awoke to a bright light in my eyes. No, not at the end of a tunnel. An examination light suspended above my head.

I tried to sit up but found I couldn't. Restraints held my chest and arms and legs to the table or stretcher or whatever I was laying on. My clothes were gone, replaced by a hospital gown. I could move my head, though, and looked around.

The room was clinical - it reminded me of a doctor's office or hospital operating room. A table with medical equipment sat to my left, while a chair sat to my right. An empty chair. Where was my father? In fact, the entire room was empty. No...wait...it wasn't.

A shimmer occupied a corner of the rectangular room. I squinted and the shimmer resolved into the shape of a person. The shape resolved in detail the longer I stared, until I could see a man - or woman - in black armor standing in the corner, a rifle held in their arms but pointed at the floor.

"Hello?" I asked, staring at the figure. I felt that if I moved my eyes, I would lose sight of them. I confirmed the theory when I flicked my gaze away and back and had to reacquire my vision of them. "Do you talk?" I asked sarcastically. "Where am I? Why am I being restrained."

Still the figure didn't reply.

I turned my head and looked in the other corner. Again, I had to stare for several seconds before I could make out the armed guard standing there, but it had seemed to come easier. "Will you talk to me?" I asked. "Please? I just want to know where I am."

Talking to the second figure seemed to work, for they turned their head from side-to-side as if looking for someone else who could be the target of my gaze.

"Yes, you. I see you turning your head. Where am I? Why am I here."

"One moment," the first figure said in a distinctly masculine voice, causing me to flop my head to the other side and look at him. "The doctor has been alerted that you are awake."

"Oh, lovely. The doctor. Where's my father?"

The man didn't reply.

I growled in frustration and struggled against the restraints, my muscles bulging. For just a moment, I thought the restraints were going to give way. But that must have been my imagination. Still, the guard in my line of sight lifted his rifle ever-so-slightly. Was he afraid of me?

The door to the room slid open, thankfully in my line of sight, and a man in a white coat entered. He was balding and with white hair around the side of his head. He smiled in what he probably thought was a reassuring way. "Hello, Rachel," he said.

"Hello," I said cautiously. "Where's my father?"

"He is...otherwise indisposed. He will be with us shortly, however."

"Otherwise indisposed?" I repeated. Was he dead? Wounded? Infected? What did indisposed mean? I clenched my fist in frustration.

"How are you feeling?" Dr. Sinclair asked, declining to elaborate.

"Like a prisoner," I said honestly. "You've got me bound like I'm in a psychiatric facility."

"It's for your own safety, I assure you," he said, stepping toward her. "What do you remember before passing out?"

I fell silent for several moments as I struggled to remember. "I remember I was at school. People started showing signs of infection - they started killing each other. I fled, and my friend, she shifted me home." That no longer felt quite so strange to say aloud. "Then my father said I was going to die but...be resurrected. And then he gave me something to drink and I fell asleep. Was it all a dream?" I prayed it was all a dream - though if it was a dream it was the most vivid one I'd ever had.

Dr. Sinclair's smile turned to a frown. "I'm afraid it was no dream, Rachel. Your planet was the victim of a terrible bio-weapon and you did indeed die."

"But...we're talking right now. So, if I'm dead, is this heaven? It doesn't look like the stories."

The doctor's smile returned, and he chuckled. "I'm glad to see you're being humorous about this. It is reassuring and suggests the treatment was a complete success."

"Call it gallows humor," I shot back. "What treatment?"

He sat down in the chair next to my bed and folded his hands. I knew that look. He was about to start lecturing. "When you fell asleep the virus in your body continued ravaging your body."

"Could you use a nicer verb than ravage?" I asked.

The doctor blinked and pursed his lips. "Very well. The virus spread through your body uncontested and killed you. That was the bad news."

"I didn't know this was a 'good news,' 'bad news' thing," I remarked.

"The good news is I was able to develop a treatment for the condition."

"To reverse the virus? Did you cure me?"

"Sadly, no." He didn't sound sad. "The damage done by the virus is irreversible. Your blood has been transmuted to another substance entirely. Trying to now transfuse blood into your veins would kill you...for good."

"Then what did you do?" I asked, curiosity warring with fear and anger.

"While you were dead, your brain shut down. The neural pathways in your brain deteriorated. You were, in effect, brain-dead. When the virus reanimated your body, including re-starting your heart and pumping oxygen to your brain again, your body awoke, in a sense, but your higher brain functions were inactive. Only the pre-frontal cortex remained preserved by the virus. That is the section which governs things like hunger and primal emotions."

"Hence zombies," I quipped. "The people died and were resurrected as mindless, hungry beasts, essentially."

"Correct. Unable to be reasoned with, unable to even understand language, the zombies feel only intense hunger and raw emotion."

"Then how are we having a conversation right now about this?"

"We used nanites to bridge the neural connections inside your brain." He made gestures with his hands to illustrate. "We essentially rebuilt the roads and bridges and infrastructure of your brain to model exactly how it was before your death."

"How did you know what my brain looked like before my death?"

"We scanned your brain upon arrival to the *Nightblade* when you had yet to die. Then we implanted you with a full suite of implants and injected you with nanites programmed to repair the damage caused by brain death. Then all that was left was the wait and pray."

I pointed to my head, or tried to, given the restraints. "Well, it clearly worked. The science and waiting part, not the praying." I didn't believe in any deities. If a God existed he hadn't done squat to save my mother all those years earlier, so why should I give him my devotion?

Dr. Sinclair's expression brightened. "Yes, I am pleased by the results of the experiment."

"Experiment?" I repeated. "You weren't sure this would work?"

"Well..." Dr. Sinclair stammered. "It was a hypothesis. Time was of the essence. Your father signed off on the procedure, knowing the risks. It was the only choice."

"Was I the first?"

"Yes."

"Did you treat others after me?" Were there others like me strapped down in other rooms? Did they have armed guards?

"Yes," he said cautiously.

"Did their treatments work?"

"It's too early to tell," he replied. "They have yet to awaken but were treated some time after you."

"How long was I asleep? Or how long have I been...what do I call it? Un-living? Undead? Risen?" I asked.

"We have been using the term undead. And to answer your question, it has been twenty-four hours since the treatment began."

"Wow. I slept like a baby, huh?" Not waiting for an answer, my gaze flicked to the guards in the corners. "What's with the guards?"

"They are here for your protection, Rachel." He furrowed his brow. "I was surprised to receive a report that you could see through their cloaking fields. Is that true?"

"Yes," Rachel said warily. "They looked like blurs at first, then resolved into armed guards."

"Remarkable. That suggests a significant augmentation in your ocular processing capabilities."

"If you say so. I don't feel so remarkable. I just want to see my father. Where is he?"

"As I said, he is..."

"Cut it with the otherwise indisposed crap," I snapped, eyes bulging and anger raging through me. I flexed my arm and felt the restraints creak. "Where is my father?"

Out of the corner of my eye I saw two of the guards lift their rifles, pointing them at me. "Come on, you bastards!" I shouted, flexing further. Just a little more and the restraints would give, I just knew it. I was dead already - what more could they do to me?

"Enough!" A voice came from the door. My father's voice.

My head snapped to the side and I felt all the fight drain out of me as I gazed on my father. He looked harder than the last time I'd seen him. The glint in his eyes, of silent amusement at the goings on around him, was gone, replaced by an intensity I couldn't recall seeing before. And his clothes. Gone were the casual clothes he often wore when working from home. And his current attire was not even his work uniform. He wore a...navy uniform? With emblems pinned to it and medals hanging off. "Father," was all I could say, feeling slightly embarrassed at the outburst he'd witnessed. "You're here." Tears brimmed in my eyes and I began sobbing uncontrollably - unable to even wipe the tears from my eyes due to the restraints.

My father approached, glaring at the guards in the corners that I could see and to his left. It took me a moment to realize there were probably other guards in that corner too, cloaked similarly. I did not want to be the object of that glare, that was for sure. When his gaze again fell on me it softened at once and he took my hand. "I'm here, sweetheart." He took in the restraints and looked to Dr. Sinclair, who stood next to him. "Are these restraints necessary, Doctor?"

Dr. Sinclair cleared his throat and averted his eyes before speaking. "Sir, they were a necessary precaution during the procedure. We explained..."

My father lifted a hand and the doctor fell silent. I raised my eyebrows at that. He had the power to silence the doctor? "I understand that. Are they necessary now, after the procedure was clearly a success?"

"No, of course not."

"Good." He proceeded to unstrap my arms, chest and legs. "Is that better, Rachel?" he asked.

"Yes," I said, smiling and sitting up. Not being treated like a prisoner any longer felt good. I chanced a glance at one of the guards. They were back to standing at ease, rifles hanging loose and pointed nowhere near me. "Are the guards necessary too?"

My father raised an eyebrow, as if surprised I had detected the cloaked guards. But he nodded. "Those, unfortunately, are necessary. For your protection, not for protection from you, however. They will never raise their rifles to you again." Another hard stare toward the guards followed, emphasizing his point.

"Where am I? The doctor said I was on the *Nightblade*. Is that a ship?" I felt like I had heard that name before but couldn't pinpoint it. Then my eyes fell on his uniform and I pointed at it. "And where did you get that?"

My father cleared his throat and gave one of his half-smiles. "Well, that's a long story, my dear."

"I've got all day," I said, spreading my arms wide to indicate the empty room.

"This may come as a shock to you." He sat down in the chair. "And I want you to understand that I kept this information from you for your protection, truly."

Dread settled in my stomach. "Just tell me. The suspense is killing me...again." I smirked at my wit - the whole being dead and then not thing was going to be comedy gold for years to come.

My father took a deep breath, as if he were about to tell me he was dying too. "My real name isn't Franklin Chaskey. It's Dawyn Darklance, and I am the supreme commander of the Federation military." He paused, waiting for my reaction.

At first, I didn't react. My mind spun. Dawyn Darklance? The name stirred up memories of countless stories in history books and pop culture alike. The Battle for Tar Ebon, the First Imperial War, the Battle of the Line and so many more. All featuring that name. My father's name. "That means," I began, "you're an eternal?"

My father nodded. "Yes. I am over two thousand years old."

I put a hand to my forehead, trying to process what he was telling me. "That makes me..." I looked at him questioningly.

"When you were conceived, nanites from my body became part of yours. They have been inside you since you were born."

"So, I am an eternal too?"

"Yes."

"Wow, you're really dropping the bomb shells today. What's next, my mom is alive?"

My father frowned. "I wish I could tell you she was. She died bravely, though."

"Yeah, yeah, defending a space station, so you told me. Is that even a true story?" How many falsehoods had he told me over the years?

"Every word of your mother's story was true. Even how we met was true - I just didn't tell you my position in the story."

"Deception through omission is still a lie," I said, quoting his own words back to him. "You lied to me, Father."

My father acknowledged my observation with the nod. "Yes, I did, and I regret that the deception was necessary. I chose to raise you in anonymity out of a desire for you to grow up normal."

"Real normal," I said. "Up until today. Or yesterday. Or whenever." I gestured again to the uniform. "Why couldn't you raise me as your daughter?"

"Growing up as the daughter of a security worker is different than growing up as the daughter of the supreme commander of the Federation military. You would have been in the spotlight every moment. Paparazzi, and less-than-savory elements, would target you. You would have been guarded every moment of the day, your every movement watched for your own protection." He sighed and looked at the floor. "I planned to tell you when you turned eighteen."

"So what, you were just going to sit me down and tell me all you just told me? 'Hey, Rachel, I'm an eternal and the highest-ranking military person in the galaxy. You're my daughter.' Like that?"

"Much like I just did, yes," he replied, meeting my gaze again. "I always meant for you to know - eventually. Are you angry?"

I was angry, as much as I hated to admit it. Angry and awed and confused and feeling side-swiped. I nodded, unable to speak.

"I am sorry. I will go if you wish."

"No," I said. "Don't go." A memory rose up in my mind. The memory of Isabelle fighting the undead invaders in the cafeteria. *Isabelle.* "Isabelle. You said she could take care of herself. And you weren't surprised about her shifting." The pieces clicked in my head, but I had to vocalize them to make them feel real. "She's Isabelle Thorpe, isn't she?" Images of family trees flashed in my mind. Dawyn, my father, was brother to Bridgette Thorpe, who was the mother of Isabelle Thorpe. "She's my cousin." It wasn't a question.

My father smiled. "Clever girl. Yes, she is your cousin. She was on assignment on Galatia IV and assumed the role of a high school student as part of it."

"Was I her assignment?"

"No. Another girl in your school was her target. In fact, it was quite random that she ended up at the same school as you. Do you remember the first time she came to our house?"

I chuckled. "Yeah. Your eyes bugged out. I thought it was because she was a new friend, or because of the color of her hair at the time. I was wrong, wasn't I?"

"Yes. I detected who she was the instant she entered our home. I connected to her implant and communicated with her. She was as much surprised by my presence on the planet as I was at hers."

"So much for communication among the Federation," I quipped. "You guys didn't even know the other was there? Hadn't gone to a family reunion in a few years, eh?"

"I kept your identity a secret from *everyone*, including my family and friends. The fewer who knew of your identity, and mine, the better."

"You said another girl at my school was her target." I thought back to two years earlier. She'd first met Isabelle through another friend, Kimberly. "It was Kimberly, wasn't it? She was absent today from school. Was she infected?"

My father nodded.

I swallowed hard. I had to ask, had to know. "Did Isabelle...kill her?"

This time he shook his head. "Kimberly was indeed her target, but not for that reason. Access to her allowed Isabelle ready access to her father's home. He was the true target of the investigation."

"He's some kind of scientist, or researcher, right?"

Dr. Sinclair, who I'd almost forgotten was in the room, snorted. "A monster is more like it. After what *he* did."

My father ignored the man and spoke. "He was the lead researcher at a lab on Galatia IV. The FIA had learned of top-secret experiments being performed there. Black ops, illegal experiments. She was dispatched to learn what those experiments were."

"She learned too late," Dr. Sinclair put in.

I held up a hand. "Wait. So, the virus that wiped out who knows how many people down on the planet was designed by Kimberly's *father*?

"We believe so. Or by someone on his team. Once all hell broke loose, and Isabelle had ensured your safety, she made her way to his lab. What they found there confirmed their suspicions."

"Is Isabelle still alive?" My heart leapt into my throat. The girl was still one of my two best friends in the universe, despite the new information. They weren't just best friends - they were cousins.

"She was wounded, but she will survive. She heals quickly."

"And Kimberly?"

"Her father had told her to run - he clearly had some foreknowledge of what would occur. She was hiding in the woods when Isabelle rescued her."

"So...they're both on the *Nightblade*?"

"Correct. Both are resting. They've had quite an ordeal."

"When can I see them? Am I infectious?"

"You can see them soon. And the doctor can answer your second question." He gestured to Dr. Sinclair.

The doctor cleared his throat, an action I knew all too well from my teachers at school. "While you are technically infectious, if your bodily fluids make contact with another person's bodily fluid through scratches, bites or sexual contact..."

"Gross," I said.

"The nanites in your blood are working to cleanse you of the infectious portions."

"You call it blood. But didn't you say earlier the virus turned my blood into something else?"

"For ease, we continue to refer to it as blood. But you are correct - the virus converted your blood into a sort of fluid that, while it acts like blood is far more complex. It is clearly engineered and designed to be infectious upon physical assault."

"Why not just make it airborne?" I asked, recalling all the references to zombie apocalypses I'd consumed over the years.

"They did, which is how it originally spread," the doctor explained. "But the airborne life of the virus was limited to twenty-four hours and only spread by living lungs. Once the host dies the virus moves into phase two and is no longer expelled when the host breathes, as breathing is no longer a necessary function."

"Wait, what?" I asked. I touched my chest, waiting for the inhale or exhale. It didn't rise or fall. I hadn't noticed. "I don't breathe?"

"No. The virus feeds off carbon dioxide - there is no need to breathe. Your heart still beats - it pumps the virus-laden blood through your body, but breathing is no longer necessary."

"Wow," I remarked. "That's awesome!"

The doctor smiled. "I am glad you think so, my dear. Now, if you'll excuse me, I have more patients to visit. I will be back to check on you later."

"Thank you for saving me, Doctor."

Dr. Sinclair offered a half-bow. "It was my pleasure." He nodded to my father and exited the room.

"So..." I began, "me being like royalty and all, do you think I can get a special dessert here? I'm starving."

"I think you've earned far more than that, sweetheart. But I'll have someone come in and take your order. You can have anything you want on the menu."

My stomach growled in appreciation.

Chapter 4

I was munching contentedly on a sandwich when alarms blared in the hallway outside. I looked through the transparent door to where red lights flashed. "I wonder what's happening out there," I mumbled with my mouth full. Yes, my father had taught me not to talk with my mouth full but sometimes I neglected his words of wisdom. I looked to the guards, who looked more agitated than usual.

The guards had continued to remain behind concealment screens, though I could see all four of them. They weren't a chatty bunch, as I found out when I tried to get them to talk. They would answer simple questions well enough but wouldn't tell me anything about what was going on down below or anything. Perhaps they didn't know. Or they didn't want to upset me.

My father had excused himself before my food arrived, claiming he was needed on the bridge. I let him go, accepting that the Federation did indeed need his expertise and leadership at a time like this. I envisioned armies of Federation Marines facing off against a legion of zombies on a huge field of battle, lasers burning into flesh and bullets piercing their rotting flesh. But wait, *I* am a zombie, an undead. How would I feel being shot at? That was a sobering thought.

A squad of troops ran by my door outside, heavy weapons at the ready. Then another squad ran by. Okay, something big was clearly going on now. I swung my legs over the side of the medical bed and got to my feet.

The guards in the corners stirred and took steps forward.

I focused on one of them, the first guard who had spoken to me when I'd awoken. "Listen, something is going on out there." I pointed to the door. "I just want to go outside and check it out. Are you going to try to stop me?" I don't know why I made it sound like a challenge. Clearly, they could stop me if they wanted.

"Our orders are to protect you," the guard said. "And that's what we're going to do." He walked to the door and it opened. He looked to the left and then to the right before looking back to me. "Two in front, two behind - and you run if we tell you to run. Deal?"

I was so surprised at their willingness to let me into the hallway that I could only nod. At last I found my voice. "Yes, that's fine."

The guard nodded and a second guard joined him. They stepped into the hallway, one facing one way, the other facing the other way, before waving me forward. The other two guards closed in to take up the rear.

I walked into the hallway and looked around at my surroundings. It was much wider than I had originally thought - at least a dozen people could walk shoulder-to-shoulder down it. To my right sat what looked like an empty nurses station. Across from it, black smoke billowed out of a room. "Where did everyone go?" I asked.

"Stay behind me," the first guard said. He led the way toward the nurse's station.

"Don't you guys have comms so you know what's going on?" I asked.

"We do, but there's a lot of chatter and some interference from the medical wing," he admitted.

"Not very inspiring," I said.

"Miss, don't worry. You're safe with us," he replied.

They reached the nurses station and the two front guards checked it. "We got bodies," the second guard said.

I stepped forward, intending to see them, but one of the rear guards put a hand on my shoulder. "I don't think that's a good idea."

"What, you think I'm going to puke? I'm dead." I shook off her hand. "Let me see."

The first guard stepped aside and waved toward the scene. "Be my guest. But don't say we didn't warn you."

I approached the desk. Blood on the walls portended what I would find. I screeched and started dry retching as I saw the bodies littering the floor. Medical personnel - doctors, nurses, a pair of security guards by the look of them, lay in various states of dismemberment on the floor. I wanted to look away -a part of my brain told me to look away - but another part, a primal part, looked at it with savage interest. In that moment I knew I was not the same person I had been yesterday. The old Rachel would never have been interested in such a scene - never. "What did this?"

"Whatever was in there," one of the guards said - a female by the sound. I turned and followed their finger with my eye to view the empty exam room still billowing smoke. Bodies were in there, too - these wore armor. Weapons lay on the floor at their side.

"Are we still in danger?" I asked, fear creeping in. I pictured some mutated monster tearing me limb from limb. Would I feel pain? Would I die? I presumed I would, since the other undead "died" from decapitation or blunt head trauma. I wasn't invincible.

"One moment," the lead guard said. He fell silent, likely consulting his communication array. "I'm told the threat has been contained. Clean-up crews will be up shortly."

"Did this happen elsewhere? That the clean-up crews are so busy?"

The guard stared at me but said nothing, which confirmed my fears.

"What did this? What kind of monster did this?"

He cleared his throat. "Miss, I don't want to upset you, but..." Was that *fear* in his voice?

"But what?" I asked, suddenly irritated. They needed to stop pussy-footing around and spit it out already.

"It was an infected individual - like you."

The revelation hit me like a battering ram to the chest. I took a step back. Well that explained the caution in his tone, didn't it? "What?" I said lamely, unable to come up with a snarkier remark.

"One of the patients undergoing treatment awoke and broke free of his restraints. He broke containment and went on a rampage until security forces could take him down."

I swallowed hard. "One man could do all this?" My eyes drifted back to the bloodstains on the walls.

"So we're told. He possessed enhanced speed and strength beyond even that of Marines in power armor.

"What stopped him?"

"Your father decapitated the patient."

"The assailant," another guard corrected. "He stopped being a patient when he chose to go on a murderous streak." Left unsaid was the suggestion that I should choose not to go on a murderous streak.

"I guess the treatment didn't work with him," I said, trying to make it clear it was a fluke. "Trust me, that's not going to happen with me."

"We know, miss. Your father has requested your presence on the bridge for the time being. It's the safest place you can be now."

I nodded in agreement. "Lead the way."

We made it to the transport tube, passing bodies scattered here and there, and made our way to the bridge. The door opened and I gaped at around two dozen Marines in heavy armor pointing weapons at us. "Uh, we're friendly," I called.

My words didn't immediately disarm the Marines, of course. But a few seconds later they put up their weapons and made a hole for my escort and I to pass through.

"Is it always this high of security?" Somehow, I doubted it.

"No. Special circumstances."

The blast door to the bridge cycled open and for the second time in as many minutes I gaped again at the immensity of the room before me. A pair of stairs led to a raised dais where a planet-shaped orb hung above a projector well. Around the dais computer terminals lined the walls and service men and women filled the seats. Chatter filled the air, but it was all technical mumbo jumbo and I felt the urge to tune it out. I fixated instead on the man standing atop the platform studying the map.

My father looked impressive with his hands clasped behind his back as he gazed upon the map of our world. Icons in red and green and blue and more colors swirled around the world and blinked in or out of existence on the surface. He turned and smiled at me. "Ah, Rachel. I'm glad you're safe. Come join me."

I ascended the stairs, gawking as I went. A glance behind me showed my guards setting up position next to the blast doors, augmenting the already-high security. My gaze finally settled on the rotating orb and the images and sounds rising from it. "That's cool," I said. Cool was an understatement, of course, but I didn't want to start fangirling over what I saw there. Not too much, anyway.

My father must have known I was hedging my enthusiasm, for he smiled knowingly and gestured to it. "This is a state-of-the-art situation map. It allows us a full view of the entire planet of Galatia IV in real-time. It displays population sizes, troop movements, enemy movements, everything."

"'Enemy movements,'" I repeated, eyes narrowing. "Are the infected our enemies now?"

My father's expression softened, and he sobered. "I'm sorry, I shouldn't have phrased it like that."

"With respect, Supreme Commander," a deep male voice came from behind me. "I would most definitely call the infected our enemies."

"Ah, General Hargreaves," my father said, looking over my shoulder at the newcomer.

I turned to get a look at the man. He was a thin, grey-haired man wearing a highly decorated forest green Marine uniform. He did not smile as his eyes settled on me. Instead, his gaze flicked to the holo-display behind me. "My boys are fighting, and dying, down there. If they're not enemies then I don't know who is."

My father sighed, suggesting this was a conversation they'd had before I arrived already. "General, we talked about this yesterday. The infected are enemy combatants not by choice but by circumstance. They did not choose to become infected. Your Marines are well within their rights to defend themselves - no one is disputing that. We are deploying them in positions to best minimize casualties. But we are also working to cure as many of the infected as possible."

The general sneered. "Bah, waste of time if you ask me. I say pull my boys up and nuke the shit hole. It's not worth anything."

My eyes widened and I clenched my fists and my jaw. I felt my teeth straining under the force. That was my *home* he was talking about. All my friends, teachers and fellow citizens. Fortunately, my mother's family was on another world - my father had brought me there when I was a baby - but there were plenty of families which had been torn apart or been wholesale destroyed by the virus and this idiot. I took a step forward, rational thought taking a back seat to my rage.

A hand on my chest - my father's hand - stopped me. I blinked, then shook my head. The general was watching me with a cool, disinterested expression. After a pause he quirked an eyebrow, as if wondering if I was going to insist on hitting him.

I took a step back.

"There are many good citizens of the Federation down there, General. As I said, they are victims and we will offer all available assistance to them."

"The next batch of 'victims' you bring up better be in reinforced shackles. I lost a dozen Marines to the one who got free aboard this ship." His gaze settled on me. "Until you put it down like the animal it was."

It was my turn to fear that my father would hit the general or run him through with his swords. I prepared to grab my father's arm and restrain him if necessary.

My fear was unfounded, however, for my father showed no outward sign of anger, not even a clenched jaw or fist. Instead he nodded. "I did what I had to do. But I believe, as does every scientist in this fleet, that there is hope for many of the victims. Yes, we had a setback and the treatment failed in one instance. But there are a dozen other patients who are recovering from their successful treatments. The treatment works."

The general inclined his head to my father. "As you say, Supreme Commander. I'm returning to Marine Ops. I trust you'll notify me if the tactical situation changes drastically."

"You'll be the first to know," my father replied. "Though I am curious as to what brought you to the bridge."

"I wanted to see your vaunted daughter for myself, sir." The general turned on his heels without waiting for a response and left the bridge.

After the blast doors had closed, my father's shoulders slumped, slightly. He met my eyes. "Are you okay?"

"Do all your subordinates talk to you like that?" I asked. "I wanted to hit that guy."

"He spoke with respect, as he is allowed. And if you had hit him you might have killed him. At the least you would have faced criminal charges."

"You'd lock your own daughter in the brig?" I asked, remembering military terminology from the countless television shows I'd watched over the years.

"I am bound by the law, the same as anyone," my father said patiently. "The Federation is built on law and order and if I circumvented that law and order, no matter who it was, then I would be no better than a tyrant or dictator."

"I thought the Empire was built on law and order and the Federation was built on freedom."

My father laughed. "Touché. The Federation was built with laws to protect the freedom of its citizens and to maintain order. The Empire was built with laws meant to protect the rule of the Emperor and to control its citizenry. That is the core difference."

"I know, I know," I replied petulantly. I *had* learned that in school. A school that was in ruins now. "Speaking of the Empire. Do you think they were behind the virus?"

"I honestly don't know. Isab…your cousin…is continuing to gather and review the evidence to build a case against the Empire or whatever party was responsible. Rest assured that if it was the Empire, nothing will stop me from making them pay."

"Are things really that bad down there? Are Marines dying in droves?"

"Come, have a look." He swiped and close-up images of a city on fire expanded to fill the space next to the hologram of the planet. "Many of the major cities are in chaos. In addition to the undead, looters and rioters have taken to the streets. Law enforcement gave up early in the fight and our Marines only landed twelve hours ago in force."

A different image replaced the first. Here was another city, this time with what looked like walls around it and crowds of people outside the walls. "We've set up temporary sanctuaries in more remote cities that were not yet affected by the virus. Walls were the priority, then defenses. We're ferrying the uninfected to these sanctuaries until they can be evacuated. The virus has a short incubation period, so we know within a few hours whether they're infected or not. Of course, the smell of human flesh has drawn the infected to these cities too." The image zoomed in to show hordes of undead hammering at the walls. "That is actually good, because it means we can apprehend groups of the undead with ease and ferry them to facilities for treatment."

"Do they all come to the Nightblade?"

"The early patients did," he gestured to me. "But no, now that the rest of the fleet has arrived, they're sent to dedicated medical frigates and kept separate so if one frigate falls the rest will survive."

"They're really that dangerous?" I asked. What I meant was, *I'm really that dangerous?*

"The virus grants superior strength and speed to that of a human. Do you remember the stories of vampires you used to enjoy?"

"I usually read the romance ones, but yeah, I remember. Vampires that could turn into bats and had super speed and strength and could hypnotize people. And were weak to silver and holy water."

"Well, aside from the weaknesses, and the bats and hypnotizing thing, the virus grants speed and strength akin to what vampires were depicted as possessing. An infected has lightning fast reflexes and the one I fought went toe-to-toe with three Marines in power armor - a feat that a dozen men shouldn't have been able to accomplish."

"Wow," I said. I curled my fingers into a fist. "So, I'm that strong?"

"We won't know until we test you, but the presumption is you are."

"Imagine an army of infected," I mused. "They would be unstoppable."

My father snorted. "Oh, believe me, once the general gets over his indignation at not getting to nuke a planet he'll begin thinking of the military applications. And I guarantee military contractors are already looking to get their hands on as many infected as possible."

"To turn them into weapons?"

"Probably to train them to be super-soldiers."

"Then the Federation should train them first," I offered. "Keep them in-house."

"You read my mind," my father said, smiling. "I will offer anyone willing to join the military an incentive."

"Even me?"

He blinked and stared at me, speechless, for a long moment. "You would want to join the military?"

I shrugged. "I don't know. But if what you say is true about my abilities then I'd be wasting them being an engineer or teacher or nurse or whatever."

"Well, there will be time to talk about that after the conflict is over." He was stalling for time, I could tell.

Rather than call him out in front of his subordinates, I inclined my head and said, "Sounds good."

The holo-map chose that moment to flash a bright red and start to blare a high-pitched alarm. My father spun and said, "Show me."

The serene city he'd shown me earlier was replaced by a scene of a walled city on fire. The wall was breached in one spot, which the image zoomed in on. Undead were swarming through the breach and being met by laser fire and hails of bullets. "Velmar City has been breached," a toneless voice reported. "Evacuation efforts are accelerating while defense forces buy them time."

My father hung his head. "I was afraid of this. The walls won't hold forever. We're running out of time. TacComm, give me Admiral Helsvyn."

"Of course," the same voice belonging to the tactical commander said from a raised alcove behind us, above the blast doors. The image of the burning city was joined by a second image, this time of a broad-chested Rovarkian man with long blond hair tied back. He looked younger than General Hargreaves, though age was difficult to gauge in the age of nano-technology.

"Supreme Commander, what a pleasant surprise," the man said, offering what to me looked like a vacant smile that didn't reach his eyes. I got the impression he didn't like my father. "What can I do for you?"

"I expected the third fleet two hours ago. What's your status?"

"We have almost completed resupply, sir. Then we will join you at Galatia IV."

"The situation has become dire, Admiral. We need your additional ships to aid in the evacuation effort now. Can you send your transports on ahead now?"

"Sir," he drawled in his thick accent, "I don't think that is a good idea."

"And why not?" I heard the undertone of irritation in my father's voice. He hid it well, but I had heard it before when he was irritated with me about one thing or another.

"We are their protection, sir. If I go sending them off into the void without defenses..."

"They're coming to what is right now one of the largest congregations of Federation warships outside of Tar Ebon. If they're not safe here, where will they be safe, Admiral?" my father challenged.

The admiral blinked, whether at the ferocity of my father's words or as a side-effect of trying to think of an answer. "I see your point. I will order the transports to depart within the hour."

"Within the half-hour," my father amended.

"Of course, sir."

"That will be all, Admiral." My father swiped and the display vanished. "Bring up Velmar City command."

A new display appeared, this time showing an improvised command center with many personnel talking at once. One Marine stood out and was the one to look into the display. "Supreme Commander," he snapped, saluting.

"Commander, what's your status?"

"Not good, sir. The undead are closing on our position. I'm unsure how long we can hold out." His gaze hardened. "But I can assure you we will be the last ones out."

"I expect nothing less. You're doing good work, Commander. We're dispatching all available transports to your location and have more on the way. Just hold on a little longer."

"Thank you, sir." The commander saluted. "Velmar City command out." The image faded.

"Have there been any other breaches, TacComm?"

"Not yet, sir."

"Let me know the instant there is. And the instant Admiral Helsvyn's transports arrive."

"Of course, sir."

My father looked over at me. "The burden of command."

"The what?"

"The burden of command," he repeated. "The burden of standing here watching brave men and women die and commanding from afar when I would rather be there, on the front lines."

"It doesn't sound like much of a burden," I said. "Other than on your conscience." A dark thought struck me. "Did you call it the burden of command when my mother died in your service?"

"Rachel," he began, pain showing in his eyes. "What happened to your mother was a tragedy that to this day I wish could have been prevented. We got revenge, but no amount of revenge could ever replace her smiling face." He cleared his throat. "But yes, my burden was to watch the video feed as the station she commanded self-destructed to keep dangerous plans out of Imperial hands."

"Better her than you, right?" I sneered. "Wouldn't want the vaunted supreme commander to die."

"Rachel Marie!" he scolded.

I blushed, though not out of shame. Anger coursed through me and I clenched my fists. "It's not fair!" I shouted.

"Stop acting like a petulant child," my father said in a harsh whisper. He looked around, as if daring his subordinates to say something about me. Or was he worried about what they would think? "This is neither the time nor the place to have this conversation." He smoothed his face. "Now, I've arranged for more comfortable quarters for you. Your guards will show you the way. Rest and wait for me there and we can continue this conversation when this conflict is over."

I glared at my father, anger growing, as a voice in the far back of my head tried to calm me down. *Don't make a scene,* the voice said. *This is your father - show him respect. You're not a monster.* I shook my head - whether to banish the voice from my head or to shake some sense into myself I'm not sure - and settled for nodding. "Fine," I said through gritted teeth. Then, not wanting to give my father the satisfaction of slinking away, I held my back as straight as possible and stalked down the stairs and through the blast doors.

My guards must have been apprised of the situation or had good hearing, for they didn't seem surprised in the least at my appearance. "This way to your rooms, miss," the first guard said.

"What are your names?" I asked, not moving.

"Pardon?"

"If you're going to be my babysitters, or jailers, I would at least like to know your names."

"I'm Terrence," the first guard I'd spoken to upon waking said.

"Phillip," the second guard said.

"Eleanor," the third guard said.

"Delenn," the final guard said.

I nodded, trying to memorize all the names. It was like when my teachers would quiz us on all the provinces on the planet or all the planets in the sector. Heaven forbid anyone try to memorize all the planets in the Federation. "Thank you." I gestured. "Lead the way."

Terrence nodded. "Same formation as before."

"But there's no danger now," I pointed out.

"Better to be in the habit of constant vigilance than allow complacency to be our downfall," he pointed out.

"Yeah, your dad would have our heads if we let anything happen to you, darlin'," Phillip said. I found his candor refreshing.

We returned to the transport tube and they punched in the coordinates for green sector.

"What sector was the medical bay in?" I asked, curious.

"Red sector," Terrence answered.

"So, what is green sector?"

"Take three guesses, the first two don't count," Phillip said.

"Shut up," one of the women, Delenn, said.

"What?" Phillip said trying to act innocent even as he held his rifle at the ready. "Green is associated with money - or used to be - right? So, it makes sense all the rich passengers would bunk there."

"That's not why they call it that," Terrence interjected.

"Not officially."

I snickered. Ask them their names and they seemed to open right up. "You guys are funny."

"He's funny," Eleanor said, pointing at Phillip. "The rest of us, not so much."

Phillip shrugged. "Gotta have some levity in the squad, right?"

The doors of the transport opened before anyone could respond to Phillip. The squad of guards led me down almost-deserted corridors. "Where is everyone?" I asked.

"Not many dignitaries aboard the *Nightblade* right now," Terrence replied. "And all the officers are out commanding."

"That make sense," I said.

After walking for a few minutes, we arrived at a set of doors. "These are your quarters." The door slid open and the guards spread out to inspect the room. Once they were satisfied, they filed toward the door and stopped just inside it. "All clear. Two of us will be outside at all times if you need us."

"Will any of you be in here with me?" I asked.

"Not unless you want us to or we believe there is reason to be in here. We value your privacy."

"That sounds like it should be on an FIA bulletin board," Delenn answered. "'We're the Federation Intelligence Agency. We value your privacy.'"

Eleanor snorted.

Phillip made a fist and held it out. "Sick burn. Put 'er there."

Delenn extended her arm and slapped the man in the helmet. "Let's go. I'm sure she wants to get some rest."

The guards slipped outside, still bantering, and the door slid shut to muffle their words.

For the first time since I'd awoken, I was alone - truly alone. My shoulders sagged. "Well, this is your life now," I told myself. "Better get used to it." I looked around the chambers. They were far more lavish than what I'd been accustomed to back in Silver City. I stood in a front room or parlor. I passed through a doorway and found myself in a hallway lined with several doors. I peeked into each one and found four bedrooms and two bathrooms. "So much space for just me," I muttered. At least I would have my pick of rooms. I chose the room at the end of the hall on the right and flopped down on the bed. It wasn't long before sleep took me.

Chapter 5

I don't know how long I slept, but boy did it feel good. There's something about natural sleep that is so relaxing compared to medically-induced comas or dying.

I opened my eyes and drank in the silence. There was a slight hum of machinery, but for the most part silence reigned. I left and made my way to the common room of my suite. Then I screamed.

A person was sitting in a chair, their back to me. I couldn't tell at first whether they were male or female. They didn't stir at my scream. Were they dead?

The door slid open and my guards looked in. "You all right, miss?"

"There...there," I stammered. "There's someone right there." I pointed at the occupied chair.

The guards exchanged glances. "Yes?" he said quizzically. "We let her in."

"Who?" I asked frantically, preparing to fight. Were my own guards betraying me? Was this an assassin, sent to finish the job?

My fears evaporated a moment later as the woman rose and turned to face me. She wore tight black leather armor and combat boots.

I gawked. "Isabelle?"

One of my best friends in the universe smiled at me in that moment. "Hey, Rachel. I just wanted to yank your chain." She looked toward the guards, her smiling receding for a moment. "You can go."

She looked back to me as the door slid shut behind them. "You look a little worse for wear."

I blushed, looking down at the hospital gown I still wore. I'd been so tired I hadn't bothered to seek out a new outfit. "It's been a long couple of days," I admitted. I sat down across from her.

Isabelle shrugged. "I admit I cleaned up before I came up here. You wouldn't have wanted to see me covered in blood and guts."

"None of it yours, I presume," I said, looking her up and down. There were no bandages on her and no cuts on any of the skin showing.

She smirked. "I had a few cuts, but my nanites healed it."

"Any caused by the infected?"

She snorted. "Ha, those lumbering idiots couldn't hit a tortoise."

I frowned. "My father said the undead are fast."

"There's a difference between the zombies and undead," Isabelle began, sounding like my father. "The zombies are mindless. They have strength, but no coordination. It's like having a powerful speeder but a stupid as hell driver. Their speed is useless for anything but running since all they do is flap around fast. The undead," she pointed at me, "have that strength and speed *and* coordination, which makes them dangerous."

"Is that what happened with the undead who," I swallowed before continuing, "rampaged through the medical bay?"

"So I'm told. He was so distraught at his condition that he went into a psychotic rage. The doc said he had a psychotic break, but who knows. My father is on his way to double check Dr. Sinclair's work and try to prevent more undead breakdowns."

"Your father is Jason Thorpe, correct?"

"Unfortunately."

I furrowed my brow. "Unfortunately?"

"My father is obsessed with his work. He has been for as long as I can remember. It doesn't leave much time for family."

"Oh," I said, at a loss for words. For as long as I'd known Isabelle, she had had mysterious parents. She never talked about them, and it turned out they were fake. Now it seemed she didn't want to talk about her real parents either. At least her father. "And your mother?"

Isabelle shrugged. "She's the head of the Federation Intelligence Agency, so she's as busy as you'd expect. She was building her network of spies while I was growing up. Then by the time I went to the Tower she was busy sailing around the world hunting down the Cult of Rae. She hasn't stopped."

"But you joined her in the FIA," I pointed out. "Surely you two see each other sometimes."

"The known galaxy is a big place," my friend pointed out. "And it's filled with dumpster fires waiting to be put out. So, it's rare that we're in the same place for long. In fact, it's been over five years since I saw her in person."

"Is she going to come here, to help with...whatever all that is," I pointed toward the floor, symbolizing Galatia IV.

"No, she's got bigger fish to fry right now. Her words were, 'this is your mess - you clean it up. I have complete confidence in you.'"

I winced. I never knew my mother, but I imagined a stinging rebuke like that would hurt, no matter how old a person was. My curiosity got the best of me. "What did she mean, your mess?"

"I wasn't on Galatia IV to cultivate a friendship with you," she began.

"I know that. My father told me. But he didn't tell me much about your mission."

Isabelle nodded. "Well, it all began three years ago when my mother briefed me on a lead the FIA had about a virus that a shadowy organization, the Xanos Reapers, were working on. They'd raided an archaeological site on Tar Ebon and stolen some important genetic material. It was the dubbed the 'primordial strain.'"

"Wait," I said, "this virus hit Tar Ebon?"

"Around two thousand years ago, yeah. It's not in the official records, and it never will be. It was deemed too dangerous for anyone to know about."

"You can tell me though, right?"

Isabelle smirked. "Of course. The Isle of Patmos was the name of the island. A friend of the family, Favio, returned from there telling tales of the dead walking. So of course, my family had to investigate. We found a city besieged by the walking dead. They only came out at night, though, but they swarmed the island. We eventually defeated them - we destroyed every one - but it was one hell of a fight."

"Someone dug up the bones of the dead you defeated, and reverse engineered the virus?" I hadn't been in the top of my biology class for nothing.

"You got it. I followed all the leads along the way, but I kept hitting dead ends. Finally, I heard whispers of a Doctor Hague operating in a shell corporation on Galatia IV. I manufactured an identity for myself, delegated my responsibilities in the FIA and assumed the life of a teenage girl - again. I must say there was more death and destruction this time around...and that's saying something."

I had to chuckle at her grim humor. I imagined it hadn't been easy growing up in the age of wooden ships and primitive technology. That said volumes about what she'd seen on my home world. "Kimberly was the key?"

"Yes. I needed access to her father's home so I could try to collect evidence and gather clues. It didn't work out as planned, however. Remember how many times we were invited to her house?"

"Like two," I said, thinking back.

"Yeah. And I didn't get anything those times either. And their lab was shielded with an energy nullification field which blocked both my power and any surveillance equipment I deployed. It took me a lot longer to do my job and I wasn't fast enough."

"Don't beat yourself up," I said. "You couldn't have known how far along they were to producing the live virus."

"Tell that to my mother," she replied sardonically.

"I will, if I ever get to meet her. My aunt."

"She knew you existed and never told me. Some trust."

"She did?"

"Yep, from the moment you were born, I suppose. She didn't tell Dawyn, but she wasn't surprised when I told her you existed. I pried the truth out of her that she'd known for as long as you'd been alive."

"Wow. She really is a woman of secrets."

"Secrets and misdirection. She won't lie to her family - not directly - but she's the master of omitting information or answering the question you didn't ask."

"I suppose that makes her a good spy," I countered. "Need I remind you that you lied to me for two years."

Isabelle laughed at that. "If you'd asked me if I was your cousin I would have answered with the truth, but touché, you're right, I'm not that different from my mother." She frowned, as if considering the implications of that truth.

"Where is Kimberly, anyway?"

"Her father sent her to go hide in a tree."

"A tree," I repeated blandly.

"That's why she didn't answer you that morning. Her father sent her into the middle of nowhere."

"Because he knew the virus was going to get free?" I asked.

"Or knew it had already been unleashed. I'm still trying to piece together the timeline of events. In any event, after I dropped you off I detected a beacon from her and went with a team of Marines to rescue her. Then we stopped by her dear old dad's laboratory."

"Was he there?" I asked, finding myself sitting there with bated breath.

"His corpse was," my friend replied as if reporting that it had rained that day. "We found his logs and a monstrosity created by the virus. That's how *I* sustained my injuries, from slamming into terminals repeatedly, and a little friendly fire. Kimberly was hurt in the fighting but she's recovering in the medical bay."

That explained why my other best friend hadn't come to visit me along with Isabelle. "I assume Kimberly knows about you." I hesitated, though I wasn't sure why. "Did you tell her about me?"

"That's not my secret to tell," Isabelle replied. "You can tell her when you see her again."

"Was she infected?" I swallowed hard. "Did she die?"

"Surprisingly she didn't. Apparently, she was inoculated against the virus at the hands of her father."

"There was an anti-virus?" I prompted.

"Not so much an anti-virus as a vaccine. It prevents a person from contracting the virus but does nothing to stop the virus if you're already infected."

"I guess that's good. If it destroyed the virus it would be a bio-weapon to be used against people like me."

Isabelle raised an eyebrow. "You're thinking like an FIA operative there, cousin."

"I guess dying made me smarter," I joked.

"Or at least more cynical."

We both shared a laugh at that. For a moment it felt like old times - as if we were sitting on my bed talking about boys or studying for a test together. But then reality crashed in and I remembered things would never be the same. We would never sit on my bed talking about boys again or studying for tests. My childhood had been ripped away from me before I was ready.

The old me would have cried in that moment - or at least teared up. But the new me, well, the new me didn't have time for tears. It was done and over. I could no more go back to the way I'd been two days earlier than I could fly. "Where are you going next?"

"Back to the bridge to see what my dear uncle needs from me. If nothing, I'm going to follow the trail the Reapers left." She hesitated. "Kimberly is joining the FIA."

I perked up at that news. "She is?"

"She feels there's no place for her on Galatia IV, not after what her father did. In the FIA we can scrub her history and she'll just happen to share the last name with a mass murderer, instead of being his daughter. For the record, I wanted to change her name entirely, but she is attached to it."

"Can I go with you?" A scene flashed in my mind of the three of us fighting faceless bad guys in space.

My best friend shook her head. "Your father would have my head if I endangered you any further. Stay here, get adjusted to your new social status and keep your head down."

"That sounds so exciting," I said while rolling my eyes.

"Think about this. It's fun being rich."

"Just how rich?" I asked, smirking.

"Let's just say your father's had funds gathering interest for two thousand years. You do the compound interest math." She smiled and stood. "We'll chat again soon, but duty calls."

"I'll go see Kimberly after you leave," I said, standing and embracing her. "Stay safe."

Isabelle nodded in agreement and a moment later had turned to the purplish mist I'd seen in my school and was gone. That was so cool. I wished I had a super power like hers.

Chapter 6

My guards insisted on following me to the medical bay. The nurses station had been repaired and was staffed by nervous-looking nurses, coordinators and doctors, despite the armed guards now stationed at every corner. They clearly didn't want a repeat of the slaughter from before.

"Is it really necessary for the four of you to follow me everywhere?" I asked. "Couldn't two suffice?"

"It's standard procedure," Terrence said.

"'It's standard procedure,'" I mocked. "That's your common refrain, you know that, right?"

"That's because it's typically the answer for the questions you ask," he shot back.

We stopped in front of the door I'd been directed to. Door 666. If that wasn't ominous, I didn't know what was. I didn't recall my suite number. "Will you at least wait outside while I talk to my friend?"

"After we check the room." He gestured and two of the guards, Eleanor and Delenn, I think, though it was hard to tell them apart, entered. After several moments they emerged and gave a nod.

"Thanks," I said sardonically, not waiting for Terrence to verbalize what the nods symbolized. The door opened at my approach.

Kimberly, who had obviously been alerted by my guards intruding, smiled at seeing me. "Rachel!" Her smile faded. "Sorry if I don't get up. I'm still recovering."

I smiled back, feeling genuine warmth toward my other best friend. "Hey. Isabelle told me about what happened to you. Dick move on behalf of your father."

Kimberly blushed. "You mean a deadly move. Something a terrorist would do. I'll never live it down."

"Hey," I scolded, "you had no way of knowing your dad was working on a deadly virus. You're not to blame." I continued to approach and put my arm around her in a sisterly embrace. "Chin up."

Kimberly smiled. "You always know the best ways to encourage me." She pulled away and pointed toward the door. "What's with the heavy security? Personal guards?"

"Well," I began, hedging, "You remember how Isabelle told you who she really was?"

"Yeah," Kimberly said. "That was a shocker. Second highest person in the FIA - can you believe it?"

"I could believe it...after I found out who I really am."

Kimberly blinked, her face scrunching up in a confused expression. "'Who you really are?' Who are you?"

I took a deep breath, more from habit than a biological need. "I am the daughter of Dawyn Darklance. The supreme commander."

Her eyes went bug-eyed and her mouth dropped open. She snapped it shut a moment later. "Are you serious?"

"As a heart attack," I replied. "Well, I'm not sure how heart attacks would affect someone like me, but you get the point."

"And you didn't know you were his daughter? Were you raised by a different family or something?"

"No, no, my father, the man who raised me, *is* the supreme commander. He went into self-imposed exile to raise me after my mother died."

"Wow. So all those times I was at your house...I was at the supreme commander's house? Why didn't Isabelle tell me this sooner?"

"She said it was my secret to tell. There's something else."

"What? Was your mother the crown princess of Monta Nallie?"

I rolled my eyes. "I wish. No, I...died."

Kimberly stared blankly at me. "But you're standing right in front of me."

"I know. But, here's the thing. The virus killed me...and then reanimated me."

"My father's virus? The one he helped create," she amended.

"The same."

"Wow. Do you feel any different?"

I shrugged. "A little more apathetic? Maybe a little smarter - I can't tell."

"You seem like the same friend I always knew," Kimberly mused.

"Well I'm not," I said, a little snappier than I would have preferred. I let out a sigh. "I'm sorry, I shouldn't have snapped at you."

"No, it's okay," she replied, looking at the floor. "I don't mean to diminish what you went through. I get what you meant about heart attacks, though."

"Anyway," I began, wanting to change the subject. "Do you know any more about what happened to Silver City in particular?"

Kimberly shook her head. "No. I tried reaching out to my remaining family down there but no luck. Obviously the news isn't reporting anymore and the military isn't telling me anything." She nodded toward the door, beyond which my guards waited,

"I'll see what I can find out," I said. I was curious to see what remained of my house, my school and the town in general. How many had survived? Our town had been suburban. It wasn't as densely populated as the more urban locales, but it still housed thousands of people and I had seen many die and rise again before my eyes. "I guess I don't need to study for that test tomorrow." I laughed.

Kimberly joined me in laughing. "With who you are you can go to any school in the Federation now." She frowned. "Meanwhile I'll be a pariah."

"No, you won't," I reiterated. "Nobody has to know you were the daughter of the mad scientist."

"Isabelle offered me a job at the FIA - if I can make it through basic training. I think that might be the route to go - to disappear like a ghost."

"If anyone should be called a ghost, it's me," I said.

"We can both be ghosts," Kimberly replied. "You physically, me figuratively." She nodded as if the matter were settled.

I smirked but didn't argue further. What *would* I do, anyway? My ambitions of being a nurse had just gone up in smoke, hadn't they? Nobody would want an undead nurse around them, and the daughter of the supreme commander couldn't be a common nurse. *Stop it*, I scolded mentally. *You're the same Rachel - nothing is beneath you, no matter who your father is.* If only I believed my self-talk.

My friend and I lapsed into a long, comfortable silence. How could we talk about mundane things like clothing, boys or the latest reality TV shows after what happened? It felt like our innocence died along with my body because of the virus. The weight of adulthood, and all the dangers therein, had fallen upon us.

I decided to change the subject. "I didn't ask what you're in here for. What injuries did you receive?" A sheet covered most of her body below her chest.

"My legs were burned in the explosion."

"Explosion? At the lab?"

"Yeah. Who knew that when Isabelle shifts it's not your whole body in one instant? She shifted us but not before the explosion burned my legs." She shrugged. "They're treating the burns and the doctors say I should make a full recovery."

"Oh, that's good," I said. Isabelle hadn't looked like she had any burns - but then again, she had been wearing a skin-tight armor of some kind that probably absorbed energy, if the holos were to be believed. "Did any of the Marines with the two of you die?"

Kimberly averted her eyes. "Yes. A lot. There was this monster - it was some kind of mutated test subject. It was three times as tall as a man and twice as wide." She met my eyes. "I saw it crush a Marine with one motion, armor and all. Lasers had no effect and bullets barely penetrated."

"How did you kill it?"

"Orbital strike." She paused, waiting for me to catch on. Then, seeing the lack of understanding in my eyes said, "That's how I got the burns. Command sent a tactical nuke down to sanitize the site and kill the thing."

"You were burned by friendly fire?" I asked, aghast.

She shrugged. "Technically. But they also saved my life. When I was in that tree a bunch of the walking dead were closing on me. If Isabelle and her Marines hadn't arrived, I would have been zombie chow."

"True," I conceded. Still - why would her father have authorized something like that - knowing his niece and daughter's best friend were down there, not to mention the Marines? "Did the remaining Marines die?"

"No, Isabelle shifted the survivors out."

I blinked. "Oh." I knew next-to-nothing about shifting. "She can shift more than one person at a time?"

Kimberly raised her eyebrow. "Didn't you pay attention when we were watching a documentary on shifting a few months ago?"

"No," I admitted. "I mean, I was but I don't remember seeing that."

"How did you think they shifted ships if they could only shift one other person at a time?"

"Shift the ship and it shifts everyone within?" I guessed.

"No, it doesn't work like that. If she shifted only the ship, then everyone inside the ship would instantly be exposed to vacuum and die." Her voice took on a lecturing tone. "That's what happened once in the early days of space flight - Flight 102. Bridgette shifted a transport ship into orbit and then back down. Only, some people didn't come with it. She had forgotten two children were aboard and her mind didn't encompass them. Historians say that set the space program back thirty years and led to a branching in faster-than-light research."

"Why did it set it back?"

"They said because it scared people. Bridgette became a recluse for a time, Isabelle didn't dare try it and public opinion of Eternals and shifting in general fell to an all-time-low. It wasn't until after the Prometheus disaster that Jason invented the..."

"Oh, I know this, I know this," I interrupted. "The shadow drive, right?"

"Yeah, the shadow drive made it possible for ships to shift without the need of a human mind. This removed any chance for error."

"Wow," I said. "I never knew the history of it."

"History was never your thing."

I smirked. "Not much of any subject is my thing, right?" I paused. "I don't even know why I wanted to be a nurse - I wouldn't have the grades for it."

"Don't beat yourself up. You wanted to help people - that's what counts. Who cares about grades?"

"Uh, the school," I pointed out. A somber thought struck me then. "I don't even know if they'll allow the undead to go to school."

"Why wouldn't they?" Kimberly asked. "You're no different than you were before and you're in your senior year. You need your degree." She stroked her chin. "Though I guess your father could probably hire tutors for you and you could just take the exam."

"I meant college," I said.

"Eh, college is overrated. Besides, do you really think our planet is going to recover from this?"

"You think we'll be refugees?"

"I think a lot of people will be either dead, undead or living and left to flee to another safe world. It stands to reason the undead would be fleeing too."

"I hadn't thought of that," I admitted. Once again, the reality of the situation hadn't fully hit me. I hadn't thought of the implications on a planetary scale and how that would affect my home world - the only place I'd ever known. A thought struck me, along with a melancholy feeling. "It won't matter to you though, will it? You're going off to train with the FIA, right?"

My friend shrugged. "Yeah, I guess you're right. I'll be away for years training and I don't really plan on coming home, either. There's nothing left for me here."

I remembered her tales of how her father was the only family she had on the entire planet. Her mother had died when she was young, and both her mother's and father's families were on another planet in the Federation far away. The thought brought the feelings of loss regarding my mother to the surface and I swallowed a lump in my throat. "I should be going. I'm going to check on my father and see how the war effort is going. I'll check in with you later."

My friend smiled. "It was good to see you, Rachel. Thanks for visiting."

"Of course." We shared one last embrace and I left the room.

"Where to now, miss?" Terrence asked as the door to Kimberly's room slid shut.

"To the bridge," I said, enjoying the feeling of command - perhaps a little too much. I started leading the way toward the transport tube. I hoped I could catch a hint of what Isabelle wanted to speak to my father about.

"But your father said he would call for you when the fighting was done," Terrence pointed out.

"Well, I'm impatient and I want an update," I replied.

"Atta girl," Phillip said.

Chapter 7

The doors of the transport tube opened, revealing the bridge ahead of us. The guards posted outside didn't try to stop us this time.

"Well, that's refreshing, not being challenged like before," Phillip noted, putting words to my thoughts.

The door to the bridge slid open and the cacophony of organized chaos met our ears, much like before. Only this time, it felt more desperate. I couldn't quite put my finger on it, but the voices sounded worried.

My father stood there, his back to me, animatedly gesturing to the holo-map.

Isabelle, who I could scarce believe was my cousin, stood across from him, scowl on her face. She noticed me first, but her expression didn't change as her gaze shifted back to my father.

Feeling slighted, I approached, noting Terrence and the others again stayed in the hall on the other side of the doors. I would have to ask if there was some silent command or established protocol that required they stay outside. "What's going on?" I asked.

My father's head jerked around as he acknowledged my presence. "Rachel." He didn't sound particularly pleased to see me. "I thought I said we would meet after this conflict was resolved."

"You did," I replied, bucking up my courage. "But I got bored. And I wanted to see for myself how things were going."

"You got bored," my father stated in what I had to admit was the flattest tone I'd ever heard him use. "You got bored?" This time his voice had heat to it, and his cheeks were growing redder by the moment. "Well excuse me while I call in a circus to entertain you," he said it in the same heated tone, with a heavy helping of sarcasm, though the volume hadn't increased. "*Children* get bored and go places they aren't supposed to. You led me to believe you were an adult. Which is it, Rachel?"

Around the bridge, chatter of humans present in the room stopped, while reports from humans on the ground, or their AI, continued to pipe through speakers, a stark reminder I was interrupting the war effort.

I would have blushed furiously if I wasn't...you know...dead. "I..." I stammered, waffling between an angry and humble reply. On the one hand, I wanted to shout, to slam my fist into his face, but the reasonable part of my brain said that wasn't how a daughter treated her father, no matter how angry she was. And they certainly didn't do it twice in twenty-four hours in the same exact place. I inhaled out of habit and tried again. "I'm sorry. I wanted an update on the war effort. If I'm being a bother, I can go." There, play the guilt card.

"Let her stay," Isabelle chimed in from behind my father. She smirked and winked before smoothing her face into a neutral visage. "She *is* the daughter of the supreme commander. She may need to know this stuff one day."

My father heaved a heavy sigh, face still red, then blew it out slowly. He eyed my cousin from the corner of his eye, then nodded and met my gaze. "Your cousin is right. Perhaps I should have included you from the start." He gestured to the holo-map. "Please, observe."

It wasn't *quite* the apology I'd been expecting, or at least hoping for, but it was as close to one as my father would give while in public. "Thank you," I said in my best imitation of a meek mouse. I stepped up to observe and told myself I wouldn't ask too many questions. That admonishment died as I saw how much the map had changed. "Are we losing?" I blurted before I could stop myself. I cringed, expecting a glare from my father.

Said glare never came. Instead, my father seemed to deflate slightly and heave a defeated sigh. The kind of sigh when as a child I would draw on the walls after he told me not to for the umpteenth time. Like that, only lives were on the line. "Unfortunately." He pointed and the holo zoomed in on one city. "Velmar City has fallen, which is not wholly unsurprising, but the speed at which it fell is. We lost dozens of good Marines and hundreds of citizens while they awaited transport." The image panned out at a gesture, showing a sea of red peppered with blue islands. "Any place not walled has fallen hours ago and even those cities with walls are feeling the strain as the undead form human siege ladders, climbing on top of one another to reach the tops of the walls."

"Did the transports from that one admiral ever arrive?" I asked, the admiral's name forgotten.

"Admiral Helsvyn. Yes, they arrived a few hours ago and we put them to use, but it's still not enough. Add to that multiple transports being hijacked and destroyed by the undead and we're almost back to where we started."

"They were improperly transporting the undead," Isabelle pointed out. "Probably in their haste to get out of the danger zone. Not that it did them any good."

"Wait," I said, holding up a hand. "The undead stole a transport?"

"Hijacked may have been a poor choice. They broke free and killed everyone aboard. We were forced to destroy the transports en-route rather than risk exposing a capital ship to a ship-full of unrestrained undead."

"So, the nuclear option is looking more probable," I guessed, a sick feeling settling into my stomach. If they nuked the planet, would they also eliminate any of the "cured" like me?

"Unfortunately," my father admitted. "Once all the living are evacuated we will have decisions to make. Her father," he tilted his head in Isabelle's direction, "believes he may be able to develop an air-borne nanite concoction to 'cure' the infected much like they did with you. But that solution may come too late. There's pressure from the senate to end this conflict quickly."

"You mean sweep it under the rug," Isabelle pointed out. "Pretend an entire planet just disappeared? What, say it was a gas explosion or something?"

"I never said it was ideal," my father replied, sounding defensive. "But if we cannot cure them without endangering more lives than we'd save we have to take steps to ensure these weapons don't end up in the wrong hands."

"You mean Imperial hands."

"Imperial, free agents, Commerce Sector, anywhere would love to have hordes of mindless undead to unleash upon unsuspecting worlds. It would be an apocalypse waiting to happen, second only to the actual virus itself being unleashed in airborne form again."

"I won't let *that* happen, at least," Isabelle replied. "I will find who was responsible and bring them to justice."

"I trust you, but you'll excuse me if I don't hold my breath," my father said. "It *was* your agency that kept the virus a secret from me."

"What would you have done if you'd known?" Isabelle asked. "Marched up to that lab and demanded they destroy the virus? They would have packed up shop and we'd be fighting for a *different* world. Better the enemy you know than..."

"...the enemy you don't," my father finished. "Yes, I'm aware of your mother's morally gray logic. Her idea that the ends justify the means doesn't sit well with me and you know it."

"It's gotten us this far," Isabelle shot back.

"I'm not positive that's such a good thing," he replied. "But that's neither here nor there." He waved as if to wave away my cousin's arguments. "If the airborne cure isn't ready by the time those evacuations are complete," he pointed to the islands of blue from before, "we'll be out of time." He paused. "I'm sorry."

I wasn't understanding what he was apologizing to me for, but I felt I needed to offer a reply. "I will understand, regardless of the action you take." That didn't mean I would offer myself up as a sacrificial lamb, of course, but I chose not to say that.

"Sir, we're receiving an urgent tight-beam broadcast from the *Cheville*," the tactical commander reported from his perch above the blast doors.

"Display it on my holo," my father called back.

"The *Cheville* is a medical frigate," Isabelle said in answer to my silent questioning eyebrow.

The holo-map morphed into a female officer wearing a harrowed expression. "Supreme Commander, I am Captain Eleanor Yrvesse of the *Cheville*." She didn't wait for my father to acknowledge her before continuing. "The undead we brought aboard to administer cures have breached containment and are rampaging through several decks of the ship."

I half-expected my father to bend over and place his head on the console, but he kept his composure. "How many are we talking, Captain Yrvesse?"

"Four had cures administered and twelve more were awaiting treatment when the breach occurred."

"Twelve are on the loose?"

She shook her head. "Two of those cured were conscious as the attack began. They attempted to help but were overpowered and..." she stumbled. "...torn to shreds. They took one of the uncured with them."

This time my father closed his eyes. "That leaves eleven remaining. And the other two cured?"

"Surveillance video shows them still in medically induced comas while the cures take effect."

"All right. Your priority is to contain the outbreak. Have you sealed the decks?"

"Of course, sir, but they have ripped through deck plating to breach other floors."

"Bloody hell. How many floors?"

"Seven of our eighteen floors are compromised. They're directly in the middle, cutting the top six off from the bottom five."

"And you're at the top," my father said. It was a statement, not a question. I suspected he knew the interior layout of *every* ship in the Federation. He paused for a long moment before speaking. "Abandon ship, Captain. Order all crew members to escape pods. The rest of the fleet will assist with recovery efforts."

The captain on the other end of the holo seemed torn between relief and disappointment. As though she were relieved her crew was being rescued but disappointed her ship was being scuttled in the process. She saluted. "Of course, Supreme Commander. I will remain on the bridge until the last crew member is off."

I held my breath, not that it mattered, since I didn't *need* to breathe. Habit, I suppose. This captain was prepared to make the same sacrifice my mother had all those years earlier.

For the briefest moment, I thought my father's gaze flicked to me. But then the moment was gone, and his steely voice spoke. "Get yourself off the instant the last crew are away. Go with the rest of the bridge crew if you can. But Captain...if you can't...know your sacrifice has not been in vain."

"Thank you, sir," the captain replied. The holo faded a moment later.

My father turned to Isabelle. "Can you shift over there and rescue the two in a coma? The cured ones."

Isabelle didn't hesitate. "Of course. But why?"

"Men and women are dying so that those who are cured can live. I will not allow their sacrifices to be in vain if I can prevent it."

Isabelle nodded. "Let me grab my gear and I'll be off." She passed through the blast doors and I caught a glimpse of her disappearing into shadowy mist before they closed again.

"Is shifting not allowed in here?" I asked.

"No. There are energy nullifiers hidden between the wall plates. They disallow any energy manipulation, including magic and shifting, while inside this room. The nullifiers are disabled when the shadow drive engages."

"It's a defense mechanism?" I guessed. "To stop assassins?"

"Something like that," my father said. He didn't elaborate, instead barking orders a moment later. "TacComm, send a message to the fleet. Message is as follows. 'All ships, the *Cheville* is being evacuated. Aid in retrieval of escape pods but employ maximum quarantine protocols when handling them. There is a chance of infected crew being aboard those pods. End message.'"

"Message has been sent," the tactical commander acknowledged.

"Now we wait," my father said.

The display had returned to the map, showing icons of various ships in the system. As I watched, the icon labeled the *Cheville* spewed forth smaller icons, with each immediately being identified by the computer as escape pods and assigned a number. Forty-eight pods.

Icons indicating starfighters streamed toward the hurtling pods, circling them in pairs and working to stabilize their trajectories. "Do they have tractor beams?" I asked, thinking of the holo-dramas where they used them.

"Some of the newer models of starfighters are equipped with grappling lines. It allows them to launch and attach cables magnetically to other metallic objects. It can aid with salvage operations, like this, or it can be used to apprehend fleeing ships, slowing them down until a capital ship can catch up. It's applications in combat are still being explored, but the general theory is they can be used on objects to change the fighter's direction rapidly. Such as around capital ships or in asteroid or debris fields."

"Oh," I said, head spinning. I had never really paid attention to the war holos and how realistic or unrealistic they were. I'd had a general sense of the capabilities of Federation ships, but little more than that.

"The capital ships do employ magnetic tractor beams designed to latch on to magnetic objects and drag them closer, but those generally use the much greater mass of said capital ships to make it work and have limitations."

"Sir, we're receiving a message from the *Eucharist,*" the tactical commander put in before I could respond.

"That's Jason's ship," my father mused. "Show us."

A middle-aged man with a full head of messy brown hair and a scraggy beard appeared on the holo. "Dawyn," he said, bowing his head briefly out of respect. When he lifted his head, his eyes shifted to my face and a quizzical look flashed across it before morphing into a more analytical look like what I'd seen in Dr. Sinclair.

"Jason," my father said, inclining his head slightly less. "It's good to hear from you. I'm hoping you have some good news to share." I suspected *I* would have had desperation in my voice at this point, but my father didn't.

"I do," Jason said in a voice one might report on the weather in. "We, Dr. Sinclair and I, believe we have created a stable airborne nanite mist that can be deployed over Galatia IV."

"That would be wonderful news," my father said, bowing his head in relief. "How soon can it be ready to deploy? The situation is getting dire down on the planet."

"We're not one hundred percent certain," Jason continued. "It's our theory that the treatment will work, but there's a chance it could fail. We want you to know all the risks."

"I understand that if this treatment fails we have no other recourse but to vaporize every unliving thing on that bloody world."

"The treatment could fail to work," Jason went on to explain. "Or it could prove fatal to the infected, killing them instead of curing them."

"Which is exactly what we *don't* want to happen," my father noted.

"I agree."

"It's worth the risk. How soon can we deploy?"

"Within the hour. I recommend evacuating all living personnel and civilians from planet-side before we deploy."

"Is the cure dangerous to the living?"

"Not necessarily, but it could cause unwanted side effects if the living are exposed to it."

"I'll ensure Marine Ops is informed," Dawn replied. "Thank you, Jason, your news came at an ideal time."

"It was my pleasure," he replied. Without further fanfare, the holo evaporated, to be replaced with an ever-updating tactical map.

"He's a man of few words," I observed. He'd only answered when strictly necessary and was short and to the point. I could see why Isabelle clashed with him.

"Jason has always been an intellectual man of few words," my father explained. "But he has been my friend and brother-in-law for many, many years and he is a good husband to Bridgette and a good father to Isabelle."

I suspected Isabelle would disagree with the last part. According to her, Jason hadn't always been an attentive father. Could you be a good yet inattentive father? I decided there were bigger fish to fry in that moment and simply said, "I see."

"TacComm, contact Marine Ops and relay an order from me requesting they evacuate all military personnel and civilians possible within forty-five minutes."

"Of course, sir," the tactical commander replied. His monotone voice irked me, so robotic. From what I'd seen in pop culture, tactical commanders were humans melded with AIs in some way to interface with the ship computers. I shivered at the thought. I wanted to ask my father about him, but, like Isabelle and Jason's relationship, now probably wasn't the best time. A moment later, he spoke again. "Sir, I also have Agent Isabelle Thorpe waiting on the line."

"Put her through. God knows she hates waiting."

Isabelle's image did not appear. Instead, her voice emanated from the projector as if she were there, but the map remained. "I've deposited the first cured survivor from the *Cheville* in room 660. It appeared empty. You might want to post some guards in there."

"Of course," my father replied. "TacComm, see that a squad is dispatched."

"Right away, sir."

"And the other survivor?"

"I'm grabbing her...shit!" a loud crack that sounded like an explosion rocked the channel, vibrating the air around me. "I've got company!"

"Get out of there!" my father shouted. I reflected it felt silly for him to say such a thing in that moment. As if she would stay and fight...oh, yeah, it was my crazy secret agent cousin we were talking about. Maybe she *needed* a reminder to save herself.

Isabelle didn't reply right away, which caused a pit to form in my stomach. I heard grunts and moans and the sound of blasters discharging and what sounded like metal on metal. At last, several moments later, she grunted "got her" and the line went dead.

"Can we track her location?"

"Attempting to locate now, sir."

I held my breath before realizing such a gesture was pointless. I didn't *need* to breath. It was a habit my body carried out, but which was not technically required for me to live. Holding my breath out of nervousness lost its meaning. I'd have to come up with a new nervous gesture. Maybe gnawing my fingers off? They'd grow back, right?

"We have her. She is aboard the *Nightblade* in room 662."

"Dispatch medical and security teams at once."

"Yes, sir."

"I'm going too," I said, turning before my father had even acknowledged me.

"Rachel, wait."

I half-turned, meeting my father's gaze. "What?"

I expected him to forbid me to go. To tell me it was too dangerous or to wait for the professionals to clear the area. The length of time he paused for told me he was warring with such statements himself. "Just be careful. Let your guards go first."

I blinked in surprise, then nodded. "Of course." I smiled in what I hoped was a reassuring manner. "My guards have been taking good care of me."

Chapter 8

I arrived back at the medical floor of the ship and found it crawling with security forces and medical personnel. I found room number 662 where Isabelle stood outside the door, blood spattering her armor but looking alive. Three medics attended to her while she grumpily answered questions from an officer, judging by the symbol on his shoulder.

I made my way toward her and found several security guards turning their weapons toward me. "Halt!" one of the guards demanded.

Terrence, who had been leading the way with Phillip, put a hand out in front of me and then stepped wholly in front, blocking any shots. "If you know who she is and value your job, lower your weapons."

"Boys," I heard Isabelle mutter. "Let her through," she said more loudly.

Terrence stepped aside and I found the guards had lowered their weapons.

I approached my cousin while my guards hung back. "Are you all right?"

"Yes, despite what the presence of three bloody medics would suggest."

"What happened? I was worried."

Isabelle snorted. "Don't waste time worrying on me. But thanks. I was just about to grab that chick," she indicated room 662 with a thumb over her shoulder, "When the door shattered inward. I barely avoided the shrapnel. Then I had to kill three of the pock-faced shit heads before I could lay hands on the girl and shift out."

"She survived?"

"Yeah, she's still in a coma, but she survived."

A moaning sound emanated from the room we stood in front of - room 660. The same room Isabelle indicated she had deposited one of the unconscious undead survivors from the *Cheville* into.

"Who's in there?"

Isabelle shrugged. "I don't know, and frankly I don't care. I need to get this blood washed off my armor and unwind. Catch me later down at the gym and we can spar or something."

"I will," I said, distracted by the repeated moaning. "I want to see who's in there first."

"Suit yourself." Isabelle disappeared in a cloud of shadowy smoke.

"Miss, I advise against this course of action," Terrence cautioned.

"I want to see who Isabelle rescued." The windows were opaque, but I tapped the control panel to turn the glass transparent and peered in.

A young man, my age by the looks of him, lay thrashing and moaning in a hospital bed, his mop of brown hair flopping violently as he moved. Restraints on his chest, arms and legs strained against his strength. That told me he was undead. I spotted four guards for him too, just like in my room.

"Is he someone special?" I asked. "He's got four guards too."

"Not that I am aware of," Terrence responded. "Four guards are standard for dangerous prisoners."

"Oh. And here I thought I was special."

"You are special, princess," Delenn said. "It's also standard for important dignitaries."

"Oh," I said, feeling slightly mollified. "I want to speak to him."

"That's not a good idea, miss. He's under guard with good reason. He could hurt you."

I looked Terrence in the faceplate and cocked my head to the side in my best recreation of the 'really?' pose. "I'm dead - what more can he do to me? Kill me?"

"He could crush your head like a watermelon," Phillip offered. "Then you'd be dead dead."

The mental image his words gave me caused me to chuckle. "Thanks for the positivity. I'm going in." Without waiting for permission, I tapped the button to open the door and went inside.

I had taken two steps into the room when all four rifles pointed at me. Only the emergence of two of my guards gave them pause. They must have exchanged silent communication of some sort, for a moment later their rifles were again pointed at the ground. "Hello, boys. Or girls," I amended. Until a person in full armor and a helmet spoke it was impossible for me to definitively tell what their gender was. The armor didn't distinguish.

"Please be careful," a male voice came from the far right corner relative to the door. "The patient is unstable."

The patient didn't look unstable in that moment. Instead, he stopped thrashing and watched me, a wary look mixed with what I imagined might have been hope in his eyes. Hope for what? That I would save him?

"Help me!" the boy screamed, resuming his straining against the restraints. "They're going to kill me!"

"He is delusional," the original guard said. "The restraints are for his protection."

And their own, most likely, I thought. I had seen the strength of those creatures. Four armed guards might have been hard pressed to take a fully feral undead down, and wouldn't a fully conscious undead be even more dangerous? One who didn't charge straight toward them but used tactics? I filed that thought away for future consideration, as I wasn't a fighter. Yes, my mother had been, and my father was, but I wasn't.

"May I release him?" I asked, resisting the urge to look to Terrence for permission. He may have been the squad leader of my protection detail, but he would have no jurisdiction in that room. Instead, I settled my gaze square on the first speaker.

The man stood still as a statue and silent as a lamb, a dead lamb, for several moments. Probably communicating with his team, though I noticed no movement from them either. At last a noise that sounded an awful lot like a sigh emerged from his helmet and he gestured. "Be our guest." He inclined his head.

I squinted, not sure if he was serious or not. Was he being sarcastic? Would they shoot me if I tried? Was he daring me? This time I did look to Terrence. "Well?" I asked.

"It's safe," he said to me in some semblance of a whisper, assuaging my unspoken fears. "Well, safe from them."

"I have nothing to fear from him," I said, pointing at the boy who once again was watching me in pensive silence.

Despite my words, six rifles leveled on the boy. Insurance, I told myself. They had just heard the news of the *Cheville* being attacked and abandoned due to undead breaching containment. Things could change in the blink of an eye. They wouldn't shoot him, hopefully. But my father would *not* be pleased if his daughter died *again*.

I approached him and started by undoing his leg restraints. Then the arm restraints and, as I reached for the chest restraints his hand snapped up and covered mine, pressing it against his chest. Of course, I couldn't feel a heartbeat, but it was still mildly romantic, I guess. I would have blushed if I'd been alive. Instead, I cleared my throat and thought of something to say. *Play it cool*, I thought. "So...where did you go to school?" I asked lamely.

I half-expected to hear gloves hitting faceplates behind me as my guardians cringed at my lame first question, but no one moved and no sounds emerged from them. Granted, Phillip was still waiting in the hall. I knew he would have given me an earful.

"Verkref High, in Everdeen City," he answered. "You?"

"Her Lady of Grace High School, in Silver City," I replied.

"Is that in the Gunshan province?"

"Yeah," I said.

"Pretty cool. I hear they produce the best clothing on the planet."

"Yeah, they're good at that," I said. I remembered one year during the holidays my father gifted me a hand-knit sweater made there. It was the warmest and softest sweater I'd ever owned.

"So..." I began again, thinking hard as to the reason I had come into that room. At first it had been because he seemed like he was in pain. Then he said they were trying to kill him. The guards said he was delusional, but was he? "Why do you think the guards are trying to kill you?"

He glanced around at the four guards in the corners and then at my escort, new suspicion in his gaze. "They kept pointing their weapons at me."

I avoided the urge to turn my own gaze upon the guards. "They were doing that for their protection, and the rest of the ship."

"What do you mean?" he asked, looking at me with narrowed eyes.

"Well," I began, feeling awkward. "There was an attack earlier today on the ship. Someone like...us...escaped and started attacking and killing people. And there was another..."

"You say escape like we're some kind of prisoners," he said, accusation in his tone.

"I also said 'us,'" I fired back. "I'm just like you."

His eyes widened. "You mean...you..." he placed a hand on his chest, over his heart. "You died too?"

"Yes," I said, realizing I had become comfortable with admitting I was among the undead now. "And I'm not a prisoner."

"But you have guards."

"They are for *my* protection. I'm..." a cough came from behind me, "not a prisoner." Were they warning me against revealing my lineage? I couldn't exactly ask them right then.

"What's your name?" he asked.

"Rachel," I said. "Rachel..."

Again, the out-of-place cough came.

"Perigren," I finished. I assumed that was what they wanted, and no additional coughs came.

"I'm Orin Strahl," he offered.

I blushed, realizing that hadn't been my first question. "I'm sorry, I didn't ask you what your name was earlier. I just launched into my questions." I rolled my eyes at my lack of manners. "Ummm...what do you like to do in you free time?"

He chuckled. "You mean pre-virus?"

"Yeah, what did you like to do, before the virus?"

He sighed, as if remembering better times. Which, to be fair, the times pre-virus *were*. "My dad was a mechanic. We worked on cars together."

"Oh, that's cool," I said, not knowing what else to say. My father had worked in IT, at least in his cover job, and I'd never seen him working on our car. That said, he was over two thousand years old, so chances were he *had* worked on cars at one point in his life. I would have to ask him sometime. "Did you enjoy it?"

He shrugged. "It helped focus my thoughts. Being out in the garage, turning the bolts and taking things apart and putting them back together. It was better than being inside with my mother and the alcohol."

"Oh. I'm sorry. Did you have any siblings?"

"No. I'm an only child."

"And did your parents...?" I trailed off, unsure of how to approach the status of his parents. "They're dead dead," he replied, answering my unfinished question. "I don't know how the virus chose who to reanimate or to let lie, but mine weren't the lucky ones." He chuckled harshly. "I'm not sure *I'm* all that lucky, though, to tell you the truth."

I didn't know how to respond to that. It was great to be conscious, but if there *was* an afterlife, like many religions suggested, was I denied eternal life and peace? "Yeah, I see what you mean."

Silence fell for several long moments. I spent the time staring at the foot of his hospital bed.

Behind me, one of the guards, Terrence, I thought, cleared his throat. "Miss, you said you wanted to get to your quarters soon?"

Terrence with the excuse, I thought guiltily. It wasn't that I didn't want to talk to Orin, I just was at a loss for words. I needed time to think. "Yes, you're right, Terrence," I replied, looking to the side where I could see Terrence in my peripheral vision. "We should go." I looked back to Orin and met his gaze. "I'm sorry, but I really should get to my quarters."

"Why?" he asked, the fire of suspicion re-igniting in his eyes.

"Well, my father is helping with some IT stuff and I'm going to visit him now that he's out of work."

"Oh," he said, sagging. Was he sagging in relief or disappointment?

"But we can talk sometime soon," I said hurriedly. "Let's exchange numbers."

Orin perked up at that, giving me a handsome smile. "I would like that."

"Well here, let me give you my communicator number." I grabbed a pad of paper and wrote down my number. "Talk to you soon," I said with a smile.

"Bye," he said, waving.

Out in the hall, I rounded on Terrence. "What was all that coughing about?" I demanded. I ignored the fact that several security guards remained in the hall, many turning to stare at me.

The team leader looked down at me. "You shouldn't disclose your identity to every random person you meet."

"Why didn't you tell me that before we went in there? And isn't that what you did when you stepped in front of me earlier?"

"I did that to potentially save your life. Let's keep walking, shall we?" he prompted, gesturing down the hall toward the transport tube.

"Fine," I said grudgingly. It wouldn't do for me to be seen arguing with my protection detail in front of Orin, or the security guards. Not that Shadow Watch Guards necessarily cared what random security guards thought of them. "You can talk as we walk."

"The more people who know who you are, the more likely it is that threats will arise," Terrence continued. "For the time being, it is the recommendation of the Shadow Watch Guard that you maintain your cover identity until no longer sustainable."

"What situation would warrant 'no longer sustainable?'" I asked.

"If your cover identity was correlated to your true identity by too many people, such as hitting the headlines on GNN or FNN, it would be pointless to maintain the charade."

"But we don't want to leak my identity to the press?" I asked.

"We don't want to put you in undue danger without compelling cause."

"I guess that's comforting," I said. "Are we really headed back to my quarters?"

"We don't *have* to go anywhere," Terrence said, stopping in front of the transport tube doors. "We could go back to the bridge."

"No, I don't want to be in my father's hair again. Where does Isabelle go to train? Or spar? She mentioned a gym?"

"There's a gym down three decks. That's the most likely one, as it's for officers and above."

"Do you think I could get in?"

"All the officers are busy leading the assault on Galatia IV," Phillip replied. "They're too busy to care right now."

"It's an evacuation now," I muttered.

"What was that?" Phillip asked.

I blinked. They hadn't heard? "Ummm...my fa...the supreme commander..."

"There's no one around," Delenn pointed out. A reminder I didn't need to use the cover story in that moment.

"I know. But I should probably get used to it." I cleared my throat and continued. "The supreme commander ordered the Marines to pull out and evacuate all remaining civilians they could within forty-five minutes."

"Why?" Terrence asked.

"They're unleashing an airborne cure for the infected. They're hopeful it will be a cure, anyway, but they didn't have enough time to test on living patients."

Phillip whistled. "They're just throwing down some untested gas or something?"

"It's a nanite-infused airborne thingy," I said, using my best scientific-sounding words. "I don't know. Jason...,"

"Doctor Thorpe," Terrence interjected.

"Right. Doctor Thorpe said he had a high confidence it would work just like it had with me." Okay, so maybe I exaggerated his confidence level a little.

"Well, either way, we're going to have a bunch of pissed off adrenaline-riddled Marines returning soon, so maybe the gym isn't the best place for a pretty little thing like you to be right now."

Delenn punched Phillip in the shoulder. "Shut up, you chauvinist pig. Did you forget she's a bloody undead killing machine now?"

"Potentially," I said as way of explanation or defense. "I don't have any training in fighting."

"Neither did the one who tore up the medical wing a little bit ago," Delenn fired back. "Or those who forced the *Cheville* to evacuate. Don't underestimate your new abilities."

"All the more reason to learn my limits sooner than later," I said. "To the gym."

Chapter 9

The transport doors slid open, revealing the gym. Despite my guards' claims, there were quite a few soldiers there already. They sparred on mats spread throughout the large chamber. Melee weapons of so many types I didn't even know them all sat on racks along the walls. In the distance, I could hear muffled coilgun and laser shots, suggesting a firing range nearby.

"Are you positive about this?" Terrence asked.

"Yeah. There can be some rough types around here," Phillip pointed out.

"Isabelle said to meet her here," I pointed out.

"Yeah, but she didn't say how long she'd be."

I shrugged. "Then teach me to fight while we wait."

Phillip burst out laughing. "What, you expect us to just teach you to fight in an afternoon?"

"You could teach me the basics," I said, feeling slightly hurt by the comment. "I felt helpless during the attack," I explained. "Isabelle had to come to my rescue. I don't want to feel helpless again."

"Well, your dearest cousin has thousands of years of experience, dear," Philip replied.

"I just want to know some self-defense moves."

"Fine. Who wants to teach her first?" Terrence asked.

Surprisingly, Eleanor, who rarely spoke to me or the rest of the squad, raised her hand. "I'll give it a go."

Terrence nodded and gestured to an open mat. "You're up, then."

I followed Eleanor out to the mat and faced her.

"Pick your weapon," the guard said.

"You're going to fight me in armor?" I asked, eyebrow raised.

"She has a point," Phillip chimed in from the doorway.

If Eleanor was annoyed, she showed no sign of it. Instead she nodded. "Fine." A click and hiss emanated from her suit and her armor *melted* away, retracting to a point behind her.

"Wow, that's a neat trick," I said, marveling at the technology on display.

"Nano-armor," Terence explained. "Standard issue for Shadow Watch Guards. It can retract into a backpack-sized lump on our backs and deploy to our full bodies in under three seconds."

"But Marines don't get this type of armor?"

"It's too expensive for Marines to get standard issue. Some of the special ops groups, like the Rangers, will get the armor as part of their kit too."

"Oh. Cool."

"Let's get on with it," Eleanor said.

For the first time, I studied Eleanor. The under-the-armor Eleanor. She had dark red hair cropped short, green eyes and a thin yet muscular build. She was about my height and studied me with a cold expression. Did she not like me? Her gruff speaking suggested not. But what had I done to offend her? Now wasn't the time to ask.

I spread my legs in my best imitation of what I'd seen in fighting holos. No one corrected me, so I assumed perhaps I had done it right. I assumed wrong.

Eleanor advanced with a cool, calm confidence I admired. Then, she lashed out, seeking to slap me. When I went to bat her hand away, she body checked me, sending me stumbling back. Before I could recover, she lashed out with a leg and I felt myself falling. Pain in my butt confirmed I'd hit the ground. I'd barely let out a moan when her knee was on my chest and her outstretched hand was at my throat, imitating a knife. "You're dead."

"Ow," was all I managed to say. "That hurt."

"You have to use your speed to your advantage," the guard said, getting off me and not sounding out of breath in the slightest. "You're shorter and skinnier than most men, use that to your advantage. You couldn't even hit me."

"But if she had, you could be dead right now," Phillip said. They'd moved to a point along the wall, in front of the electro-staffs. "She has super strength, remember?"

"She's supposed to have super speed, too," Eleanor shot back. "How much good did that do her?"

Phillip could only shrug.

"Again," Eleanor said, taking up position on the opposite end of the mat even as I struggled to roll over and get to my feet with a groan. "This time you come at me," she commanded.

"Yeah, like that won't end badly," I said sarcastically, balling my hands into fists and preparing myself, mentally and physically, to attack her. I imagined my attack in my mind's eye. I could turn her own moves against her, or grapple with her and use my superior strength. Or maybe do a jumping strike to tackle her to the ground or...

A snoring noise jolted out of my thoughts. I looked over to find Phillip with his head down, mimicking sleeping. A loud noise emanated from his direction again.

"Phillip?" I asked

"Oh, sorry, lass, you were taking so long I fell asleep waiting. You gonna make a move?"

Anger and embarrassment warred within me and I was left with my mouth open wide. At last I snapped my mouth shut and laughed half-heartedly. It was a joke, after all. "Okay, here I go," I announced.

"Don't forget to announce that to your enemies," Phillip shot back. "So they can be prepared and all...to kill you."

"Shut up," I said in a higher tone than I intended. Without further commentary, I advanced. I chose to try the same move she had used, aiming to slap her with an open palm.

She had other plans, of course, and leapt back, dodging my slap. Then, with my arm still outstretched, she grabbed my wrist and twisted.

I yelped in pain and surprise, though I maintain it was more surprise than pain. In that moment she brought her leg up and kicked me square in the chest while simultaneously releasing my wrist. I toppled backward but didn't lose my balance this time.

Instead of pursuing me, she stood there bouncing on the heels of her feet, ready to move in any direction.

Gritting my teeth, I planned my next move. Clearly the frontal attack wouldn't work, and we weren't using weapons yet. What if I used her own strategy against her?

I approached again, forcing myself to look apprehensive. She watched me with a lazy expression, her posture indicating I was not a threat. When I swung my arm to slap her like I had the first time, she grabbed my wrist, just like last time. She grinned savagely as her leg lifted again.

For a moment, everything seemed to slow. Her leg moved at a crawl, or so it seemed to me. It moved slow enough that I was able to grab onto her ankle with my other hand, halting her blow.

There we were, my wrist in her hand and her ankle in my other hand. She hopped on one foot, trying to reposition herself.

I smiled triumphantly. "Got yo..."

My words were cut short as she let go of my wrist and, taking a big hop, swung her *other* leg around to wrap around my neck. Her weight, now on my neck and in my hand, hit me in that moment but I continued to hold on to her ankle. Her weight seemed more insignificant than I would have thought.

But then the blows landed, for her leg around my neck had given her a height advantage, and she was making the most of it. She slapped the top, front and back of my head with both hands, causing me to wince and release her ankle, then fall forward as she fell backward on purpose, dragging my head toward the floor.

I smelled sweaty synthetic fabric as my chin met the mat with her leg still around my neck.

"Do you submit?" she asked.

I thought about pushing up, trying to buck her off like a bronco. Or reaching up and grabbing her, but I realized I'd lost. If she'd had a knife or a pistol, it would have been over for me.

"Yes." I sighed with resignation as she unwrapped her leg from around my neck and came to a standing position once more.

"That wasn't bad," she commented. "You're learning."

I blinked, as much caught off guard by her comment than if she'd punched me in the gut. "Uh, thanks?"

"Now let's try with weapons," Eleanor said, pointing toward my guards. "The electro-staffs."

"Oh," Phillip said, moving aside and grabbing two staves, then tossing them to us. "This oughta be fun."

"Set them on the lowest setting," Terrence cautioned, arms crossed.

"Yes, father," Eleanor said. "Taking all the fun out of this."

"Her father would not be pleased if his daughter were electrocuted on her second day in our care," he replied.

His subordinate shrugged. "He might understand if we told him it was during training."

"Lowest setting," Terrence reiterated. "That's an order."

Eleanor gave a half-hearted two-finger salute and hefted her staff. "You ready?" she asked, looking over at me.

I lifted the staff, its weight feeling unfamiliar to me. I'd never even played with *wooden* staves as a kid, let alone electro-staffs. "How do I...oh," I said, the charged end, consisting of two metal rods flanking a central spike, spinning to life and throwing off electrical sparks as I found the on button. The opposite end of the staff boasted a wide butt but no spikes or damage-inflicting elements from what I could see.

"That's the one-sided variant," Phillip called.

"There's a two-sided kind?" I asked, skeptical.

"You betcha. You don't want to slam *that* into a metal deck by your feet. Trust me."

"You speak from experience," I said.

"That may or may not have happened to me," he said.

I chuckled, his levity welcome. "Good to know." I wiped the grin off my face and focused on tactics I could use with the staff. I could use it like a spear, seeking to stab her with the shocking end. Or I could swing it like a halberd, basically an axe attached to a spear handle, like I'd seen in the classic holos. I could throw it like a javelin, too, if I wanted to risk her swiping it out of mid-air and having *two* of the weapons. No, nix that idea.

Eleanor, sensing my hesitation, decided to show off and her skills by spinning her staff, causing it to form what appeared to be a seamless glowing circle of blueish white light, framing her. It was like looking at a person standing behind a spinning fan. She strode toward me, staff continuing its spin unabated.

When she was a few feet from me, I thrust with my own staff, hoping to break the rotation of her staff and throw her off guard. Like if you stuck a knife into a fan while it was spinning.

Unfortunately, when I thrust, she was ready. The rotation stopped immediately, and she held the haft of the staff up to catch my staff head between the central post and one of the spinning rods. The rods protested, as their motion was arrested, and sparks flew as electricity arced between the rods and the staff haft. How she was not electrocuted was beyond me. Granted, the staves were on the lowest setting.

I pushed with my staff, hoping to overwhelm her with my strength.

She let go of the staff with one hand, letting her staff swivel in her hand. Faced with the lack of counter-pressure, I stumbled forward. Before I could turn, I felt a poke on my back and my muscles seized as a low current surged through my body. My knees buckled and I slumped to the floor, staff still clutched in hands that couldn't let go.

The poking sensation on my back ceased and the current running through my body went with it. "And you're dead," Eleanor said in what I considered a smug tone. "Or would be soon enough, once you're incapacitated."

"Ugh," I said, waiting for the sensation to pass so I could regain control of my muscles. Surprisingly, it happened quicker than I thought. Maybe it had to do with the nanites they'd injected into me. Moments later I was standing up again, even if I leaned against my staff for support. "I'm up, I'm ready. Let's keep going."

A slow clapping from my right caught my attention. I turned to look and found Isabelle there.

She wore a tight-fitting black synth suit with a utility belt around her waist. A pair of long daggers and two full holsters hung from it, along with a variety of pouches. "Bravo," she said with a smirk. "Good try."

I felt embarrassed that my friend had to see me fail so badly, but then I remembered she was more than my friend. She was my cousin, and a secret agent. That would be like a child being embarrassed at being dropped in front of a trained soldier while playing with toy swords. "Thanks," I said. "Just trying to get some self-defense pointers."

She nodded slowly. "Well, to start you need to learn your limits. You have speed and strength beyond normal humans, but you're not using it."

"I did use it," I protested. "Earlier."

"Well, you're not using it to your fullest extent," my cousin shot back. "You need to know how far your body can go before you get into a situation where you'll need it to."

"You mean like combat?" I asked. "I don't plan on being in combat any time soon."

"Sometimes combat finds you," Isabelle said cryptically.

"That should be on a poster," Phillip called from where he stood with the other guards.

"Shut up," Isabelle and I said at once. Just like old times, when we told Nelson to shut up when he'd try to say pithy things in class. It made me smile. Just like old times. Perhaps the only thing that *was* still like old times.

"As I was saying, sometimes you can't avoid situations where you might need to know how to fight, how to truly fight."

"I'm going to school to be a nurse," I pointed out. "I doubt I'll see much combat in a hospital."

"You should consider joining the military," she said bluntly.

I shook my head vehemently. "No, that's not my place. I want to help people."

"Hey," Phillip protested. "We help people."

"As do I," Isabelle said, eyebrow raised.

"I didn't mean it that way. I don't want to hurt some while protecting others."

"We usually hurt the bad guys," Isabelle pointed out.

"I know, but still," I said, not willing to contemplate joining the military. "It's just not right for me." I neglected to mention the real reason why it wasn't right - that I feared dying like my mother. That

I was angry at the Federation for taking my mother from me and leaving me believing my father was someone he wasn't.

"Well, if you ever change your mind, they'll be happy to have you. In the meantime, let's give you some more practice. First, let's test your agility."

Without warning, Isabelle withdrew a knife from her belt in one smooth motion and tossed it toward me.

Time seemed to slow as the knife pierced the air. Then, when it was a foot from my face, I snatched it out of the air, blade in my hand. "Ow," I said, dropping the knife and looking at the blood dripping from the wound I'd gained grabbing the knife. But as I watched, the wound healed, leaving drying blood on my palm.

"You should grab it by the hilt," Isabelle said.

I rolled my eyes. "Thanks, next time I'll use my super-human speed to grab a different part of the knife."

"Yes, you will," she replied. Then she snapped her fingers and pointed toward my three guards still in armor. Eleanor had rejoined them but had yet to armor up again. "You three, charge her and dog pile."

"Us?" Terrence asked.

"With our armor on?" Phillip asked.

"Yes, you three, and yes, with your armor on. Don't worry, she has super strength."

I groaned. If this was what she called practice, what would she call real training for the military? A stampede? Bullets instead of knives?

"Get going," Isabelle prompted.

"Sorry, kid," Terrence said. He charged forward, the other two following.

I braced myself, throwing one leg behind me and thrusting my arms out in front of me, as if I could block the three armored Shadow

Watch Guards barreling toward me, albeit in slower motion due to my enhanced reflexes.

Terrence was the first to hit, tucking his shoulder and ducking beneath my outstretched arms. The impact lifted me off my feet and moments later I lay on my back, the breath slammed out of me. Then Phillip and Delenn joined in the dog pile. I felt like a thousand pounds lay on top of me. Despite that, it didn't feel as heavy as it should have. I remembered one time when a football player slammed into me and fell on top of me, and that had been a scrawny one. It had felt far worse than this.

"Now push them off," Isabelle instructed, though it sounded muffled beneath the bodies of my faux attackers.

Gathering my strength, I placed my hands on Terrence's chest plate and pushed, grunting. At first, nothing happened. But then, Terrence, and Phillip, and Delenn, lifted. By the time my arms were fully extended, Delenn had fallen to the side and Phillip had stood.

I bent my arms again and then *pushed* with all my strength. Terrence flew toward the ceiling of the gym and slammed into it. Then, nothing holding him up, he plummeted back to the deck, landing on his stomach. He emitted a loud groan.

I covered my gaping mouth with a hand and gasped. "Terrence! I'm so sorry!" I ran to where he lay and grabbed his hand.

"Careful, darlin'," Phillip cautioned. "Wouldn't want to crush his fingers."

A slap against what sounded like armor came from behind, followed by an "ow" from Philip. Likely one of the ladies had slapped his helmet.

I ignored him. "Squeeze my hand if you can hear me," I said.

Terrence squeezed my hand. "You've got some strength there, kid," he wheezed. "Good thing you weren't trying to kill me." He let out a hoarse, sick chuckle.

I joined in, laughing louder than I should have, considering I probably broke a rib or two of my lead protector.

"See?" Isabelle said, not having moved from where she stood, arms crossed. "You have speed and strength greater than you know."

"Yeah, and I almost killed a man."

"Pfft, his armor absorbed most of the blow, didn't it, Terrence? Nano-armor is flexible, whereas Marine armor would have cracked."

"Yes, ma'am," Terrence replied, rising but holding a hand to his ribs. "Just might need to visit the med center."

"Might as well move in there," Phillip chimed in, walking over to put an arm around his squad leader. "You okay alone, Delenn and Eleanor?" he asked.

"Yeah. And I have Isabelle here too," I said. She could hold off an army.

"We'll be back quick as a whistle," Phillip said, leading Terrence out.

"We'll give you two some privacy," Eleanor said, leading Delenn toward the transport doors to stand watch.

I turned to Isabelle. "So..."

Isabelle held her hand up to forestall me, a distant look in her eyes. A moment later her eyes re-focused on me. "I have good news. Great news, actually."

"What?" I asked.

"My father came through. The anti-virus or cure or whatever they call it worked."

My eyes widened. "They're cured? All of them?"

"For the most part," Isabelle replied. "Some died from the cure, the rest are unconscious and we're waiting to see if they wake up. The few that have appear to be back to normal."

"Well, that's great news," I said. "Maybe our planet can finally get back to normal."

"It'll be years before the planet is back to normal," Isabelle cautioned.

"So, I'll probably have to go elsewhere to finish school?" I asked.

"Most likely," Isabelle said.

"But you don't need to finish, obviously," I said.

"Correct. I did my schooling at the Tower two thousand years ago."

"I guess I'll be on my own, then. Kimberly's off to what, train with you?"

"There's not much choice there," Isabelle said. "She's famous enough that even with a new identity someone could identify her, and her life would be in danger. Just like I trained you to defend yourself, I'll train Kimberly to fight for herself."

"Will I see you guys again soon?"

"We'll be around," she replied, cryptically. "And now, I should be going. Time to start to hunt for the monsters who created and unleashed this plague upon the galaxy."

"Safe travels," I said.

"You too. Don't get too bored with school and living the high life."

I snorted. "Thanks for the pep talk."

Isabelle smiled. "Any time." She faded to shadowy mist and was gone.

Chapter 10

The first day of school. Well, the first day back to school. Three weeks had passed since I awoke as an undead super human. Three weeks of watching as Galatia IV slowly came back to life, with the people starting to rebuild their lives. Three weeks of watching mass burials of those who hadn't made it, either because they'd been eaten by the infected, been shot by the Marines or killed permanently in some other way.

The fleet had dispersed, and things started calming down. Then my father asked me where I wanted to go to school. He'd offered private school, with tutors coming to me. Yet life on the *Nightblade* was boring, even with Orin to speak to. I chose Gerald Raverdeen High School on Xaros III, one of the designated refugee planets chosen for those affected by the disaster on Galatia IV. It was rated highly from the research I'd done.

I was looking forward to continuing my senior year, I really was. But the bigots had other plans.

I showed up at school that morning in my nondescript speeder. I had insisted to my father, in no uncertain terms, that I did *not* want my identity as his daughter being known. He had agreed, reluctantly, and even told my guards to back off after I pointed out how suspicious it would look to have four Shadow Watch Guards dropping me off or hanging out waiting for me all day. I was alone at last.

That may have been a bad choice on my part.

A crowd had gathered, but until I got out of my speeder, I didn't know why and assumed they were there to wish their children well for their first day. Nope. They were there to protest the undead. Me. How do I know? The signs telling the dead to go to Hell or go frack themselves gave it away quickly.

Police officers held the crowd back, leaving a small pathway that the normal students walked up on their way into the high school. The students gawked at the gathering but there was no fear in their stances as they ascended the stairs and passed a cordon before entering the school. At closer scrutiny I recognized the cordon as part of a National Guard perimeter around the school. Someone was serious about security.

I wasn't the only undead starting at Gerald Raverdeen High School that day, either. A group of nervous-looking students stood huddled to one side, looking dejected. The difference was they had their parents with them, and those parents were ushering their wards back to their vehicles. They weren't eager for a confrontation.

I opened my mouth to shout to my fellow undead, but snapped it shut. They wouldn't hear me, and they were the ones doing the smart thing. I turned, preparing to leave myself.

"Rachel?" A male voice said from behind me, half question, half recognition.

I spun around, feeling momentarily dizzy from doing a three-sixty in less than as many milliseconds. "Orin?" I smiled despite the situation. A friendly face, at last. "I didn't know you were enrolled here."

He shrugged. "You mentioned it in a text, and I wasn't committed anywhere else, so I figured I'd enroll where I would have a friend around." He gazed at the hate-filled crowd being held back by police. "I don't know that it will matter, now."

"There were more," I said. "They took off."

"Yeah, I was with them. I tried to convince them to stay, but they were scared."

"Why aren't you scared?"

He shrugged. "Not much left to live for. They've got families." He waved his hands to illustrate the now-fleeing students and their families. "I don't have someone who will miss me."

"I'll miss you," I blurted before I could let rational thought stop me. I would have blushed if I wasn't pale as an albino horse. I cleared my throat. "I mean, you don't think we'll die today, do you?"

"I certainly hope not. Your guards aren't around by any chance, are they?"

"I don't want them around," I said sternly. "You have no idea how much of a fight I had to convince my father to have them keep their distance."

"It might have been a mistake," he pointed out in a matter-of-fact tone.

I straightened my back and faced the sidewalk head on. "No, it wasn't. I've got to prove I can stand on my own two feet. Besides, they're not going to do anything more than spew hateful words. The police and National Guard will keep us safe."

"I hope you're right," Orin said ominously. He held out his hand. "Shall we?"

I smiled for the second time since seeing him. "Through the valley of death."

"Ironic."

"I know." I started walking and he matched steps with me.

At first, the crowd didn't notice us. They kept shouting aimlessly about how the dead should have all sorts of awful things done to them or, more tamely, go home. But it was inevitable that someone would notice us. And they did, when we were about halfway to the stairs.

"There's two of 'em!" a shrill voice rang out, somehow cutting through the din. "There's two of them undead!"

I continued forward, not daring to look around for fear my knees would turn to jelly or I would turn tail and run. *Don't be afraid, don't be afraid,* I chanted mentally. I jerked to a halt and shuddered as a hand touched mine before I realized it was Orin.

"Sorry," he mumbled, smiling down at me. "Do you mind?"

Another time, another place, I would have smiled sweetly, maybe even shyly, while taking his hand. Here though, I grabbed the proffered hand and held on as if I were drowning and he was the only person who could pull me out of the water. Only this was a sea of hate. Steeling my nerves again, I started forward, friend at my side.

We had gone another ten paces when something hit the back of my head. Something warm and slimy. "Ugh," I grunted, touching the point of impact and bringing my hand back in front of my face to view the results. A red fruit of some sort sat dripping in my hand, mocking me as its remnants slithered down my back.

"Scum!" a voice cut through the air.

"Go home!" another voice came.

"We don't want you here!" a third came.

"You should have stayed dead!"

"Death to the undead!"

The voices continued, becoming a torrent I struggled to ignore. I let go of Orin's hand and raised my hands, preparing to cover my ears, before stopping myself. "No, I won't let them win," I muttered. I wouldn't give them the satisfaction of showing weakness. Sticks and steel could break my bones, but words could never hurt me went the childhood rhyme on my world. Oh how wrong that rhyme was.

I shook my hand to rid it of the red fruit but chose not to share the remnants with Orin. Instead, I clenched my fists, the only outward sign I would allow of my stress and continued. "Let's go.

We'll be safe beyond the cordon." I continued on, though we'd only made it a short way.

Emboldened by the first thrown fruit, more followed. Fruits and vegetables flew through the air and slammed into the ground around us and onto our bodies. A moment later I felt sharp jabs of pain. I looked down to see rocks littering the ground. They were throwing rocks at us? The police would stop them, I was sure of it. Boy was I wrong.

The torrent of rocks did the exact opposite of slowing down. They accelerated and soon the rock storm became a rock hurricane, with dust rising from the points of impact, obscuring my vision and causing me to cough and my eyes to water. Our progress halted again as I pulled my shirt up to block the dust. I mean, I was undead so it shouldn't have affected me, but it did. Orin too, by the look of his tear-filled eyes.

"Tear gas," he shouted with a gasp before hiding his mouth and nose again behind the fabric of his shirt. For all the good it would do.

I realized too late that the smoke rising from the rocks was indeed a gas, for my eyes went from watering to burning. I looked to the side, expecting to see the police turning to push the protesters back. Instead I found the police pointing their gas launchers toward *me*. "No!" I shouted. I wasn't the bad guy!

They paid me no mind, and another volley of gas canisters soared through the air. The growing haze forced me to struggle to see the hate-filled crowd, though I could still hear them. That didn't last long, though, for the sounds of my surroundings were quickly being quashed by the sound of blood pounding in my ears. I was panicking.

Through the tear-inducing mist I saw the police line part, not break, part like gates opening, and the crowd flood through. Their target? Orin and I.

My nose and mouth still in my shirt, I tried to cover my head as more projectiles slammed into me. The gas began drifting away, blowing in the wind, but the view it left filled me with terror.

Protesters had us surrounded. Their shouts filled my ears and disoriented me, leaving me staring at the swarm like a deer witnessing a herd of hunters charging it would. For a moment we stood in the eye of a hurricane of flesh, for all the projectiles stopped and only the shouting remained, like wind in the eye. It didn't last, though, as the first protester took a step forward.

He was a big man, towering above even Orin, who wasn't short by any means. But where Orin was twig-thin, this man was enormous. His muscles bulged as he cracked his knuckles. "Not so tough now, undead, are you?" He sneered and the crowd cheered at his comments.

"We don't want any trouble," I shouted over the crowd. My vision had cleared somewhat, likely aided by the virus in my blood, or the nanites that had healed me, but I still squinted as the man had the early morning sun behind him.

"You asked for trouble the minute you stepped on this path," he said gruffly. He gestured and several other men, and even a few women I might have mistook for men, stepped forward. "We're here to teach your kind a lesson they'll never forget."

Part of me wanted to run. To cower in fear and beg for mercy. I wanted to bargain, to tell them if they let us go I would pay them. I wanted to throw my father's name around. One sentence naming Dawyn Darklance as my father and the crowd would part. But something held my tongue. Fear? Pride? Even to this day I don't rightly know. In that moment I felt only a white-hot rage boiling up. "We. Won't. Back. Down," I said, biting out each word. I felt Orin take my hand again, a silent show of solidarity.

The man's sneer turned into an evil grin, like the devil made flesh. "Just the way I like it. Let's get 'em, boys!" He suited action to words and advanced.

Before I knew what happened, a fist slammed into the back of my head, jerking me forward and dragging Orin with me. I let go of his hand a moment later but before I could turn to face my attacker, the man who had done all the talking was upon me. He made to punch me. I lifted my arms to block, remembering my brief training session aboard the *Nightblade*, but he kicked me in the stomach. While I doubled over, he kneed me in the face, causing a spike of pain and a sickening crunch sound.

I lost track of Orin in the fighting, though I heard him shout "leave her alone" over the din.

The protesters, my enemies, now, were laughing as I was punched again, this time in my kidney, and cried out in pain. "Please," I pleaded through tears as blood streamed from my nose and dribbled into my mouth. I could fight, but no, that would make it worse. The memory of me sending Terrence toward the ceiling flashed in my mind. I didn't want to hurt them.

"Look at her blood!" one of my foes shouted. "It's green!"

"Freak!" another said.

I had no time to dwell on what color my blood was. I was fighting for my life. I opened my mouth, intending to shout out my identity. I reeled backward as a fist slammed into my mouth as soon as I straightened.

In that moment, I heard a roar of primal fury. I tried to turn my head, but it hurt too much. As I turned my body and I saw Orin holding one of the big men by the throat. His red eyes flicked to me and I felt a moment of fear mixed with awe. He'd gone feral. Some of the newly-cured had done similar in the weeks since the mass curing of Galatia IV.

The big man squirmed in the grasp of my undead friend, but to no avail. He pounded at Orin's arms and tried to kick, but Orin may as well have been a statue.

A statue that snapped the man's neck a moment later. He then tossed the corpse into the protesters and lunged toward the ones surrounding me.

For their part, the remaining men backed away, some stumbling over those behind them and falling to the ground. One such unlucky soul became Orin's next victim as he leapt on them and tore out their throat with his teeth.

"Put him down!" one voice shouted, then was taken up by the crowd moments later.

A bang resounded and Orin's head exploded, teeth and green blood plus pieces of skull and brain matter flying out.

"Orin!" I screamed, lunging toward my now truly dead friend. But before I could reach him, I felt an impact in my stomach and found myself flying through the air. Someone had kicked me. I lay there, crumpled and bleeding, feeling like I was dying all over again. I tried to rise, but a blow to my back slammed me back into the ground and my chin hit the concrete. At the same time, I lost all feeling in my legs.

Panic settled in then as I struggled to comprehend my lower body being paralyzed. Anger rose up, too, and for a long moment I felt as though I would lose control like Orin had. *Must keep it together*, I thought, knowing that staying calm was the only thing that might possibly keep me alive.

Activating emergency repair protocol, a voice in my head said, cutting through the din around me. *Sending emergency Code Indigo to all available resources,* it went on.

"What?" I tried to say, though I must admit it came out more like a moan than actual words. I hadn't heard a voice in my head before.

The voice in my head didn't answer me. Then it dawned on me. It was the voice of my implant. They had installed one after my run in with the virus but had neglected to tell me how it functioned. *You're my implant?* I asked, this time in my thoughts. Even my thoughts sounded weak. I felt my will to live fading.

Correct. My designation is IM-8-LNT, but you may name me whatever you choose.

I'm not exactly in a position to be naming you right now, I thought back. *What is a code indigo?*

Before my implant could answer, however, a boot descended toward my head and, after a violent burst of pain, my world went dark.

Chapter 11

An alarm blaring awoke Captain Wilson. "General quarters, general quarters," came a muffled mechanical tone over the loudspeaker from the squad's ready room.

He rolled out of his bunk and activated his comm. A message request waited for him. "Captain Wilson here."

"Captain, this is the tactical commander. Please prepare your rangers for emergency orbital drop."

Captain Caleb Wilson's brows furrowed. "Emergency drop? Aren't we still in orbit around Xaros III?"

"Correct. There has been a Code Indigo issued. Tac Comm out." The link closed before he could respond.

"Shit!" He swore, leaving his quarters and joining the rest of his team in the ready room.

"What's up, Cap?" Lieutenant Vranson asked.

"Code Indigo," he replied.

"What's that?" The question came from Private Derikson, the rookie of the squad.

"High level target in imminent danger," Captain Wilson explained as he activated his synth suit and went to his locker, opened it and began gearing up. "We drop as soon as the ship breaches atmosphere."

As if waiting for his announcement, the tactical commander's voice filled the ready room. "All crew prepare for atmospheric drop in ten." A heartbeat later... "Ten, nine, eight..."

The room shuddered, almost throwing the rookie off his feet, as the *Solace* made its descent into atmosphere. They'd trained for this scenario countless times, and deployed in such ways several dozen times, but it felt strange to be deploying on a Federation world and have it not be a drill. *Like a damn invasion*, he thought.

"Let's get to the pods. Move it people!" Captain Wilson reminded his rangers.

They descended faster than usual, Captain Wilson noted. Under normal circumstances the ship would have taken several minutes to stow cargo properly and prepare. But under such emergency circumstances Caleb knew only the essential procedures to prevent loss of life would have been followed.

He made his way to the pods, fully geared now, rifle in hand, and entered his designated pod. The other four rangers were already there, strapped in and waiting. They nodded to him and he returned the acknowledgment. It felt strange being with a new squad. But after the garrison on Galatia IV fell to the infected, and he almost died after becoming infected himself, he was lucky to have been returned to his former rank and given his commission back. Hell, he would have died aboard the *Cheville* if not for Isabelle Thorpe saving him. Still, his squad mates were inferior to him. They didn't have his *power*. They hadn't survived death. He knew that was why the Federation had kept him around - because of what he could do. Or perhaps they were afraid of him. They had reason to be.

Less than a minute later the light outside in the hangar turned red and the pod door closed. Their pod was picked up and shuttled to the launch chute. Then, seconds later a *thump* came from beneath the pod and the g-forces shoved him back into his seat as they plummeted toward the planet below. The planet's gravity had them, so they did not float weightless, which was one of the reasons for launching from atmosphere instead of orbit - they didn't have to deal with as strenuous of a re-entry procedure. There were cases where orbital drop ship launches were required, such as in a war zone where it was unsafe to descend, but standard operating procedure called for them to descend to atmosphere first.

As they hurtled toward the planet at high speed, the external sensor array displayed a view of the ground and a zoomed-in view of their landing area. A massive crowd of people had gathered around what looked like a school. Their LZ was a rooftop near the square, while their target was obscured by a mass of people. Refuse of assorted colors of green, red and yellow littered the ground. Captain Wilson only hoped they wouldn't be too late for whoever it was. If they warranted this level of response, they must be extremely vital to the Federation.

Chapter 12

I awoke some time later, though I didn't know how long, to find the same horrific sight greeting me. Angry-looking men and women staring down at me. I still couldn't feel my legs, and although the pain had subsided a little it hurt to breathe. *I wish I knew how to stop my body from wanting to breathe*, I thought. I didn't need to breathe, but how to get my body to stop doing something I'd been doing since birth?

Something caught my eye in that moment as I blinked against the morning light. A large object in the blue sky. Now, I was no stranger to air ships and starships and the like, but this was unusual enough that even in my disoriented state I noticed. It wasn't a small star yacht or star fighter. No, this was a warship. A cruiser, if I had to guess, and it had descended into atmosphere. I knew nothing about military protocol, but the sight kindled a tiny, insignificant hope in me. My implant had said it sent out a signal. Could the ship in orbit have heard, and cared?

The angry mob, having finally noticed I was awake, started kicking me again. One man pointed his pistol at my face. "Go ahead, bitch, turn feral and we'll put you down like the animal you are. I dare you."

I flinched away from the gun but couldn't even scurry backward to avoid my assailants. On top of that, a part of me *wanted* to rage out and chew on people's legs or, better yet, rip out their throats. But the rational part of me knew that would be suicide, even if I *could* feel my legs. I had to stay calm if I wanted any hope, no matter how slim, of surviving.

Another barrage of blows came, almost pushing me over the edge. The pain to my upper body worsened. My implant screamed warnings at me about nanites being deployed to heal me, yet clearly the nanites were being overwhelmed by the damage to my body. I'd been told that being undead meant the virus healed me rapidly - well, not that rapidly, apparently. The nanites and virus were overwhelmed.

I felt blackness again closing in on me when a *thump* sounded in the distance and reverberated through the ground. Another followed, and then another and another and another. On and on the thumps came, throwing up dust from atop a building in my line of sight. I lost track of how many but could now see ships flying overhead as well. Starfighters, this time, silhouetted against the now ever-present warship maintaining its orbit.

The crowd had noticed the thumps and aerial activity too by this time, giving me a welcome respite from the constant pain and allowing my virus and nanite-laden blood to affect at least a few repairs before they noticed me again.

And notice me they did. "Shoot her and let's get out of here," one of the men said to the man holding the gun pointed at my head.

That man hesitated but then something seemed to click inside his head, and he focused it rock-steady on me. His finger went to the trigger.

I refused to back down. I stared straight into the man's eyes, daring him to do it. If I had been confident of my voice I would have shouted at him to do it, but it probably would have come out as a squeak or a whimper. Instead I braced myself for dying a second time - this time for good.

A shot rang out, but not from my assailant's gun. The bullet struck flesh, but not my flesh. Instead it struck the gunman's hand, ripping it off and striking one of the on-lookers in the stomach. The gun intended for me toppled to the ground. All this happened in a flash, then the screams started as people looked around for the source of the bullet.

The source made itself known an instant later as four black-armored figures hurtled through the air and landed with powerful thuds around me. Each carried a rifle and they took up stations in the four cardinal directions around me, guns pointed at the crowd instead of me, for once. "Back up!" A mechanically-amplified voice bellowed. Terrence's voice. Hope surged in me and tears sprung up.

"Or you can charge us. I'd like a good fight," Phillip quipped even as he lunged toward two protesters who hadn't moved fast enough. They stumbled back, with one falling as they did.

"You're all right now, hun," Delenn's voice came from behind me. "Medevac is en-route and so are the rangers." She leaned over and pressed a cylinder to my thigh. A hiss indicated medication being injected.

Support nanites detected, announced my implant.

As for the rangers, I kept my eyes on the building I'd seen dust rising from and watched as dozens of figures leapt off the top of the four-story building and landed on the concrete below, becoming lost in the crowd.

"I'm sorry," I said, my first time speaking since my protectors arrived. "I should have let you come." As expected, my voice came out as a sickly croak. But the words had to be said. I was feeling better already, and I wiggled my toes. "I can feel my legs," I announced.

"Good," Terrence said, not taking his eyes off the crowd. "As soon as we get a stretcher we'll get you to a transport."

The crowd, startled at first by the appearance of four Shadow Watch Guards, were emboldened by the chaos. Several of the men threw rocks at the armored figures, though it wasn't clear if their target was me or my guards. A few more charged forward, some wielding make-shift clubs. They were rebuffed with fists to the face or gut, which I knew was showing restraint.

A disturbance among the throngs of people caught my eye. Moments later a stream of armored rangers passed through a forced opening and started to spread out, shoving rioters back.

"Form a perimeter!" Terrence ordered, voice still amplified. "Protect target Indigo at all costs."

"Target Indigo," I mumbled. "That's what my implant sent."

"Yes. Code Indigo is reserved for Eternals and their kin," Terrence explained. "There's no higher alert - not even for the president of the Federation."

"Wow. That makes me feel like an even bigger fool," I said. "All this attention for me."

"You almost died," he scolded me. "Your implant sent your vitals along."

"I'm already dead," I pointed out.

"She's got you there, Chief," Phillip said.

"She's *un*dead," Delenn scolded.

"Tomato, tomahto," Phillip said, stressing different vowels in his words.

The rangers finished establishing a perimeter before we'd even finished talking. The protesters, intimidated by more than four soldiers, started to disperse, though many still shouted hateful words as they went.

A second ruckus in the crowd revealed a medivac team breaking through and racing toward us.

"Here's your ride, princess," Phillip said. "You think you can walk?"

I nodded and took his hand when he offered it. Standing wobbly to my feet, I turned to look at the school. Despite the police and protesters retreating, the national guardsmen hadn't budged. If anything, they made the school look more imposing.

Bracing myself, I pointed to the school. "I need to go there first."

"What?" Phillip asked, startled.

"Have you lost your mind," Terrence said. "You *need* medical attention."

I turned to face the squad leader. "And I'll get it. But not yet. I need to walk up those stairs."

"Why?" he asked, point blank. He hadn't said no yet.

"It's important. If I back down now the bigots and haters win. But," I held up a finger, "if I walk up those steps I show them that *I* ultimately won, not hate."

"This isn't the time for symbolism," Terrence growled.

"I think it's noble," Eleanor said, shrugging.

"I'll have you four, and the rangers, the entire time. No one will hurt me."

"You bet they won't," Phillip said.

Terrence was silent for a long moment, looking around at the assembled rangers and at the medivac team and the ships still swarming overhead. News media had arrived too, with their recording drones filling the sky. Even now he was likely on camera. "Fine," he said, relenting. "But you don't leave our sight for even a second, you understand?"

"Yes," I said, putting as much innocence into my voice as I could.

"And if things get too hot you listen and obey when I tell you to evac, yes?"

"Of course."

He walked away to talk to the medical team, clearly telling them to wait in the wings until I'd accomplished my mission. When he returned he pointed toward the stairs. "Eleanor and Philip, take point." He looked straight at me, helmet down-turned to face me. "Don't make me regret this."

"I won't," I promised. Then, turning and throwing my shoulders back, in addition to wincing and almost doubling over when my ribs protested with twinges of pain, I walked through the line of encircling rangers and toward the stairs.

If the national guardsmen were nervous they didn't show it. They maintained their blockade of the school I intended to enroll at.

I reached the foot of the stairs and looked behind me. The rangers had fallen in to form a corridor on either side of the sidewalk, with the medical team not far behind me. While most of the protesters had departed, several hundred remained off to the side, chanting behind a police barricade. It seemed the police would do their jobs when all eyes were on them.

Seven steps to reach the top. I took the first step, then the next, wincing at the momentary pain. But compared to what I'd just endured, this was nothing.

At last, I reached the top. My four guards stood behind me, while a straight-faced national guardsman stood in front of me, arms crossed. Six guards stood at his back. "I would like to pass," I said, resisting the urge to say something more aggressive, like "you're in my way" or "move."

"I'm sorry, we have our orders," the guard said, eyes dull. If he feared the Shadow Watch Guards and rangers at my back, he didn't show it. "You're not allowed into the building."

"By whose orders?" Terrence asked.

I held up my hand, forestalling him from speaking more. This was my fight. But he had a point. "Who ordered you here to keep me out?"

"The planetary governor," the guard replied.

"So, you won't leave until the governor calls you off?" I asked.

"Correct."

I thought furiously. We could fight, as I knew my guards and the rangers could handle the guardsmen handily, but that could turn into a bloodbath on live holo, something I didn't really want. I could turn and walk down the stairs into the custody of the waiting medics. But then the bigots would win. The crowd would cheer if I did that. I didn't want them to cheer. But what other option was there?

"May I speak to the headmaster?" I asked.

"One moment," the guard said. He pressed a finger to his ear, likely activating a comm, and moments passed as he stared toward the sky. "He's on his way. But don't try anything," he warned.

"That goes double for you boys," Terrence shot back. "Lay a hand on this girl and you'll have a war on your hands."

The lead guard didn't reply, nor did he look scared or impressed. "You don't have jurisdiction here, and you'll be gone soon enough."

"What's he talking about?" I asked, not turning my head as I scanned for the arrival of the headmaster.

"Federation forces have no law enforcement jurisdiction on Federation planets," Terrence explained. "It's to prevent the military from being used as police forces and to prevent vigilante justice when we're on shore leave. It's a check and balance."

"So, you're here illegally?"

"There's one exception to that rule," Terrence went on. "And this jerk may not be aware of it, so I'll spell it out. The law states that in the event of a Code Indigo emergency being declared, all Federation forces are automatically deputized in the system the emergency was declared. So, *friend*, we are here legally."

"We'll see," the lead guard said, though I thought I saw seeds of doubt sprouting in his eyes.

Sirens in the distance drew my attention. Police forces had arrived and set about forming a perimeter. Their SWAT officers formed a perimeter around the rangers, weapons faced *toward* them. Whoever was commanding the police forces was an idiot for escalating the conflict.

"Idiots," Terrence growled, echoing my thoughts. "They're just making it worse."

We stood in silence for several long moments before the door of the high school creaked open. A pot-bellied, shorter-than-average man with glasses stepped out and strode haughtily toward me. Four National Guardsmen followed him. He pushed his way through the guards in front of me and stepped up next to the lead Guardsman. "What is the meaning of this disturbance?" he sneered at me.

I swallowed a snarky retort, instead clearing my throat. "Well, the National Guard here won't let me into your school. Would you mind telling them to let me in?"

"Why would I ever do that?" the headmaster asked. "I'm the one who called for their assistance."

I had been expecting such a response. "Well, call the governor and tell him to call off his wolves."

"I will not do that."

"And why not?"

"Because your...*kind*...do not belong here."

I took a deep, calming breath. *Don't punch him, don't punch him,* I repeated internally. "Sir, I am alive, as alive as anyone else. I can think, and I have feelings. What makes me less than human?"

"The fact that you are *not* technically alive means you are not technically human. You are...something else...something sub-human," the headmaster explained.

I gaped, flabbergasted. This was the headmaster of a school, a supposedly educated man, and he believed I was less than human because of a circumstance beyond my control? "I respectfully disagree, and again request admittance to your school."

"Request denied," the headmaster replied immediately. "You have one minute to leave the premises or the National Guard will have no choice but to forcefully remove you."

"Over our dead bodies," Terrence growled.

The headmaster paid him no mind. "You can end this conflict."

The words reverberated in my head. If I just walked back down the steps, walked away, there would be no more chance of bloodshed. No more people would die, the hostilities would die down. *But then the bigots win*, my inner voice said. Which was true. They would proclaim victory from the rooftops. It would present a precedent whereby bigots could justify denying people like me services, entry to buildings and more, backed by the history of this day. "No," I declared. "I will not back down."

The headmaster glared daggers at me but shrugged. "Very well. Commander, remove her please."

"With pleasure," the commander said, motioning to me.

Four of the guards standing behind him approached, moving past the headmaster to stand in front of him and their commander.

My own guards stepped forward, forming a wall of flesh. "Back the frack down before you get hurt," Terrence said. Behind us, I could hear weapons being readied. I looked behind and found the rangers raising their weapons to point at the police forces facing off against them. What would it take to get them to back down?

The answer to that came a moment later as thunder boomed in the distance. Only it wasn't thunder. My eyes tracked skyward toward the cause.

There, descending through the clouds, supplementing the one already there, were a dozen or more ships of that size. Clouds of ships, looking like gnats from afar, swarmed toward the surface...toward me.

A shadowy cloud materialized behind the ranger lines, materializing into two people. The first looked remarkably like Isabelle, who, along with her ability to shift, suggested this was Bridgette Thorpe, Isabelle's mother and my aunt. For her part, she returned to shadowy mist and disappeared. Who knew where she was off to.

The other person was my father. I wasn't one to weep, I swear, but again tears formed in my eyes. He'd come for me.

The National Guards had stopped at the sound of thunder and stood tensed across from my guard detail. Uncertainty had finally caught up with them.

My father looked around, at the assembled rangers and the counter-acting police forces, then up at the National Guards and finally settling his eyes on me. He smiled and ascended the stairs, giving me a hug. "Rachel, I'm so glad you're all right."

"You have impeccable timing," I remarked. "Things were just about to blow up, possibly literally." I chuckled at my own grim humor.

"I came as quick as I could," he replied. "I brought the *Nightblade* and the rest of the fleet."

I pointed to the sky. "Yeah, it's pretty impressive."

"Now, who's in charge of the idiots keeping you from entering this school?"

"I'm glad everyone agrees they're idiots," I responded. "The headmaster is right there," I gestured over my shoulder with a thumb. "But the governor is the one who authorized them being sent out."

"Yes, the governor," he said, in a ponderous tone. "I'll be dealing with him later." He stepped past me and approached the National Guard line. "Headmaster?"

The plump man, barely visible behind the line of guards, spoke, "Who are you?"

If I'd been drinking something, I would have spit it out. I guess he hadn't seen who shifted in. Or maybe he'd missed the new ships in orbit. Either way, he was proving the idiot title fit.

"*I* am your worst nightmare," my father began. "I am Dawyn Darklance, supreme commander of the Federation, Sword of Justice and a dozen other titles I don't care to recite right now. What matters is an entire fleet is at my command in orbit and *you* facilitated the circumstances in which my daughter almost *died*. So, you will understand if I am angry." Despite saying he was angry, he'd said everything in a deadly cold tone that could have frozen fire and sent a chill up my spine despite the heat of the morning sun.

"I...I...didn't know," the headmaster stuttered, still hiding behind the guards. "Your daughter...I didn't...of course she can enter. Get out of the way!" he shouted, presumably at the National Guardsmen in front of him. "Let her through, let her through!"

The guards moved out of the way, with only their commander standing in the way. He looked from my father to me and back, face pale. It was as if he hadn't realized I was someone important before that point. He stepped back, turned crisply and marched away. He must have given a silent order to the remaining guards, for they fell in and soon the entire company forming a perimeter around the high school were marching away from the grounds.

With the guards gone, the headmaster stood there, alone.

I glared at him, the reality of what just happened crashing into me like a wave. *He* was the reason for the violent mob. It was *his* fault Orin died, senselessly. My hands balled into fists and red encroached on my vision. I let out a guttural growl. A vision flashed in my mind's eye of me lifting the headmaster up by the throat and crushing it.

A hand on my chest returned me to reality. "There's been enough blood shed today," my father said. He stepped in front of me and stared into my eyes. If he feared what I would do to him, he didn't show it. Then again, the history books said my father could slow or even stop time. If I *did* reach for him, he would just stop my motion and move out of the way. Probably. I hoped I would never find out which of us was faster.

I shook my head to clear it and held his gaze. "You're right."

"Now, if you're ready, I'll walk you into the school."

"No."

"No?" he asked, perplexed.

"I've decided I don't want to go in. There's been enough drama for one day, and there's no way the students and teachers will accept me after what just happened. And..." I looked back to the rangers forming a perimeter and the transports even now landing companies of Marines around the campus as the police retreated. "...I've decided I want to help people in a different way."

My father nodded slowly. "I take it you've decided to change your career choice."

"Are you upset?"

"If you're referring to joining the military then no, I'm not upset. In fact, I'm proud."

"I figured you'd want to keep me safe."

"Sweetheart, I do. But there comes a time when parents must let their children leave the nest. They have to admit their children are ready to face the world and then watch them fly away. In your case, I will quite literally watch you fly away in a shuttle."

I smiled. "Thanks for the vote of confidence in me." I cringed as my implant informed me the temporary injected nanites had run their course. Pain flooded me an instant later. It was less than before, thankfully, but still caused me to yelp in pain. "But I'd really like that med-evac right about now."

Chapter 13

I awoke an indeterminable time later and flinched at the bright white lights overhead while my mind struggled to banish my dreams and remember my past. "Can someone turn those down," I said aloud, pointing toward the ceiling.

The lights dimmed a few seconds later. "Glad to see you're awake." Terrence's voice. I turned and saw him, standing by the door. The other three members of his squad were present as well. None of them wore armor, instead wearing tight black synthetic fiber suits like what Isabelle wore.

"Is..." I stopped, my memories returning in a flood. *I was about to say Orin,* I realized with a wave of sadness. The boy who'd died protecting me. If not for him, I could have died before help arrived. "Is my father around?" I asked instead as I sat up and fussed with the hospital gown.

"He's still *talking* to the governor," Terrence said. "He said to notify him when you woke and he would return soon."

"I'd be doing a hell of a lot more than talking," Phillip put in. "I'd be kicking ass and taking names."

"And *that* is why he's the supreme commander and you're a grunt," Delenn pointed out. "There's a time for force and a time for diplomacy. Women know that, and some men do too."

"That's only because women are the weaker sex," Phillip replied. "They have no choice but to...oof..." he grunted as Delenn punched him in the gut. He found himself on the floor as Eleanor swept his legs out from under him.

"Wanna revisit that statement?" Delenn asked.

"That's not fair," Phillip mumbled. "It was two on one."

Delenn snorted. "Keep telling yourself that."

"Why aren't you wearing your armor?" I asked.

Terrence shrugged. "It gets uncomfortable, sometimes. Yes, it's more comfortable than rigid Marine armor, but it still traps heat and moisture. And, since there's no danger right now, we can afford to not be armored up."

"Yeah, it chafes," Phillip said as he rose to his feet, unaided by the women.

Not wanting to picture Phillip scratching himself, I changed the subject. "We're on the *Nightblade* again?" I asked.

"You got it," Terrence replied. "Don't you recognize it?"

I chuckled. "You got me there. I've spent more time in a hospital room in the last three weeks than I have in my entire life." I sobered. "Was there any more bloodshed after I evacuated? How long was I out?" The last thing I remembered was loading into the transport and being injected with a sedative they warned would knock me out. They'd explained I had to tell my implant to allow the sedation to proceed. Speaking of. *Are you there?*

Yes, miss, I am always at the ready. How may I assist you today?

Why did I only just hear from you when I was dying?

A failsafe, miss. I was dormant in your brain. However, emergency protocols dictate that in the event of life-threatening wounds, I activate the appropriate alerts.

How did you know I had life-threatening wounds? I'm dead.

There are still signs of life present in you. Your infected blood still pumps, only it does not require breathing, and hence no oxygen. The synapses still fire in your brain, and the pain receptors still activate in much the same way as they did when you were alive. There are many other signs if you'd like a comprehensive list.

No, that's all right. I hesitated, feeling awkward. *Thanks for saving my life.*

No thanks are necessary. I was doing what I am programmed to do.

"No, the police forces cleared out after your father's show of force and Federation personnel made their way back to the fleet a few minutes after you evacced. You've been out for a couple hours now."

Terrence's voice surprised me. I'd had a relatively lengthy conversation with my implant in the second or two before Terrence replied. Interesting.

"Orin," I began, clearing my throat and continuing. *Don't cry, don't cry.*

If you'd like, I can cease tear production and halt tear distribution temporarily, my implant offered.

Not right now, thanks, I said.

"...was his body recovered?"

Terrence nodded. "It was recovered, but we recommend a closed casket funeral. Your father was going to speak to you about making arrangements."

"He had no family," I said. "None living anyway."

"As the records indicated. You can bury him tomorrow, most likely."

I fell silent then, images of Orin filling my mind. Guilt welled up, choking me. If I hadn't gone down there, he wouldn't have walked with me. If he hadn't walked with me, he wouldn't have died defending me. *I* was the reason Orin was dead. Now tears did well up. *Let them fall,* I ordered my implant. *I still don't know your name,* I pointed out.

I did explain my designation is IM-8-LNT.

Yes, but I can't call you that. I need an easier name.

I am quite responsive. Even calling me "implant" is an acceptable input.

Well, I want a more human-sounding name. A name floated to the top of my consciousness. A name I'd heard in many holos growing up. *How about Jarvis?*

I am amenable to any name you assign. I do not have an opinion either way.

Tone down the enthusiasm. That's a joke, I hurried to add, before he actually turned down an enthusiasm setting. Not that I thought one existed, but just in case. *Fine, Jarvis it is.*

A fine name, miss.

Before I could ask my implant, Jarvis, any other questions, like what his full capabilities were, the door to the room slid open and my father entered. I smiled widely at him. "Hey."

"Hi, sweetheart," my father said. "How are you feeling?"

"Well, they said it's only been a few hours, but I'm not feeling *any* pain. The doctors must have given me some insane treatments."

"They did, actually," he replied. "I don't know all the details, as medicine always bored me, but from what I understand the amount of nanites they dumped into your system while you were sleeping would kill a normal person. It's only when a patient is sedated that that volume of nanites can be used."

I can confirm your father's words, Jarvis chimed in. *I counted ten billion one hundred million and...*

That's enough, Jarvis. I don't need an exact count.

Of course, miss. I'll return to standby mode until you require my assistance again.

Thanks. "Thank goodness for modern medicine," I said aloud.

"And thank goodness for your unique physiology," my father said. "Without the virus working together with the nanites natively in your blood since you were cured, you wouldn't have survived until help came." He clenched his fists. "Which reminds me. I had a nice *long* talk with the governor and made it clear, in no uncertain terms, that any mistreatment of the undead on his planet will have me knocking on his door to hold him personally accountable. I think I put the fear of God into him."

I chuckled. "Now to get the rest of the galaxy to fall into line. You can't believe it will only be one planet that is bigoted, can you?" My father wasn't *that* naive, was he?

"No, of course not. But we set an example today and drew a line in the sand. *You* set an example. The video of your actions today has already gone galactic and I've received messages from countless senators indicating their support for civil rights legislation protecting the rights of those infected by the virus. Change is coming."

"That's good," I said, sobering up as my thoughts turned darker. "Dad...do you ever feel guilty?"

"Guilty about what?"

"About people who died at your command, or under your command, or because of an action you took or a decision you made."

He nodded slowly. "I'm guessing this is about Orin. Am I right?"

I nodded. "Yes." It wasn't worth denying. "I'm feeling a lot of guilt right now over his death. I keep replaying it in my head, over and over, thinking about what I could have done differently."

Several long moments passed as my father studied the floor. "To answer your question, I did feel guilty, long ago. Can you guess when?"

He'd said long ago, so I guessed he didn't mean my mother. Further back? "No," I said at last, not trusting myself to elaborate and berate him for not saying he felt guilt over my mother's death. It hadn't technically been his fault, even indirectly, but still.

"Two thousand and some years ago, at the Battle of Pelinor Field. The woman I loved died, Anwyn, cut down by the Krai'kesh during their final assault on Tar Ebon."

I remembered the history lesson now. Anwyn had been a druid, but her powers were nullified by the Krai'kesh crystal and she'd died protecting my father. "That's when you went into a rage, isn't it?"

"Yes. The only time I can recall stopping time completely. I became so angry that my power exploded outward and all time, or as far as I could see, stopped. That momentary freezing of time allowed me the time, literally, to destroy the magic nullification crystal the Krai'kesh hauled along with them. Destroying that crystal allowed the mages of Tar Ebon, including your uncle Jason, along with John and Ashley, to finally use their magic to turn the tide of battle. Her one sacrificial act won the day."

"But you still felt guilty," I prompted.

"Yes. For years, centuries, I blamed myself. Intellectually I knew it wasn't my fault - her blood was on the hands of the Krai'kesh. But emotionally, I continued to ache."

"What changed?"

"I met your mother," he said, smiling wanly. "For centuries I'd avoided love, attachment and relationships. When I met your mother, I felt an irresistible pull. For the first time since Anwyn's death I didn't feel that twang of guilt when I looked at her. Then the impossible happened."

"What?" I asked. I hadn't heard this story before. Not surprising, considering my father had led a secret life right under my nose.

"I was on Icarus Station with you mother when, and I know it sounds insane, but I *saw* Anwyn."

My eyes widened. "You saw her?" He was right, it did sound insane. "Like a ghost or spirit or something?"

"No. In the flesh. I touched her. Hugged her. She was as real to me as you are."

"Did anyone else see her?" I asked, skepticism creeping in.

"No. I saw a flash out of the corner of my eye and there she was. I pointed to her, but your mother couldn't see her."

"Was it a hallucination?"

He shook his head. "No. It was real. Security footage afterward showed a distortion of some sort. But your uncle was able to filter it and it showed Anwyn, as clear as day."

"Wow," I said, impressed. "What did she say?"

"She didn't know she was deceased. To her, she had just fallen asleep in the tavern we were staying at on the way back up to Tar Ebon to fight the Krai'kesh."

"Wait. She time traveled or something?"

"Your uncle called it astral projecting. He said the druids told stories, which we always presumed were just myths, about projecting their consciousness forward or backward in time. Well, it seems it was true, in a sense."

"Did you tell her about her future?"

"Yes, I did. I realized it was foolish and that it could possibly change things, but I told her. Then she did something that reminded me why I fell in love with her all those years ago. She smiled that irresistible smile and told me she would willingly sacrifice herself if it meant saving the future Federation."

My mind reeled at the revelation. "When she died, she *knew* she was going to die?"

"In retrospect, I think she did." My father sighed. "Thinking back, I remember the morning after, when she awoke with night sweats and brushed off my concerns, claiming nightmares. She also wouldn't hear a word about not joining the fight. Of course, your uncle believes my memories were possibly altered by my interaction with her past-self but it doesn't matter now. I still couldn't save her, yet my guilt over her death was assuaged once and for all that day."

"Well, Orin isn't going to come back from the dead," I said. "How do I stop feeling guilty?"

"Focus on the good that came from his death," my father suggested. "Think about the calls for equality rising from across the

Federation. Even the Empire is denouncing the actions of the governor." He chuckled.

I joined in with his laughter. "You know it's morally bad when the Empire is denouncing it." I forced a smile. "Thanks, Dad, I'll try that."

"You'll be honoring his memory, also, by joining the military," he pointed out. "You can be part of a force responsible for protecting trillions of citizens."

"I guess you're right," I said, pushing aside thoughts of Orin for the moment. The grief wouldn't leave that easily, I knew, but my father's words would make the grief bearable in the days to come, I thought. "So, when do I join the military?"

Part Two

Chapter 14

Avylon II, the official military training planet of the Federation. I watched out the viewport from my seat as we neared it. It glowed in the light of its primary star, while the ships, shipyards and stations lay in orbit around it.

Two months since my "death," just over a month since my run-in with bigots on Xaros III and here I was, joining the Army.

I turned to my companion. "Thank you for coming with me."

Terrence, dressed in civilian clothes, not a synth suit or weapon in sight, smiled at me. "Of course." He handed me a chip. "Here's your ID card, Rachel Halbert," he spoke my new last name with deliberate emphasis. "It's loaded with a significant amount of credits."

I smirked. "They do say my father is one of the wealthiest in the Federation. It's the least he could do."

"Indeed. But remember to stick to your cover story."

I sighed. "Yes, my father is Decklin Halbert, the CEO of Elbion International, a multi-planetary shipping conglomerate headquartered on Galatia IV. My father was killed during the outbreak. I survived due to the brave action of Marines and want to give back by joining the Army." I recited the details of my cover by rote, after being grilled by my guards *and* three FIA agents, none of them Isabelle as she was on mission somewhere, to make sure no cracks appeared in the cover. I brushed away a lock of blond hair and touched my cheek. They'd given me a program for my implant which rearranged my face. I now looked like, in my opinion, an uglier version of myself, and a stranger on top of it. But I was assured the change would fool facial recognition, while ocular implants changed my retinas and nanites re-drew my fingerprints. Absolutely nothing remained to connect me to my former self until I chose to revert it.

"Good. Are you nervous about basic training?"

"Considering you've told me nothing about it...a little," I admitted.

He smiled devilishly. "That's the fun of it. You get to experience it *all*."

I rolled my eyes. Even Terrence was becoming more comfortable with me. In the months since the incident I'd become quite close with my guards. I felt a pang of regret that I was leaving them for a ten-week training program.

Twenty minutes later we were docked and passing through security. I considered holding my breath while passing through the scanners, but my fears were unfounded. The FIA had done their job well. Security didn't give me a second glance and didn't question my identity in the slightest.

Terrence passed through too, under the false identity of my rich Uncle Morris who'd inherited the business after my father's death. He was my father-figure surrogate if any duties required it. He would stay on-planet for the duration of the training, until my graduation, to make sure no true danger happened to me.

I'd been afraid that my guards would be punished after the debacle on Xaros III, but my father had been understanding. No one could have foreseen a horde of bigots waiting for me, and it didn't do me any good to be kept in a gilded cage, safe from all dangers.

"Well, kid, this is where we part ways," he said, eying the entrance for recruits before meeting my gaze. "Don't try to stand out, or the drill sergeants will find their new favorite person to pick on - you."

It was my turn to smirk. "Was that actual advice about what to expect?"

He grunted, a slight upturn to his lip the only sign he found my joke amusing. "Call it a freebie."

I hugged him, which surprised me and might have surprised him, for he delayed putting his arms around me to return the embrace for a couple heartbeats. "Thank you," I whispered while my head was next to his. "For everything."

"When you get done, you'll be saluting me," he said, changing the subject.

I chuckled. "Until I restore my identity."

"Yeah, I don't know what rank you'll hold then," he admitted.

"Supreme Daughter?"

"Undead in Chief," he said. "Maybe. I'll get Phillip thinking about titles for you."

"I can't wait," I said. Without a glance back, I passed through the gate leading to the recruit processing center.

THERE'S A SAYING IN the military - hurry up and wait. Well, I found out, the hard way, that motto is most definitely true. Over the next five hours I hurried from station to station where I waited. I endured poking and prodding for blood draws and physicals, interviews for mental stability and soundness of mind checks, citizenship and paperwork checks and more. Then of course I had to get my hair cut shorter. Not a buzz cut, not for girls, but still a lot shorter than I expected. Surprisingly, my being undead didn't even draw a raised eyebrow from the intake coordinators. Then I realized why: there were hundreds of undead there.

I'd missed it at first, but once I started looking for the signs, pale skin, lack of breath, enhanced agility and strength, and standing apart from the others, I found them quickly. *Well, that didn't take the Federation long to realize their potential as weapons. Who wouldn't want super soldiers with strength and speed and near unlimited stamina?*

After passing all the tests, I assembled with the rest of the recruits in the assembly hall. While we waited, I decided to try to talk to my fellow recruits.

One girl, standing in the corner, with tattoos, numerous piercings and a buzz cut, caught my eye. She looked to be around my age, and undead, judging by her super pale complexion. She watched me approach with a raised eyebrow.

"Hello," I said, more timidly than I wanted. I cleared my throat and tried again. "Hi." There, more confident.

"What do you want?" the girl said, sneering.

My confidence threatened to fail in that moment, but I forced a smile. "I'm Rachel. What's your name?"

"Get lost," she said.

"I...uh...noticed we're both undead," I continued, ignoring the opportunity to say "hi, get lost, nice to meet you," like I expected Phillip would do.

"Yeah, so?" her tone suggested I had pointed out the sun was yellow. Then again, not all suns were yellow, in the Federation. It was more like I'd said space was cold.

"Well, since we're stuck waiting here, I figured I'd talk with someone."

"There are hundreds of 'someones' here," she pointed out. "Go talk to one of them."

I almost turned to leave. Almost. Instead I took a deep breath, out of habit, and pushed ahead. "I don't want to talk to them. You seem interesting. I want to talk to you."

"Why?"

"Because you seem interesting," I repeated, trying not to sound as if I thought she were daft.

"I'm not," she replied.

"Can I ask how you were turned?"

"No."

"Come on. I'll share mine if you share yours." I cringed as I realized how cheesy that sounded.

"Fine. You go first."

"Okay. I was at school and..." Shit, I'd almost told the real story. Too late now, so I'd have to improvise. "...the school was attacked by the undead, I was infected and then I found out my dad died. I went to live with my uncle, who is rich by the way. I decided to join the military to give back."

"How charitable of you," the girl replied. "And it's a boring story."

I gaped. She barely knew me and was insulting my storytelling skills. Thinking back, it *was* kind of a boring story. "Yeah, well, most true stories are boring." *Great comeback.*

The girl snorted and shook her head. "Whatever you say."

"I told you my story. What's yours?" *And what's your name?* I thought.

She heaved a big sigh, out of habit, like me, and started speaking. "I was in the bathroom, at my school, when I started puking."

I cringed. "Yikes."

"Are you gonna give a commentary or shut up and let me talk?"

"Sorry, continue."

"I passed out and, when I came to, I was in the middle of a field with a horde of other people. Our clothes were all torn and half of us were naked. It was embarrassing."

I knew the reason for that, and almost said as much, but then realized that would be knowledge this persona didn't have. I kept to my word and stayed quiet.

"It had something to do with the cure being dispersed in the air. Some cure, it gave us back our minds but couldn't restore our bodies."

"You could be dead," I pointed out. "Like permanently."

She glared at me. "That's not helping."

"Sorry."

"From there, we were moved to refugee camps to be reunited with our families."

"Were your parents...was your family...?" I left the rest unsaid - she knew what I meant.

"They all survived. Even my annoying little brother."

"That's good, isn't it?" I asked.

She shrugged. "I guess. Except they survived and didn't get infected."

"Ohhh."

"Yeah." She frowned. "You can imagine their reactions when they found they had an undead daughter. Did you see those videos of the crowd at that high school a few weeks back?"

"Uh, yeah," I hedged. "I might have seen something about that."

"Well, my parents were a bit like that. They wanted nothing to do with the undead, or me. They moved off Galatia IV the first chance they could and left me behind. They left in the night while I was sleeping."

"Shit," I whispered. That was horrible. I'd suffered physical wounds, but this girl suffered mental wounds as deep or deeper. "I'm sorry you went through that."

She shrugged, eyes focused on the floor. "It doesn't matter. I was almost eighteen anyway. I was planning on hitting the star lanes right after graduation anyway."

"Yeah, but...," I stopped. Pity wouldn't help her in that moment. I shook my head. "Never mind."

"I ran into an Army recruiter at the refugee camp. Offered a bonus if I signed up. So, no money to my name, I signed up. And here I am."

"And your name?"

"You're persistent," she observed.

I offered a sheepish grin. "It *is* common courtesy."

The girl rolled her eyes. "Julianna."

I held out my hand. "Nice to meet you, Julianna."

"Yeah right," she said, but shook my hand. "What about yours? Common courtesy and all that."

I rolled my eyes. "Rachel."

The doors to the auditorium opened as the person we were waiting for, the battalion Captain, made his way into the room. He was a shorter man with pitch black hair and a handsome face. I turned my attention to him.

"Recruits," he began, his voice amplified by the sound system in the room. "Your attention please." His voice suggested he wasn't asking. "Form into lines."

The gathered recruits looked around like sheep in a field, unsure what to do.

"Form up!" a drill sergeant at the front bellowed, un-amplified. His words were taken up by half a dozen other drill sergeants. "Straight lines!"

"I guess we don't have a choice," I said to Julianna, shrugging.

She groaned and rolled her eyes.

"We knew what we signed up for," I pointed out. "I think we do a lot of standing at attention in the Army." Terrence hadn't told me much, but I did know that, at least.

The two of us made it to the end of the last line of recruits. If you could call them lines. They snaked like string tossed by a toddler willy-nilly. If I had to guess, the drill sergeants would punish us for our ineptitude later.

"I am Captain Wilson, Battalion captain here at Camp Revery. You are here because you want to serve in defense of the Federation. We," he gestured to the drill sergeants standing at attention in front of his dais, "are here to transform you from lackluster civilians into hardened, obedient soldiers."

I nodded. I did want to serve the Federation, though they didn't know in what capacity. The Supreme Commander's daughter was sure to have special duties. The children of the other Eternals all held important positions in the Federation. I would as well, one day. Had to survive basic training first, though, or no one would respect me.

"You will embark upon a ten-week training course," the captain continued. "These drill sergeants, among others, will guide you through basic training. Obey their every word or expect to be punished." He let the word hang in the air for several long moments before continuing. "Once the training is complete, those who survive will continue on to their specialty training centers."

I shuddered at the way he said "survive." Were people going to die during training?

"Males and females will be in separate training camps, but we are also pleased to announce a further separation between undead and the living."

That caused a stir, as recruits looked among themselves, perhaps trying to identify who was undead and who wasn't. It didn't totally surprise me.

"The reason should be obvious. The undead have...enhanced...speed, strength and endurance. It wouldn't be fair to put them among the living. There will be four separate sections of the base - living men, living women, undead men, undead women."

"Why separate the undead?" one boy said in a whisper meant to be heard. "Can the females even get pregnant?"

He asked a good question, something I hadn't thought of before. But if Captain Wilson heard him, he gave no indication.

"From here, you will pass through the doors behind me," he indicated two large doors marked living and undead. "You will board transport shuttles that will take you to your assigned areas. You are *not* to leave your assigned area, under penalty of being thrown in the brig. No outside contact is allowed, including implants. Magic nullification techniques are employed to prevent use of magic. Those with magic will be allowed to use their magic when they move on to their specialty training." He clapped. "That is all. Disperse."

The ragged lines of recruits broke apart and headed toward their designated doors. "How bad can it be?" I asked Julianna.

Chapter 15

Cold mud splattered my face as I completed my twenty-third push-up.

"You call that a push-up, maggots!" my drill instructor, Sergeant Ferrez, shouted at the top of her lungs. How she didn't strain a vocal chord was beyond me. Practice, I suppose. "Just for your shoddy push-ups, give me twenty more!"

I would have groaned, but I was too tired to care. These twenty-three push-ups had followed a twenty-mile run and one hundred sit-ups. The commander's claim that the undead had unlimited stamina was shown to be a lie, or at least an exaggeration. While our bodies didn't seem to need oxygen, our muscles still fatigued from use...just slower. One day some doctor would document just how different undead bodies were from the living, but for now basic training was our metric. Normal humans were asked to go on two-mile runs - we did ten, for example. And we were warned we'd be pushed even further as training went on. We were the first class, after all, so what they learned from us would be carried forward to future classes. An image of mice in a maze popped up in my mind's eye. An apt analogy.

Out of the corner of my eye, I saw Julianna keeping her face *out* of the mud. She seemed to have adapted to military life far faster than I had.

I thought back to the day we'd dispersed into groups to be transported to our specific camp. We'd been cramped into a transport ship like sardines in a can, then told to run out of the transport. No walking here.

Next, they'd given us an impossible task - we had to learn the names of every recruit on the transport in five minutes. Despite our best efforts, with every recruit seemingly shouting their name out in unison repeatedly, I'd barely learned the names of ten recruits at the end of the five minutes - out of over a hundred.

After performing the obligatory twenty push-ups as punishment, they'd given us what little time left remained in the day to mingle with our fellow recruits and eat at a leisurely pace. Then we'd gone to bed...and found we were tricked.

The next morning they'd stormed into the barracks, a dozen drill sergeants, banging loud objects and kicking over the bunks of those too slow to roll out of bed, dumping their recruits onto the hard duracrete floors. Once the barracks was in chaos, the drill sergeants ordered us to clean the filthy barracks. Then, when the barracks wasn't clean enough after twenty minutes, they'd assigned *more* push-ups.

Couple that with surprise nighttime drills, 3-minute meals and seemingly endless marching drills, and the first four weeks had both flown by and dragged.

"Fifty-five," I grunted, forcing myself to stand to avoid flopping into the mud. I looked around, relieved to see I wasn't the *last* to complete the push-ups, but chagrined to see Juliana standing next to me, uniform virtually unblemished, grinning insufferably.

"You look like you rolled around with the pigs," she commented.

I snorted, blowing mud out of my nose and wiping my face. She was right. The front of my uniform was caked in mud, while my backside was covered in splotches where mud had splashed up. "Yeah, well, I beat you in the ten-mile run."

"Only because that blubbering idiot stumbled and tripped me," she said, glaring at Elise, who lay on her back in the mud, being lectured, loudly, by one of the drill sergeants. "I would have beat you, otherwise."

"Excuses, excuses," I jested. "You just can't accept I'm faster than you."

"Don't just stand there," a drill sergeant shouted. "Form ranks!"

I wasted no time forming up with the other recruits. To be last was to be punished in boot camp.

After the last recruit had finished doing push-ups and joined the line, and then completed more push-ups for being last in line, Sergeant Ferrez spoke. "Fall out."

She led us toward the firing range where she held up a gun.

"This," she said, "is a rifle. A *rifle*," she emphasized the word. "*Never* call it a 'gun' or 'boom stick' or any other stupid name in any drill sergeant's hearing or your whole platoon will be running ten miles. Once you're assigned your own rifle, you are encouraged to give it a name. Do *not* give your training rifle a name."

Yikes, intense, I thought. *Note to self - don't call it a 'gun.'*

I can set a reminder if you would like, miss, Jarvis chimed in.

No, that's not necessary, I replied. *I hope,* I amended.

"If 'rifle' is too difficult for you to remember, the official name of this beauty is the CG-16 rifle. Can anyone answer what the CG stands for?"

One of the women, Evelyn I thought, raised her hand. "Coilgun," she answered when the sergeant called upon her.

"Good," Sergeant Ferrez replied. "And what *is* a coilgun?"

Physics 101, I thought. Then I raised my hand.

"You, in the back," calling on me.

Now was my chance to nerd out. "A coilgun is weapon that employs a magnetic coil in the barrel. When the trigger is pulled, the projectile, called a bullet, is propelled at extreme velocity."

"Good. And why are coilguns superior to traditional chemical reaction weapons using gunpowder?"

"Because the velocity of a bullet fired from a coilgun is magnitudes greater than that of one fired from an older gunpowder weapon."

"Which allows the projectiles to be heavier and to pierce ever-stronger materials," Sergeant Ferrez finished. "One thing you will learn in war, recruits, is that as offensive weapons become more powerful, ever more powerful defenses will be created to counter those offensive weapons. Then, more power offensive weapons are designed to counter those more powerful defenses. It becomes an ever-escalating arms race. Such has been the case between the Federation and the Rakosh Empire for two millennia."

The Rakosh Empire. The moral opposite of the Federation in almost every way. The only place more morally grey was the Commerce Sector and the far reaches of the non-aligned planets where warlords ruled whole planets unchallenged. But the Empire was by far the largest opponent to Federation power.

"You will find much larger versions of coilguns aboard capital ships. They are called railguns when used aboard capital ships, while they remain called coilguns aboard smaller craft like fighters, freighters and transports.

"There are also laser weapons," she continued. "They are less frequently used, as they have far less range of coilguns and are more prone to dispersion and can be affected by strong energy nullification fields. Armor has advanced to the point where the mesh structure dissipates all but enormous amounts of raw thermal energy with no damage to the wearer, so coilguns are used to pierce enemy armor.

"And now, the parts of the rifle..." she went on to explain every part of a coilgun, from the hilt to the tip of the barrel. She showed, in detail, how to break down and then reassemble a rifle, then made every recruit follow suit for hours afterward.

We returned to the barracks for a quick meal and a cold shower. I'd gotten used to scarfing my food down in three minutes and washing as quick and efficiently as possible.

That night as I lay awake, I wondered if I'd made the right choice. My body ached, with Jarvis displaying my energy level on an overlay to my vision. The nanites in my body, coupled with the nascent virus inside me, could heal nearly any wounds given time. Yet, they couldn't fix fatigue.

"Julianna," I whispered, "you awake?"

My bunkmate and grudging friend spoke from above. "I am now," she whispered back. "What do you want?"

"Do you ever regret coming here?"

"Like joining the Army? No, I'm having a blast."

"Doesn't your body ache?"

"Of course it does. But this is greater than my aches, Rachel. It's noble and all that shit."

I snorted. "You, being noble? I don't buy it."

"Fine." She paused. "It's all I have, Rachel. It's a purpose that drives me on." I felt a thump and there she was, kneeling next to my bunk. "You have something to go back to. Me? I have nothing to go back to. I either adapt to this shit and become a soldier or I become an orphan."

I cringed. She was right. Some part of me had no fear of being booted out of the military. I hadn't been actively thinking of dropping out of the Army, but I'd known that if I failed to complete basic training I would still have a meaningful place in the Federation. I didn't have it all on the line. "I'm sorry," I said.

"Forget it," she replied, standing up and making for the ladder leading to the top bunk. "No, really, don't mention it anyone. I don't want to be seen as weak."

I had to smile at that and suppress a laugh. My friend had proved herself to be one of the toughest recruits in our camp. I doubted revealing she had nothing to lose and everything to gain by making it through boot camp with flying colors would hurt her image. Instead, I replied with, "I promise," and went back to sleep.

THE NIGHT PASSED WITHOUT incident and the next day we got to fire our rifles. It was the first time I'd ever held a rifle, but it felt right in my hands. A drill sergeant ushered me up to the firing line and adjusted my sights for me and walked me through bracing it against my shoulder, lining up my target and pulling the trigger. I missed...*a lot*, but the feeling of rightness and excitement I felt holding my rifle, even a training rifle, couldn't be dampened by inexperience.

The CG-16 was a semi-automatic weapon. Pull the trigger once and a single bullet would fire. Pull it rapidly and the bullets would come out as fast as you could pull the trigger. The magazines of the CG-16 were detachable and each magazine held one hundred and twenty bullets. The sergeant explained we would carry several magazines into combat scenarios and knowing how to change the magazine rapidly could save our lives. Staying undead was an appealing concept, so I absorbed everything like a sponge.

After all the recruits had had a chance to fire their rifles, we worked on how to march with our rifles. Holding them pressed against our shoulders, palm on the bottom of the stock, we marched back and forth for hours. Not only was it important to march with our back straight and weapon steady, it was critical that we marched in *unison*, a concept some recruits found difficult. This led to push-ups for all.

That evening, for the first time since basic training began, the sergeants gave us fifteen minutes to eat our meal. And boy did the recruits take advantage of it.

"Did you guys hear about what happened on Xaros III a few weeks back?" one of the girls, Stephanie, asked at our table. Much like everything else in basic training, there wasn't much personal space, and they crammed twenty of us at a table meant for ten.

"You mean the supreme commander's daughter?" another girl, Heather, asked. "Rachel, right?"

My head jerked up from the sandwich I was eating as slowly as possible. My goal was to take the last bite right before the fifteen minutes were up. I'd be chewing it as I ran, not walked, the drill sergeants hadn't gotten *that* lenient, out of the mess hall.

"Yeah," Stephanie answered. Then her head swiveled to me. "The same name as you."

"It's a common name," I muttered. "Galatia was small, but it wasn't *that* small."

"Don't get so defensive," Stephanie said, sniffing. "Nobody thought you were her. Completely different hair and she's *way* prettier than you."

"Gee, thanks," I grumbled. The way she described my old features, I'd gone from a beautiful swan to the ugly duckling. That didn't help my self-esteem.

"Besides," Julianna said around a mouth full of steak, "the supreme commander's daughter wouldn't be slumming it with the likes of us."

"True," I agreed, wishing the subject would change but not wanting to draw attention to myself. The perfect opportunity presented itself: two men in uniform entered the mess hall.

"Recruits!" a drill sergeant shouted. "Attention!"

I wanted to groan. We had three minutes left on the timer. But I knew a groan would end with the whole lot of us performing physical exercise as punishment. Instead, I took one last little bite, and chewed as I fell into a straight line in front of the newcomers and saluted perfectly.

I recognized the first man, Captain Wilson. But the other - I didn't recognize him. He had a hooked nose, was balding on the top of his head and had piercing green eyes that lingered on me for an uncomfortably long moment. He stood a head taller than Captain Wilson and was surprisingly buff for looking like a middle-aged man.

"Recruits," Captain Wilson began. "This is Colonel Octavius Schattler. He is the commanding officer of the newly formed eighty fifth ranger regiment, known informally as the Ghost Regiment. He is here to inspect the recruits." He looked to his superior, as if wondering whether the man would speak.

The gruff colonel continued to look over the assembled recruits. His gaze again lingered on me a second longer than the others - I didn't think it was my imagination - before speaking. "You should be honored to be here, recruits. You are the first of a new lineage of super soldiers. You are superior to living soldiers in every conceivable way - that should make you proud." He paused.

Several recruits nodded, an act I followed suit with moments later. I did feel proud, though my being "superior" was through no fault of my own. A freak accident, even *if* it had been weaponized by enemies of the Federation, my power was through no merit of my own.

"Some of you will not make it through basic training," he said, no regret in his voice, just matter-of-factness. "For those who do graduate, you will have many career options available to you. I trust that some of you will consider joining the Army Rangers." He nodded to Captain Wilson before walking out of the mess hall.

"At ease," Captain Wilson said before following the man out.

I held my composure until the two men were gone, then sagged. There had been a power in Colonel Schattler's presence and voice that awed me and scared me in equal measure. He was clearly a confident, powerful man, but I sensed you did not want to get on his bad side.

Unfortunately, our drill sergeants didn't let us finish our lunch.

TEN MINUTES LATER, we stood outside a windowless building on the far side of the camp. Signs posted on the outer walls and next to the door of the building warned of hazardous chemicals and poison. I swallowed hard.

"I hope you recruits didn't eat too much," Sergeant Ferrez said, an evil grin on her face, "because you might lose your lunch with this next training."

I resisted the urge to slap my face with my hand. Of course that's why they would allow us a relatively luxurious lunch - they wanted us to feel the most discomfort possible.

"This is the gas chamber." She produced a mask from a crate next to her. "This is a gas mask. While most armor you wear will be hermetically sealed against chemical and biological contaminants, we are using these older style masks so you can easily remove them and take a sniff of toxic fumes. Everyone form up and grab a mask on your way in. Do *not* put it on yet."

We all lined up and grabbed a mask as we passed into the building. Inside, a tile floor with bare walls and vents high above met us. When the last recruit entered, the sergeant sealed the door.

From there, Sergeant Ferrez and half a dozen other drill sergeants taught our group how to put on and clear the gas masks. After a dozen times repeating the maneuver, I felt confident.

"Now this next part may actually go in your favor. You're the first group, even before the men, to breath in this gas. While teaching you about the hazards of hazardous chemicals we are also going to test your level of resistance to said chemicals. Put on and clear your gas masks."

After we all complied, a hiss emitted from the vents and the room rapidly filled with a light green mist.

"When a sergeant taps on your shoulder, you will lift your mask and state your name, rank and FIN. Then you will replace your mask and clear it. This is to teach you to trust your masks, whether separate like these or built into your suit. Sometimes you won't have time to seal your suit before you've inhaled. Begin!"

The sergeants began, a half dozen at a time, tapping us on the shoulders. Each recruit lifted their mask, shouted their name, rank, and Federation Identification Number.

I finally felt a tap on my shoulder and lifted my mask. "Rachel Halbert, recruit, three one one seven three nine two seven..." shit, I'd forgotten the next digit. *Jarvis, are you there?* I asked in the space between thought.

I am always here, miss, Jarvis replied. *How may I assist?*

Weren't you listening? What's my fake FIN?

Ah, yes. It is three one...

I just need to know the last three digits, I interrupted. *Quick.*

Ah, it is five eight six.

Thank you. "Five eight six," I finished. Only a second or two had passed. I dropped my gas mask down on my face and clear it with a hiss. Then I felt my vision blur from whatever gas I'd inhaled.

Low level neurotoxin detected, Jarvis announced. *Deploying nanite defenses.*

Immediately, the blurring of my vision stopped as the nanites in my blood cleansed and blocked the toxin.

Others in the room were not as lucky. They stumbled around or bent over as if they were getting sick. One clawed off her mask and screamed, which only made things worse. She hadn't always been the brightest.

"Everyone remove your masks, take one deep breath and exit the building while *walking*," Sergeant Ferrez ordered.

I gritted my teeth. What was she putting us through? But I complied, because disobeying her in this moment would only bring worse pain. I inhaled deep, ignoring the alarms Jarvis sounded in my head as he warned of moderate levels of neurotoxin entering my system. Then I walked out, following several recruits who were not faring as well as me.

Once outside, I coughed as the nanites cleared out the remnants of the gas in my body while watching the other recruits hacking their lungs out and falling to the ground gasping. Did they mean to kill us?

"You're killing us!" one of the girls shouted, voicing my thoughts. I guess the other undead didn't have as many nanites, or any, as me. And the virus wasn't offering enough defense.

"On the contrary," Sergeant Ferrez replied. "We just dosed you with a neurotoxin that would kill a living man with a single breath. Normal soldiers would have died in that room without uttering their FIN. But you undead, you *survived*. And you're speaking and conscious. That is remarkable."

I stood there, stunned. They'd duped us. I mean, technically they hadn't told us which gas we were inhaling, but we hadn't expected something deadly. How many of us would have gone in that building knowing the gas being administered was a neurotoxin? How many other "tests" would they put us through, some of which were deadly to the living, before we completed basic training?

Chapter 16

The week following exposure to the neurotoxin passed relatively quick. By the end of the week the drill sergeants were trusting us recruits more and we were looking like soldiers.

Two weeks before the end of training they piled twenty of us into a transport shuttle and ferried us off-camp.

"Where do you think we're going?" I asked Julianna as the transport neared a silver tower.

"I heard something about zero-G training," Julianna whispered back. "From one of the girls whose brother went through basic here."

"Why wouldn't they just train us in space?" I wondered aloud.

Julianna offered her characteristic shrug. "Beats me."

A short time later, the transport docked and the other nineteen recruits and I marched out and entered the facility. Only when we were standing at attention inside, with a large duraglass window in front of us did Sergeant Ferrez speak. She wore gloves and space boots in addition to her uniform. A utility belt lay at her waist. She wore no armor or helmet.

"You are here at the Gerald G. Hoss Gravitation Center to participate in zero-G training," she began, confirming Julianna's intel. "The reason we are not training in space is because this facility serves two purposes. First, it serves as a research facility studying gravitation and anti-gravitation, hence the weightlessness present in the chamber beyond. Second, its walls are magically hardened and heavily shielded to allow discharging of a wide variety of light and heavy weapons, something not always feasible, usually for cost reasons, in a space station. So here we are."

I supposed cost cutting existed in government as well as in business. I'd always thought the Federation was ultra-rich, but it couldn't have been cheap to run a massive navy and administrate thousands of planets.

"We will start by entering the chamber behind me. Inside, you will be weightless. At the bottom of the silo section, the tower you saw on our approach, is the anti-gravitation generator. It counteracts the effects of this planet's gravity, simulating weightlessness."

I wanted to ask why anyone would want to simulate weightlessness on a planet. What possible use would it be to a civilization with space travel readily available? But I knew asking questions would only land me in hot water. I was still sore from our hundred push-ups the day before when one of the recruits stole a sergeant's cap and put it on. We were encouraged to not hold grudges against our fellow recruits for punishments they earned the group, but we made an exception for that idiot.

"Enter," Sergeant Ferrez ordered.

The twenty of us and four drill sergeants, including Sergeant Ferrez, filed into the chamber. As soon as we passed the threshold, we began to float toward the center of the room. It was a surreal feeling, considering even the smallest space-worthy craft in the Federation nowadays had artificial gravity generators to simulate a planet the size of Tar Ebon's gravity. If I'd been around centuries earlier, during the pioneer days, I would have been accustomed to the zero-G experience.

Once everyone was inside the chamber, the doors slid shut. I floated there, in a cluster formed of my fellow recruits and the sergeants, unsure how to move in the zero-G conditions.

Sergeant Ferrez produced a silver device shaped like a handle from her utility belt and held it in front of her. "This is a portable propulsion device, or PPD. It is a highly efficient device which uses tiny amounts of a specialized gas to create propulsion. You simply aim it in the direction you want to go and hit the button." She aimed it toward the ceiling and an instant later an exhaust trail appeared from the rear of the handle. She propelled toward the ceiling of the silo. "It uses micro-bursts to move you in your desired direction. Press the button too many times in a row and you'll find yourself with too much momentum to stop yourself and you could die."

She lifted her glove and the handle came with it. "The PPD is magnetic, so it will adhere to your gloves until you disengage the magnets in your gloves temporarily or unless enough force is applied to break the magnetic field. These devices are frequently used by maintenance crews and zero-G boarding parties. You will be assigned a PPD if you are being sent on a space mission. Marines have one as part of their standard kit."

She used her PPD to direct herself to the wall, where she replaced it in her utility belt and lifted her legs. A vmmm sound emanated and her boots clicked to the wall. She was now walking down the wall toward the door to the room. "Your PPD will do you no good when you reach the hull of an enemy ship and need to be steady to plant a breaching charge or use a laser cutter. In such cases, you'll activate these, your mag boots, and they will clamp to the metal hull of the ship. The Empire experimented with different alloys during the last war, which were not magnetic, but they were installed on a limited number of ships and bases, meaning mag boots continue to have a prominent place in any zero-G kit. They are activated using your HUD or tactical implant."

Tactical implant? I thought. *I wonder what a tactical implant is? Is it different from what Jarvis is?*

A tactical implant is an advanced version of me, Jarvis answered. *It contains military subroutines dedicated to tactics and combat. It allows complete control of a synth suit and all related articles such as mag boots, personal propulsion devices and much more.*

That sounded cool. *How do I get a tactical implant?*

Upon completion of basic training, I will be upgraded to a tactical grade implant.

I won't lose you? Your personality?

My personality shall remain intact, my tactical capabilities will merely be unlocked.

You have the capabilities now, they're just not unlocked?

Correct.

Did all the undead get that treatment?

No. Most of the undead were given simple implants with a single subroutine designed to ensure the neural pathways remained intact through use of specialized nanites. Their implants are capable of no other functions.

I'm special? Again?

Quite. You were given the top of the line implant, me, designed by your uncle personally. I can upgrade as necessary to support your skill level.

Impressive.

"The last item is the mag grapple," the sergeant continued. Only a couple seconds had passed, if that. She produced a metal pistol-looking item from her utility belt. A hook-like object sat at the tip of the weapon. "It's the simplest of the articles. You simply point and pull the trigger. A tritonium-clad cable is launched at high velocity toward the target. It attaches to any metal surface, much like the mag boots. Do not mistake simple for easy, however. It is simple to use but difficult to master. The key to mastering the mag grapple is to know how far your range is with the pistol and to only fire when you are in range. It takes time to reel the cable in - time you may not have if your PD is out of gas and you're not close enough to the enemy ship to engage your mag boots. The mag grapple can help close the gap.

"For the next hour, you are going to float here. The purpose is to acclimate you to weightlessness without other aids, which will in turn make you appreciate mechanical aids even more later. Your goal is to reach the top of the silo without any mechanical aid. You *can* use your fellow recruits."

If their point was to make us understand how powerless we were in a weightless environment, it worked. Without handholds or propulsion devices we were helpless. Even trying to link hands and form a human chain required us to all get to each other. Flapping our arms was useless - as useless as humans trying to fly by doing the same. Unlike water, where kicking your legs could propel you, in zero-gravity there was no medium to move through except air. We were essentially in free fall, only without the falling part. Like jumping out of a transport high in the atmosphere but not dropping toward the ground below.

Finally, after much pushing and shoving to bounce recruits off walls and ping-pong them into other recruits we had a twenty-woman chain formed and we bounced from wall to wall up toward the ceiling. We made it with three minutes to spare.

"Good," Sergeant Ferrez said. "Now..."

Red lights flared into life directly above our heads and interspersed along the walls of the silo in that moment. Loudspeakers incorporated into the lights blared a long tone and then a mechanical voice spoke. "Alert, alert, containment breach. Alert, alert, containment breach."

"Shit," Sergeant Ferrez swore. "Hurry, to the exit," she snapped. She withdrew the sole PDD in the room and propelled herself to the first person in the human chain. "Take my hand, Tanya. And everyone hold hands tight. Do *not* let go." Then she activated the PDD in bursts.

The PDD didn't seem designed to propel twenty people through space, for we moved much slower than the sergeant had when she demonstrated it. All the while, the lights continued to blare and the mechanical voice droned on.

I exchanged glances with Julianna. She squeezed my hand briefly and smiled. "It'll be all right," she said, though she didn't sound too confident.

We were halfway between the ceiling and the door when an ear-splitting wrenching noise came from below. Then, the metal cover we'd seen at the bottom shot into the air, propelled by a hazy wave of energy that mimicked waves of heat rising from hot duracrete. The cover stopped its ascent, floating like we were, but the wave washed over us, sending the whole lot of us floating upward again, like leaves on the wind.

I felt something in that moment, as I tumbled through the air, still clutching the hands of the recruits on either side of me. Something *inside* me.

Genetic mutation sequence detected, Jarvis declared. *Energy absorption critical.* I wasn't sure whether it was meant to be a warning or a notification, for I had no idea what that meant.

But before I could ask, the waves of energy buffeting us upward ceased and we began to fall.

Some of my fellow recruits screamed as we free fell. The silo was tall but not *that* tall. A few more seconds and we would slam into the ground only there was no ground. Instead, a black blob swirled around below us, like a whirlpool of ink.

Terror entered my heart in that moment. I felt Julianna's grip weakening, while the girl next to me let go completely, flailing her arms.

For some reason, I seemed to fall slower now. I looked over and Julianna was the only one holding my hand. Some feeling inside told

me not to let go of Julianna's hand. "Hang on!" I shouted over the
screams of the falling, who were now below us.

"I...can't," the words seemed to be a struggle to Julianna.
"Something...pulling."

I frowned. I didn't feel any force pulling me. And yet...the others
were falling. "Just hang on," I repeated, pleading with my friend as a
feeling of dread descended on me.

We continued our descent, at a much slower pace, but Julianna
pulled downward, her arms stretched to the max and my muscles
straining likewise. "Can't...hold...on," she grunted.

The first of the recruits hit the dark blob below us and I stared in
horror she was ripped apart, first skin stripping, then bone cracking
and shattering, internal organs turning to mush. In an instant she
was turned into a green streak tinged with pink and white spiraling
into the tidal wave of darkness.

No, I thought. *Think, Rachel, think! That's got to be a singularity.
A black hole.* We were falling toward a fracking black hole. But why
wasn't I feeling the pull of the singularity? Only my connection to
Julianna was dragging me down. Could I somehow save my friend?

I tried pulling, but with nothing to brace against it was futile.
I closed my eyes. What had Jarvis meant with his warning? Clearly
something had happened to me. *Jarvis, quick, what happened when
the wave of energy hit me?*

Your cells absorbed the unknown energy.

Unknown?

There is no known record of the energy in my databanks.

*Well, when it hit we all started rising, so could it have been
associated with anti-gravity?*

*Anti-gravitons are a theoretical particle and there is no record in my
databanks of them being observed by the scientific community.*

But you would have said the same about the virus that killed me, I pointed out. *You had no knowledge of the virus. Could the anti-gravitons have been hidden?*

It is possible, Jarvis mused. He fell silent. Perhaps I'd stumped him.

I decided to go with my gut feeling, and my high school physics lessons. Assuming I'd absorbed some form of anti-gravitons, did it mean I could *manipulate* them? It wasn't unheard of for people to be able to manipulate matter and energy - mages did it all the time. And my father could manipulate time, which wasn't even an energy. Then there was Bridgette and Isabelle, who could travel to a sub-dimension or whatever shadow space was.

I had to try. I opened my eyes to a horrific scene. Another recruit had reached the event horizon and I watched as it tore her apart. Sergeant Ferrez had angled toward the wall and anchored herself there using her mag boots, then held her grip on the human chain of recruits. Only, her ankles were at an odd angle and she wore a look of anguish on her face. It looked like her leg had snapped and now she was being torn between the mag boots and the gravity well. As I watched, she released the mag boots.

"No!" I shouted, trying to feel *something* inside of me. I did feel different, but I couldn't put my finger on it. I'd never heard magic explained - how it felt to mages, that is - so I didn't understand the mechanics of manipulating matter or energy.

I was left to watch as the entire chain of recruits, with Sergeant Ferrez at the tail, slithered toward the singularity, like a piece of spaghetti being sucked up by a diner. One by one they were torn apart, some dead before they reached the event horizon, the G forces bursting blood vessels and causing aneurysms.

"I can't...hold...on," Julianna protested. "Slipping..."

"No," I shouted, desperate, fist clenched. Finally, something flowed within me, spreading to my brain. I shivered as if suddenly exposed to frigid temperatures. Then, my world expanded in a flash within my sub-conscious and I could *see* something, like flecks of black, pulsing out in wave-like clusters. I looked at my hand and it glowed white.

*So, if black is gravitons and white is anti-gravitons...*I looked at my hand still grasping Julianna's hand. The white of my hand met the black of hers. The gravitons surrounded her like a black halo. If I could just extend my white anti-gravitons out of my body to encompass her...but how?

I imagined the white halo around me spreading down my arm and up Juliana's arm. It felt like times when I was downstairs and would imagine the upstairs of my house. I wasn't there, but my mind's eye showed it to me. This was similar, for when I looked down I saw the white spreading over Julianna's arm like a film, pushing back the black. It passed over her shoulder and up around her head, then across her other shoulder and down the opposite arm. It covered her chest and back, passed over her waist and at last encompassed her legs.

Finally, the strain I'd felt lifted and, since I'd been pulling with all my strength, she hurtled toward me. I let go of her hand and embraced her. "You're safe now," I said frantically, trying to be reassuring. "I promise."

Sergeant Ferrez' screams cut off as she turned to mush or goo and disappeared, the last remnants of the others in the room. Only the flashing red lights and sirens remained.

Julianna and I floated there, a white aura surrounding us both as we clung to each other.

Seconds, minutes, hours, I lost track of how long we floated there. But at last the gravity well started to shrink and within moments became a pin-prick of darkness that popped out of existence, taking the black waves of gravitons with it.

I let out a sigh of relief but an instant later the white aura around us bled away like mist in the wind and we were in free fall. The last thing I remembered was the floor of the chamber - the gravity well emitter, nearing.

Chapter 17

I awoke to light in my eyes. I blinked and tried to focus. Someone shone a flashlight in my eyes.

"You're awake, good," a male voice said.

"Can you get that thing away from my eyes?" I asked. I wasn't restrained, so I lifted a hand to brush it aside.

"Of course." The light retreated before my hand.

I blinked several times as the afterglow faded. Then I focused on the man standing next to my hospital bed. Jason Thorpe. My uncle. "What are you doing here?" I refrained from saying his name or relationship to me.

"Don't you remember?" he asked.

"I..." a flood of memories returned. The silo, the death of eighteen recruits and five sergeants. I clenched my eyes shut against the torrent. "...remember." Tears dripped down my cheeks.

My uncle said nothing, giving me the time I needed.

I opened my eyes and met his. "How did I survive?"

"I was hoping you could shed some light on that same question," he replied. "Tell me what happened, from your perspective."

"First, I want to know what made that...thing...go haywire," I gestured vaguely, not wanting to speak the name of the machine that destroyed my friends.

"The FIA believes it was sabotage."

"Sabotage? From who?"

"Your cousin and aunt are trying to answer that exact question. Right now their lead suspects are a sub faction of the Cult of Rae known as the Xanos Reapers, the Empire or a yet-unknown player."

"Could they have made it any broader?" I asked.

He chuckled. "It's in the preliminary stages of the investigation. They found the control room crew slaughtered but no sign of the attackers. The surveillance video had been wiped, even the backups."

"It could have been an inside job? Who else would know about this facility?"

"Not many people knew its true purpose, but many recruits passed through here and trained in zero-G. They just weren't told *how* the technology worked."

"Anti-gravitons," I said.

My uncle nodded slowly. "Yes." He studied me, eyebrow raised. "And I suspect they played a role in your survival. Am I correct in my assumption?"

"You could say that." I launched in to my story, leaving nothing out, not even the gory bits.

My uncle obliged me by staying silent the entire time, interspersed with numerous raised eyebrows. After a long moment, he spoke, "How intriguing."

"Intriguing?" I repeated. "You think my friends dying is just intriguing?"

He had to sense to look chagrined by my rebuke. "My apologies. I sometimes struggle to connect with others emotionally. I *am* sorry for your loss. The part I was referring to as intriguing was you seeing the anti-gravitons. I am impressed you were astute enough to guess what they were."

"My implant was of no help," I complained. "He said he had nothing about anti-gravitons ever being observed by science."

"Yes," my uncle said. "The details of our research here was highly classified, which meant it would be kept outside of any public databases. Your implant does not yet have military clearance, an oversight I should correct."

"I know what classified means," I snapped. "I'm young, not stupid."

Jason smiled. "Feisty like your aunt." He produced a data pad from his lab coat and tapped away at it for several seconds. "I just need to touch your head with this," he held up a metal wand emitting a red light, "to upload the clearance authorization codes."

"Jarvis will be military grade, then? He mentioned something about upgrading himself when I graduated from basic training."

"This will expedite the upgrade and grant you clearance far beyond what a grunt would have. However, you must use discretion in sharing this information. Share classified intelligence with the wrong people and they will ask where you obtained it from."

"Which can lead to awkward questions," I surmised.

"Indeed. May I?" He waved the wand.

"Of course."

He pressed the light-emitting end of the wand to my temple and I felt a slight vibration from it.

Update received, Jarvis announced. *Installing.* A second passed. *Update installed; military grade programming and level one security clearance unlocked.*

Awesome. So now I would be privy to all the Federation's secrets. Only fitting for the supreme commander's daughter.

"Back to the anti-gravitons," I said, a question burning inside me. "Why did *I* absorb them and none of the others? I thought at first it was because of my undead nature, but it didn't affect the others." *And they all died,* I thought grimly. *All except Julianna. I wasn't strong enough, wasn't fast enough, to save them.*

My uncle nodded. "I took the liberty of drawing blood while you were sleeping and..."

"How long was I asleep? The last thing I remember was falling to the floor of the silo."

"You were asleep for three days as the virus and your nanites worked together with emergency injections to repair the damage from your fall. You sustained multiple breaks and fractures in your legs and arms and your hip was shattered."

"Ouch," I said, wincing just hearing the extent of the damage. No wonder I'd passed out.

"Getting back to my original answer," he sounded like he didn't like being interrupted while lecturing. "Your genetic structure possesses something the other recruits did not contain."

"What?" I asked, sensing he was waiting for such a question.

"Your father's genes." He held up his data pad and a chart of several symbols and codes appeared. "This is a chart of your genetic code directly after you rose from the dead. We noticed at the time specific genes that closely matched your father's and aunt's genes. However, they were dormant, meaning you did not manifest the time-bending or shadow-walking abilities they did."

He swiped and a different chart appeared, with different content. "This is your genetic code after the accident. Those same genes are now active but *mutated*. They emit an energy I've never witnessed. My theory is you absorbed the anti-graviton energy as it pulsed out before its collapse and, because your gene were pre-disposed to special abilities, only dormant, they absorbed the energy and used it to mutate and 'awaken' in a sense."

"The sabotage mutated my genes?"

"Correct."

"The glow I saw - it was the gravitons and anti-gravitons? Black and white respectively?"

"I believe so. A similar phenomenon is observed by mages when they, we, manipulate matter and energy. If gravitons are indeed an energy source as I postulated, then it technically makes you a mage."

A highly specialized gravity mage, but a mage by the technical definition."

"I don't want to be a mage," I protested. "I want to be a ranger."

He smiled. "You can be both, you know. My niece and nephew serve in the armed forces and are accomplished mages in their own rights. Also, this newfound magic of yours saved your life."

"Yeah," I said, haunted by the realization. "I would have been mush like the others if this hadn't happened. My father will probably want me to return home after almost losing me for a second time. A third, if you count my dying from the virus."

Jason laughed lightly. "He was quite tempted to order the *Nightblade* here posthaste, or have my wife or daughter bring him, but I talked him out of it."

"Because it wouldn't do for the supreme commander to be seen caring about a single recruit, right?"

He shrugged. "It would have blown your cover, that's definite."

"How is Julianna?" I asked at last.

"She's well. She sustained less damage than you - it seems she fell on top of you - but she had fewer nanites to stem the damage in the minutes before medics arrived on the scene. She is in the room next to you."

"What facility are we in?"

"We are in the premiere military hospital on the planet."

"I can continue basic training after I recover?"

"Yes, you can. I spoke to one Captain Wilson and he indicated both you and Julianna would be welcomed back to training with no penalty imposed. However, we need to explore your new abilities."

I furrowed my brow. "You mean like how I manipulated the anti-gravitons?"

"Precisely. I hypothesize you possess the ability to manipulate both anti-gravitons *and* gravitons, like two sides of the same coin. Much like pushing and pulling, or positive and negative charges of a magnet, gravity can pull, as we classically have observed, or it can repel, as we artificially observed in this facility. Therefore, I believe you can shift your 'polarity' for ease of explanation to apply the effects of gravity or anti-gravity to a person or object."

My eyes went wide as the implications of his words sunk in. "I floated in that chamber. Does that mean I could *fly*?"

My uncle grinned wide. "Now you're catching on. And that is only the beginning. Unobstructed by the pull of gravity, and with no need to breathe, you could even fly in space. Or so I predict. We will need to run a battery of tests to analyze the full extent of your abilities."

From anyone else, the word "analyze" would have filled me with more concern. As it was, it evoked images of poking and prodding and running on a treadmill with wires stuck to me. "I hope you won't treat me like a lab rat," I warned. Special or not, I wouldn't be treated like a prisoner.

"We would never do that," he protested. "Not to you and not to anyone. You have my word."

I sighed. "I know, and I'm sorry I thought that of you. It's just that this is a lot to process."

He took my hand in his. "I understand. I felt much the same when I learned of my powers for the first time."

"You mean, you weren't born with your powers?"

"Your father didn't tell you?"

I shook my head. "We haven't exactly had a lot of time to reminiscence about ancient history yet. I've only known his true identity for a few months."

"Ah, yes, I forgot." He cleared his throat. "Well, you've heard the legends of how we arrived in Tar Ebon's greatest hour of need, yes?"

"Vaguely." History hadn't been my favorite subject. "But I assumed you just came from a far-off land."

"That lie of omission is intentional," he admitted. "The truth is far stranger and not many would have accepted it. The truth is we came from another planet."

"Like in a space ship?"

"No. That was the Founders. They arrived in ark ships that crash landed around the planet. No. My twin sister Ashley and my friend John arrived through more unexplained and mystical means. We still don't know the true means by which we were transported from Earth to Tar Ebon. Not yet, anyway. The same happened to your father and aunt twenty years before we came to Tar Ebon - they too were ripped from Earth and flung to Tar Ebon."

"Wow, that is far-fetched," I admitted. "And you didn't have magic when you arrived?"

"If we did, we were not aware of it. It was only later that we discovered our magic and went to the Tower for training."

"My father and aunt Bridgette went to the Tower?"

His face fell. "Sadly, no. Their story is quite a bit darker." He paused for a long moment. "They were abducted by an evil man and his band of assassins. Your father managed to escape, but your aunt remained in their clutches, naught to be seen for over a decade. Your father never gave up searching and joined the military of Tar Ebon. He rose to a high rank over the course of nearly two decades before finally being reunited with her. It was shortly after their reunion that the three of us," he tapped his chest, "arrived." He smiled. "In fact, I met Bridgette while she attempted to sneak in and assassinate the king of Tar Ebon."

"Really?" I asked, horrified. "Did you stop her?"

"Actually, I saved her. The king was prepared for her, and an ancient nullification field blocked her shifting abilities, so she would have been impaled by several crossbow bolts if not for my timely appearance. There is more to the story, but we will have to save that for another time. The point is, I too went through a period of adjustment to my powers."

"And then you ended summoning tornadoes during the Battle of Pelinor Fields and bringing down the storm wall," I said, recalling those two testimonies of his power from history. "It seems you adapted well."

He nodded. "And so too will you, with training and time. I did not become the powerful mage of history without much training and time. Remember that, when the path you travel seems difficult."

I smiled. "I will." Then I frowned. "I felt so helpless in that room. I barely saved Julianna's life. I can't help thinking if only I'd been stronger, or if only I'd had better control of my power..."

"Thoughts like that are slippery and dangerous," my uncle cautioned. "They can lead you down a path of despair if you are not careful. If I thought of all the people I might have saved, it would drive me mad. Focus on doing your best to save those you can and don't feel it is your sole responsibility to save everyone."

"Thank you, Uncle, that makes me feel better." I put my hand to my mouth. "Oops." I'd used his family title. If anyone was listening...

"It's fine. There are no bugs in this room. But outside we should use discretion if you wish to continue down this path with your identity. I cannot show favor to you during the testing."

"I understand. I'm used to being nobody special."

"Good. Now, if you'll excuse me, there is someone here to see you. Just remember your cover." He walked to the door and opened it.

Terrence - I mean Uncle Morris Halbert, stood there, grinning like a fool. "There's my girl!" he roared, bringing a smile to my face and tears to my eyes. He clapped Uncle Jason on the back as he passed and then embraced me as the door to the chamber slid shut. "I was so worried about you, dear, when I heard the news."

"I'm all right, Uncle Morris," I said, emphasizing his cover name. "And I have some news." I went on to relay the summary of my uncle's conversation with me.

When I finished, he whistled. "Whew, miss. First you get super speed and strength, now you can control *gravity*? What's next, you start shifting like your cousin?"

"Hah! I doubt that would happen."

He shrugged. "You never know. Do you want me to be there for your training?"

"You know that wouldn't work," I said. "I can't have my 'uncle' there for my training, no matter how much I might wish you were."

"I suppose you're right. I'll be around if you need me, though."

I bowed while sitting. "Thank you. Now, if you'll excuse me, I want to go see how Julianna is faring."

Terrence gave me a hug before departing. I rose from my bed and made for the door, but the door opened again before I reached it.

Captain Wilson, the battalion CO, stood there.

I halted, then came to attention, wincing slightly, and saluted him. "Captain Wilson, sir."

He returned my salute. "At ease. How are you feeling, recruit?"

"A little sore, sir, but on the mend."

He nodded. "Good, good. Doctor Thorpe explained his hypothesis regarding your newly developed powers. I am setting up a training facility for you to test your powers ASAP."

"Yes, sir." I'd expected no less. A potential weapon? Of course the military would want to test it out. I was only just imagining the implications.

"Here are the coordinates," he handed me a card with coordinates written on it. "Meet me and the doctor there tomorrow at oh eight hundred hours."

"Of course, sir."

He nodded, then paused. "I'm sorry that this happened to you. I believe you and your fellow recruits were targeted because of your status as undead."

"Oh," I said. My uncle hadn't shared that theory with me, but I could hardly share that intel. "I wasn't aware of that."

"Yes, the FIA believes it was sabotage, but they did not specify the motive. Hatred for our kind is high, recruit, and I find it as no surprise if that hate was their motive."

"I understand, sir. I hope the FIA catches them soon."

"As do I." Without another word, he turned and left the room.

Time to check on Julianna and get a good night's rest. I had a feeling training was going to be intense.

Chapter 18

"Again!" Captain Wilson shouted from the sidelines. We stood amid an ordnance testing ground, which struck me as odd. But I suppose it made sense considering we didn't know the full extent of my power - and considering the power of the singularity the day before.

I swiped sweat from my forehead and grunted. I'd lifted this crate over a dozen times already, and it was harder than I thought. I could do it one more time, couldn't I?

I stuck out my arm, hand spread, and concentrated. Then for the fifteenth time I envisioned the white anti-graviton energy stretching out from the center of my palm toward the crate. It obeyed my command and snaked out of my hand. It wrapped around my target and, to my eyes, the crate appeared surrounded by a white mist. Now the hard part: tightening the anti-graviton lasso and lifting the crate. *Condense*, I ordered in my mind, and the mist shrank until it formed a cube matching the shape of the crate more precisely. *Lift*, I thought and envisioned the cube of anti-gravitons rising into the air. They obeyed and the crate lifted once again into the air. I heaved a sigh of relief.

"Good," Captain Wilson said, tapping away at his data pad.

Beside him, my Uncle Jason watched, small smile on his face. He was watching scientific history being made. "How high can you lift it?" he asked.

I shrugged, still maintaining the connection. "I can find out." I turned my attention back to the floating crate and tried to direct it to go higher. It floated higher for another five seconds or so, then stopped and I felt an intense strain on my mind. "Can't...extend," I gasped. I released my hold on the lasso and the energy dissipated. The crate fell back to earth and shattered.

"Can you explain what you saw," my uncle asked.

"It's like a rope extending from my hand to the crate, then spreading out and surrounding it."

He nodded with understanding. "Ah, so it appears to work similarly mechanics-wise to the magic mages possess. Once you've encompassed the crate, try cutting the rope, as you described it, but maintaining your concentration on the anti-graviton blanket, as it were."

I frowned. "But once I cut the rope, won't that destroy the energy flow? Or interrupt it?"

"It shouldn't. If my theory is correct, your brain is visualizing a rope as a visual aid to know where to summon the anti-gravitons to surround the crate. When you cut the rope, but maintain your concentration, the anti-gravitons will continue to exist in our world. You don't need the rope to summon anti-gravitons."

"If you're correct," I pointed out.

He gestured. "By all means, proceed."

I cleared my throat. "Can I have a bite to eat and a drink first?"

He smiled. "Of course, where are our manners? Let us take a fifteen-minute break and then resume." He turned, as if remembering his manners. "If that is all right with you, Captain."

The captain looked displeased, but nodded. "Fifteen minutes. This is important training and we have no time to waste." He'd only said that a dozen times since I started earlier that morning. He stomped off toward the sole building at the top of the ridge behind us.

"Do you think I'll ever get the hang of this?" I asked as I sat down on a bench and pulled sandwiches, some fruit and a couple bottles of water from a bag. My "uncle" Terrence had gone on a food run for me, so that I could avoid military rations as long as possible. Then again, I was planning to become a Ranger, so I'd have to get used to rations. Still, I wasn't a ranger *yet*.

"It's only been a few hours, Rachel," he said as he sat next to me. He didn't eat, even when I offered him a sandwich, but he did take the bottle of water I offered. "Remember the analogy about learning to ride a bike? You won't learn to master your powers overnight."

"Tell that to Captain Wilson," I said gloomily.

"He is a rather intense man, I agree. But he's just trying to do his job. This is boot camp, after all. He's in that hurry up and train mindset."

"Yeah, I suppose." I sighed. *They'd laugh if I said not having Julianna on the sidelines bothered me.* No sooner had she woken up this morning than they'd sent her back to the base camp to resume training. She hadn't suffered any physical damage, and she didn't have any special powers after the disaster, so there wasn't any reason to either hold her in the hospital or bring her here to practice a new power. But it still bothered me to be relatively alone.

Fifteen minutes later, on the dot, we were back at it. The afternoon flew by as I continued to lift crates and other objects, metal, wood, plastic and more, into the air or practiced moving it with my mind. I wasn't moving the objects so much as directing the anti-graviton cubes surrounding the objects where to go. And it wasn't always cubes - the anti-graviton shroud could form-fit around anything.

"I want you to try to fly," Captain Wilson barked.

I opened by mouth to protest, but a sharp glance from my uncle stopped me. This is what I was here for. "I don't know how I would do that," I admitted.

The captain looked at my uncle. "Do you have any bright ideas, Doctor?" He had no idea Jason was my uncle, and we had to keep it that way.

My uncle mused on the problem for a long moment, then spoke deliberately. "You said back at the silo you started to glow with white energy after being exposed to the anti-gravitons, correct?"

"Yes."

"And it arrested your downward motion, yes?"

"Yes."

"It stands to reason if you can infuse or surround your body with the same anti-graviton energy you can render yourself weightless, allowing you to float."

"But floating isn't flying," I remarked, pointing out what seemed obvious to me. "How would I direct myself where to go?"

He stroked his chin. "Yes, that does present a conundrum. Generally, magic cannot be used to lift oneself. For example, though I can summon a platform of solid air to lift you, I cannot so easily summon one for myself and ride it around like a magic carpet. Something about the proximity of the magic to the source of the magic causes an interference. I've yet to be able to fully explain why it is not possible other than to analogize it to generally being unable to lift oneself."

I nodded thoughtfully. That analogy made sense. We couldn't exactly lift ourselves. "So, it would be impossible for me to fly?"

"Well, let us first test the theory that you can levitate. It happened before, but it could have been due to the circumstances of the eruption of anti-gravitons."

"Like a fluke?"

"Yes." He gestured. "Proceed."

I swallowed my irritation at my own uncle's impatience and concentrated, imagining the white mist surrounding *me* rather than an inanimate object. I felt my feet leave the ground. I opened my eyes and held up my arm. It glowed with the same misty white light. "I think I did it." I looked down. I floated a few inches off the ground. "I definitely did it."

"Good, very good. Now try to imagine yourself floating or being pushed upward."

"Okay." I closed my eyes and tried to imagine the anti-graviton mist risen, much like it had when it surrounded the crate.

Nothing happened.

I tried harder, clenching my jaw and expecting to feel the wind through my hair as I whooshed into the sky. How I'd get down was something I'd figure out later. After a minute or two of standing there like that, I gave up and opened my eyes. "Nothing's working."

He stroked his chin. "Hmmm." Then he snapped his fingers. "I've got it! Anti-gravitons and gravitons. They're like magnets - or they can be." He held one hand up above his head. "Imagine this is a giant positively charged magnet." He held his other hand down by his waist. "And imagine this is a smaller positively charged magnet. In magnetism, opposites generally attract."

"Yes, I know that," I said. I wasn't an ignorant school child.

"Well, what if it's similar with gravity? What if you generated a sufficiently dense gravitational anomaly in the direction you wish to go and then somehow bind yourself to it?"

"Bind myself how?"

"You described originally reaching out to the crates as throwing a rope or a lasso. Well, what if you connect your anti-graviton shell to said graviton bundle?" He brought his hands together and clapped. "The anti-particle and particle would seek to reunite, opposites attracting."

I shrugged. It was worth a shot. We'd come this far, hadn't we? Retaining the anti-gravity shell around me, I imagined a bundle of gravity a few hundred feet above me. I saw it, like a ball of pure black. No one else could see it, of course, as had been the case with all my powers. Then I lashed out with a line of white light and connected it to the ball. Instantly, my feet left the ground and I soared into the sky, though my brain tricked me into thinking I was falling. "Woohoo!" I shouted.

I reached the ball of condensed gravity and floated there. I tested dissolving the ball and I continued to float there. I didn't need the ball to float, but I did need to bind myself in the direction I wanted to "fly."

I tried again, this time binding myself to a ball a few miles away. Again, once I lashed myself to it, I hurtled in that direction, my body threatening to flip onto its side so that the soles of my feet faced the artificial gravity well I'd summoned. I arrived there and oriented myself "upright" again, feet facing toward the planet, then looked down. Now how to descend?

Releasing the anti-gravity field around myself, I plummeted toward the earth at a startling speed. This time I screamed in a mix of terror and excitement. How to stop? I had no illusions I would be in the hospital for weeks if I landed without cushioning.

Thinking fast, I re-summoned the anti-gravity field around me when I was a few feet from the ground. I halted immediately, stopping perhaps five feet above the ground. I released the field and fell gracefully to the ground. "Ta-da!" I said, throwing my arms up like a gymnast might after landing a perfect move. The anti-gravity field faded away.

My uncle started clapping, while Captain Wilson wore a satisfied smirk.

"Well done, Rachel," Uncle Jason said. "Though I would like to see you attempt landing more gracefully."

"Yes. In a combat situation, stopping to float for even a moment could mean you're an easy target for anti-air defenses," Captain Wilson said.

An idea came to me, then. "What if I could bind myself to a moving ball of gravity?" I illustrated with my hands, making a fist represent the gravity ball and my other hand, unclenched, represent me. "I could follow the ball of gravity, maintaining a set distance from it, to allow it to drag me along."

"Like a grappling hook," my uncle mused. "Yes, that could work."

"Try it," Captain Wilson demanded. Did nothing please that man?

I nodded and complied, summoning a ball far above me and re-summoning my anti-gravity field, binding myself to it. I flew toward the ball, but this time I *moved* the ball higher. I continued to fly toward it. Then I moved it to the right and my flight path arced to follow the ball.

What if I needed to change direction in flight? What then? I thought about the problem as I moved the ball toward the ground. If I needed to make slow arcing turns a single ball would be fine, but if I needed to make a 180 turn, what if I released the first ball while simultaneously envisioning another ball behind me? In an instant, I flew backward, grunting at the jarring change and feeling an intense pressure. I turned as I flew toward the new ball. That would take some getting used to. To finish things off, I tossed the ball to the earth and flew down, settling more gracefully to the ground this time.

Even Captain Wilson clapped this time around.

"Better," my uncle said. "And I'm impressed you were able to turn so rapidly. If a pilot tried that, the g-forces would rip him apart without inertial dampeners. Your power must give you built-in inertial dampening."

"That's good, right?"

"Very good," he replied. "You're like a pilot, only without need of an engine."

"And bearing no weapons," Captain Wilson noted. "Also, how is she going to do when faced with a combat scenario, like anti-aircraft fire?"

"All in good time, Captain," my uncle assured him. "Let her keep practicing flight. There will be a time for tactical aerial fighting later."

The captain grunted but did not argue.

I STUMBLED INTO THE barracks right after lights out. Hours of training left my body aching.

I passed empty bunks on the way to my own and my thoughts turned unwittingly to those recruits lost. Killed in action before they'd even graduated. Killed by an enemy they'd never had a chance to fire a shot against.

The loss of the sergeants hadn't hit me as hard. I knew being tough or mean was their modus operandi but still, it was harder to mourn the loss of women who'd screamed at you for weeks on end.

I reached my bunk and whispered, "Julianna?"

A shape moved in the dark and I heard rustling sheets as Julianna practically leapt out of bed and scaled down the ladder of our bunk bed. "Rachel!" she said in an excited whisper. "You're back!" She embraced me.

"Yeah, they let me sleep," I said. "I wasn't sure they were going to." That was a lie, but still, it felt like we'd been training for days on end. Yet it had been just over twelve hours and they'd given me a break for lunch and dinner. There would be more training tomorrow, and the day after, and then a week later we would be graduating from basic training. "They cleaned the deceased bunks out quick," I observed. It had been four days since the attack. I guess I could call it an attack considering saboteurs had been involved. Had I missed the funeral?

"They had a funeral for them yesterday," Julianna said, answering my unspoken question. "That's when they cleaned up their bunks."

"Oh." Now I felt bad for thinking the military wouldn't give them proper burial.

"Things still haven't been the same, though," my friend continued. "Everyone's been quiet, the remaining sergeants haven't been screaming as much. And everyone, recruit and sergeant, is jumping at shadows. The night patrol has been doubled, from what I heard."

"I guess word that it was sabotage spread pretty quick," I said. So much for keeping that classified.

She shrugged. "You know how they say bad news travels faster than anything. Do you...do you want to talk?" She asked in an awkward tone, unused to expressing friendly sentiments. I guess my friend did still have a heart.

I shook my head, grateful for her asking. "No, I just want my bed and a decent night's sleep. We have what, a week and two days till graduation? And I have two more days of this special training." I doubted the sergeants would take it *too* easy on us, regardless of the circumstances. The shock of the attack would wear off and things would go back to normal. I hoped. Then where would I go after basic training? Which specialty would I choose?

Chapter 19

I stood at attention along with thousands of other recruits. Every eligible recruit, be they living or undead, male or female, was gathered here. Before us, a ceremonial stage held several officers and a podium. My father stood at the podium.

"Distinguished guests, ladies and gentlemen:

"As Colonel Schattler put it, what a joyful day for our graduates here this morning; for the families that have nurtured them and raised them to take on these challenges.

"And it is a great honor to be here today on Avylon II, one of the foundational keystones of our great military, and to join you on behalf of the president of the United Federation of Planets, to pay his respects, and the respects of the Federation people, to this military graduating class.

"I would never have imagined, ladies and gentlemen, when I joined the military at age twenty-one some two thousand years ago that I'd be standing here, nor can you graduates anticipate where you'll be many years from now.

"Before this class was walking, the Federation had been thrust into a war by maniacs who thought that by hurting us they could scare us. We don't scare, and nothing better represents the Federation's awesome determination to defend herself than this graduating class.

"Every one of you could have opted out. Many of you were recently infected by a virus that turned your world upside down," his eyes settled on me for a long moment before passing on. "There was no draft, but you heard the call to serve the Federation regardless.

"Today in honoring you graduates, in celebrating your achievements and giving thanks for your commitment, we can see clearly your role in our galaxy.

"For today, as Colonel Schattler said, you join the ranks of those whose mission it is to guard freedom and to protect the innocent from all threats, foreign or domestic. And make no mistake, the Krai'kesh *are* coming, and we shall meet them when that day comes."

I resisted the urge to roll my eyes. Yes, I believed the Krai'kesh had attacked Tar Ebon thousands of years ago - I was not a Krai'kesh denier - but my father had likely been warning of, and preparing for, the Krai'kesh for centuries and they'd yet to show their faces.

"We must never permit the Empire or their allies to define our time or warp our sense of the normal.

"This is not normal and each of you cadets graduating today are reinforcing the ranks of our army, bringing fresh vigor, renewing our sense of urgency and enhancing the army's lethality needed to prove our enemies wrong. You will drive home a salient point: that free men and women will volunteer to fight, ethically and fiercely, to defend our experiment that you and I call, simply, 'the federation.'

"You graduates, commissioned today, will carry the hopes of your individual planets, and the federation on your young shoulders.

"Your oath of service connects you to the line of soldiers stretching back to the founding of our government...and in the larger sense, it grows from ancient, even timeless roots, reflecting the tone and commitment of youth long ago who believed freedom is worth defending.

"In terms of serving something larger than yourself, yours is the same oath that was taken by the young men of ancient Tar Ebon. They pledged to defend their city, what would soon be the capital of the Federation, from the evils of the Krai'kesh, the Empire and all others who would threaten her.

"After ten harsh weeks, you understand what it means to live up to an oath; you understand the commitment that comes with signing a blank check to the federation people, payable with your life.

"In fact, many brave recruits lost their lives a week and a half ago, not in a battle, but while training. They were casualties of war nonetheless, a shadow war against an enemy hidden in the shadows.

"My fine young soldiers, a few miles east of Tar Ebon, where I often visit, at the Pelinor Battlefield Cemetery, is a statue of a Federation soldier at rest, and overlooking his comrades' graves. It is inscribed with the words, 'Not for themselves, but for their country.'

"To a high and remarkable degree, the federation people respect you. But for those privileged to wear the cloth of our nation, to serve in the United Federation Army, you stand the ramparts, unapologetic, apolitical. And you hold the line.

"You hold the line, faithful to duty, confronting our nation's foes with implacable will, knowing that if there's a hill to climb, waiting will not make it any smaller.

"You hold the line, true to honor, living by a moral code regardless of who is watching, knowing that honor is what we give ourselves for a life of meaning.

"You hold the line, loyal to country and defending the constitution, defending our fundamental freedoms, knowing that loyalty only counts where there are a hundred reasons not to be.

"Rest assured that nothing you will face will be worse than the Battle of Pelinor Field. Nothing can faze the United Federation Army when our soldiers believe in themselves.

"For when destiny taps you on the shoulder and thrusts you into a situation that's tough beyond words, when you're sick and you've been three days without sleep, when you've lost some of your beloved comrades and the veneer of civilization wears thin, by having lived a disciplined life, you'll be able to reach inside and find the strength that your country is counting on.

"Now you are privileged to be embarking on this journey because you're going to learn things about yourself that others will never know.

"And we can all, in this stadium today, see the storm clouds gathering. Our enemies are watching. They are calculating and hoping the federation's military will turn cynical. That we will lose our selfless spirit.

"They hope our country no longer produces young people willing to shoulder the patriot's burden, to willingly face danger and discomfort. By your commitment you will prove the enemy wrong. Dead wrong.

"You are a United Federation soldier, and you hold the line.

"Now, I may not have had the pleasure of knowing each of you personally, but I have high expectations of you.

"Fight for our ideals and our sacred things. Incite in others respect and love for our country and our fellow citizens...and leave this country greater and more beautiful than you inherited it, for that is the duty of every generation.

"To the families here today, I can only say: Thank you. Thank you for the men and women you raised to become soldiers.

"For duty, for honor, for our galaxy...hold the line."

The entire stadium erupted in cheers in that moment, clapping reaching a thunderous crescendo. I looked to Julianna, who stood next to me, and she wore a grin.

My father knew how to inspire a crowd. I felt the urge to ascend the stage and embrace him but resisted. It wouldn't do for a random recruit to be seen embracing the supreme commander. It would spark unwanted questions and likely blow my cover if people put the pieces together. As it was, rumor had it that the real me was in seclusion, but several conspiracy theory groups didn't believe it.

The band started to play as the onlookers descended on the field to congratulate their graduates.

Terrence found me quickly - he must have had an eye on me the entire time. "There's my niece," he said, hugging me.

"Thank you for coming, uncle," I replied. "This is my friend, Julianna." I wanted to include her, as she had no one.

He smiled wide and held out his hand. "Congratulations, Julianna."

"Thank you, sir," she replied, taking his hand and smiling in a more subdued manner. She looked around, then at me. "I'm gonna get out of here. No reason for me to stay. I'll let you catch up with your uncle." She started to back away.

"No, wait," I said, reaching out and taking her by the hand. "Please stay. You're like family to me now."

"Oh," she said, seeming taken aback. "Okay."

We mingled for a bit, talking to other recruits, living and undead, and observing the organized chaos that was basic training graduation. The next phase of our lives would be different. We would go into various jobs and specialties, spread out across the Federation, with a singular purpose of holding the line.

"Private Halbert?" a voice came from behind me.

I turned to find Captain Wilson standing there in his dress uniform. I saluted. "Yes, sir?" Even though we'd spent three rough, long days training with the man, I kept my distance.

"At ease, Private," he said, returning the salute. "I wanted to speak to you about your plans after graduation. Do you have any?"

"I was focused first on getting through basic training," I replied. "I figured I would determine my specialty after that."

He nodded. "Good, that's good. Because I have an offer for you that I think you'll find hard to refuse."

I stood there, waiting. I didn't want to sound disinterested or appear too eager.

"I want to offer you a position in the 7th Ranger Battalion," he said.

I felt my eyes widen. "An army Ranger?" I asked.

"Of course. We were watching you throughout basic training and you're quite impressive. That, coupled with your unique physiology makes you an ideal candidate for the Rangers."

Of course, it came down to my powers. I was surprised the entire planet of Galatia IV hadn't been forcefully recruited in to the Federation. If the planet had been in Imperial territory I'm sure they would have been.

"I would be honored, sir," I replied, unable to reasonably say no without revealing myself. An ordinary recruit would jump at the honor to join the Rangers. "When do I start?"

"Right away. Report to Fort Helen near the city of San Rivel one week hence. Fort Helen is about three hundred and fifty miles north of here."

Here I was thinking Ranger training would have its own planet. But then I remembered Avylon II was the training planet of the Federation and that meant every branch of the military would call this their headquarters. It therefore stood to reason that the special operations teams would too. "Of course, sir," I said, saluting.

He nodded as if he'd expected nothing less than my complete obedience, then turned to walk away.

"Sir?" I said, a thought coming to me. "I have a special request?"

He turned and raised an eyebrow. "A special request? You already agreed. Now you want to negotiate?"

My face warmed, an unusual feat for an undead person, but I kept my cool. "I only just thought of it, sir. I would like my fellow recruit Julianna Severstein to also be recruited into the Seventh. She's undead too," I hurriedly added.

"Yes, I remember who she is. She was in the silo with you when it exploded." He contemplated for a long moment, stroking his chin. "Fine, she'll be accepted too."

"Thank you," I said. Only then did I realize I hadn't asked Julianna what she wanted to do with her career in the military. For all I knew, she could have already planned a career in communications or some other branch. But I crossed my fingers mentally that she would agree to follow me into the Rangers.

"YOU WANT *me* to join the Rangers with you?" Julianna asked, incredulous.

"Yes. I know, I should have asked you first but..."

"I'd be honored," she cut in.

To the side, Terrence nodded, seeming to approve of my choice of group to join. I think the only group he would approve of more was the Shadow Watch Guard. I'd have to ask him sometime how one joined their elite ranks.

"It's settled then," I said, excited. "We have a week leave before we report to Fort Helen. Want to have some fun first?"

"I thought you'd never ask," my friend said, offering a wicked grin.

Chapter 20

"**P**repare to jump!" Captain Wilson shouted over the sound of the wind as the H-1000 gunship cut through the atmosphere.

I clutched the strap of my parachute and avoided looking down. Granted, I was the last person who should fear heights, considering I could literally fly, but I still felt slight discomfort contemplating the dizzying height. *It's only training*, I thought, *and it's only my first time.*

Three other Rangers stood in front of me in line. They gave me confidence to know I wasn't going to be the first out of the gunship.

"Go, go, go!" Captain Wilson shouted.

One by one the three Rangers preceded me out into the expanse of atmosphere, disappearing from sight. When it was my turn, I felt the chilly air whipping me wildly and for a moment I panicked. But then I remembered the lesson Captain Wilson had hammered into our heads and focused on the ground, orienting myself. Out of the corner of my eye, I saw the other Rangers ahead of me in their descent.

Fifteen, sixteen, seventeen, I counted. At twenty, I pulled the rip cord and felt a tug as the parachute deployed, slowing my descent. *That wasn't so bad*, I thought.

HAVING MASTERED JUMPING out of a gunship, I now faced off against Julianna on the training mat.

"Begin!" Captain Wilson shouted.

Julianna moved first, charging at me and preparing to bull me over and tackle me to the ground. I side-stepped her charge, pushing her head down, but instead of sliding into the ground, she twisted and swept a leg out, tripping me and sending me into the air.

In that timeless moment before I fell, I surrounded myself with anti-gravity and halted my descent, floating there weightless. Then I summoned a ball of gravity above me to orient myself perpendicular with the ground, standing up, and immediately canceled both spells, landing on my feet.

My friend stood there, arms crossed. "You done showboating? While you were floating like a possessed person, I could have strangled you, cut your throat or shot you in the head."

"Gee, thanks for the descriptive ways of killing me. Do you think about that a lot?" I asked.

"She's right, Private," Captain Wilson said. "If you're going to show off with fancy tricks, you need to do it faster than your opponent can react."

I sighed. So much for trying to fight smart. "Yes, sir," I replied, setting my feet for the next round of sparring.

BODY SORE FROM DOZENS of rounds of hand-to-hand combat, I stood with a dozen other Rangers-in-training watching as one Dr. Hervera demonstrated the use of an injector.

"As you can see, the injector is light-weight and straightforward to use. You simply press to the skin and pull back on the trigger." She demonstrated on one of my fellow trainees. A hiss emanated from it. "Each standard dosage contains one thousand nanites programmed to spread out and cluster near any wounds, infections or damaged organs. Obviously, more severe wounds will take more nanites, and several severe wounds will need many doses, otherwise a single dose will focus on one wound at a time, which may be too slow to save a dying person. The nanites are also only active for about thirty minutes before they die and are absorbed into the bloodstream. They're later flushed out when the patient urinates."

"Are we allowed to use more than one dose at a time?" one trainee asked.

"While not recommended when there are several wounded, if there is a single severely wounded soldier you may use up to three without overly taxing their system. More than that could start clogging up their arteries and cause cardiac issues.

"When nanites are not available, or when there are more wounds than nanites, you have to go old-school and bandage the wound." She held up a roll of white bandages. "Now pay attention to how..."

I yawned. This was going to be a long day.

"THREE ASSAILANTS," Julianna whispered from half a foot away. "Two o'clock. Wind speed, ten kilometers per hour."

Happy to be away from learning how to use injectors and bandage wounds, I lined up the shot, taking wind speed into account. I then released my breath and steadied my sniper rifle, preparing to pull the trigger. It was easy to release my breath considering my kind didn't need to breathe like the living. I pulled the trigger and the ground next to one dummy target flew into the air. *Damn, I missed.* Without missing a beat, I adjusted and fired again. This time the chest of the dummy exploded from the impact of the coilgun shell.

"That's better," I said.

"Keep shooting," Captain Wilson said through the squad comm. "One shot, one kill. In a real situation, by the time you lined up the second shot your target would be diving for cover or you'd be receiving counter-fire, most likely both."

"Yes sir," I replied, sighing.

"THIS," CAPTAIN WILSON began, "is a rocket propelled grenade launcher, or RPG. Unlike traditional rifles, which were improved by adding electromagnets, the mechanism of this weapon has remained the same for centuries. However, the grenades it launches have improved as armor has increased. For instance," he turned and launched a grenade toward a metal shack in the distance. It landed a few feet from it and then exploded a moment later, peppering the metal shack with dozens of holes. "This specific grenade is known as an armor-buster grenade. It contains dozens of titanium balls and double the explosive material than an ordinary grenade. This makes it weigh more, but it does more damage to armored opponents.

"Then there are EMP, or electromagnetic pulse, grenades. They disrupt electronics for a brief period of time. This can include internal comm devices if the EMP is strong enough or if the internal device is not shielded. Most military-grade implants are shielded from all but the strongest EMPs."

Are you shielding, Jarvis? I asked.

Of course, miss. I can withstand everything below a class 6 EMP wave.

How many classes are there?

Six.

Oh. So that's pretty good.

Yes, miss.

"This next weapon is a heavy machine gun," Captain Wilson hefted a long-barreled weapon with holes along the barrel. "It uses coilgun mechanisms..."

This training session held my attention.

SIXTY-ONE DAYS. SIXTY-one days of nineteen point five hours of instruction per day. I'd jumped out of a gunship, become an expert in hand-to-hand combat, become a competent marksman, learned to mend the wounded under pressure, learned about heavy weapons and infiltration and so much more.

Now I stood graduating once again – this time from Ranger school. There were noticeably fewer Rangers than had graduated basic training, which made sense considering there were many specialties to go into. I also only recognized a few of them, because the undead and living had generally been kept separate. Captain Wilson said it was because the living were jealous, or perhaps scared, of us. I could believe it, after what I'd witnessed, though I thought soldiers would be more willing to accept different people.

Julianna stood at my side. It filled me with confidence to see my friend there. We'd been through Hell together but we'd come out on top.

Now on to the real missions.

Chapter 21

I looked through the viewport as the *Daedalus* shifted from shadow space into real space. A set of three rings spun perpendicular to the central axis. A large ship sat docked to one of the rings, while two smaller ships, about the size of the *Daedalus,* also lay docked, though they were detaching themselves as I watched.

Captain Wilson had explained the *Daedalus* was an assault corvette. It boasted a "stealth" suite of sensor-jamming and sensor minimizing arrays while also being combat capable against ships of its own class. Two dozen starfighters sat in its hangar while four gunships waited, unable to be used for long in the vacuum of space. They were designed to be dropped into low planetary orbit, near where the atmosphere began, and descend from there, if the *Daedalus* was unable to enter atmosphere itself or time was of the essence.

"Pirates," I grumbled to Julianna. "Looks like they've spotted us."

"No, not us," Julianna said with a grin, pointing. "Look, beyond the station." She tapped on the viewport and the smart display zoomed in to where she tapped. A cruiser and two frigates had emerged from shadow space and were deploying fighters.

"Bait?" I asked. "Why do they need us?"

"Because we want the hostages *alive*," Captain Wilson answered tersely, having overheard me. "While our colleagues in the navy hold their attention and drain their station of every available spacecraft, we will slip in, dock and get the hostages out before anyone notices."

A favorite saying of my father came to mind just then. No plan survives contact with the enemy. Would our plan?

"What kind of hostages are they, sir?" Julianna asked with a modicum of respect. She'd learned, the hard way, to speak respectfully to commanding officers or she'd earn latrine duty or some other menial punishment.

"Hostages with rich families," he replied. "The Federation doesn't negotiate with terrorists, but their families are happy to pay the Federation to risk our lives to save them."

"Oh," I said. So it wasn't an altruistic mission? Not that I regretted saving innocent civilians, but the exchange of money suggested we were putting the lives of the rich above the lives of more deserving citizens with fewer resources.

The *Daedalus* streaked rapidly through space as the battle began in earnest on the far side. Streaks from tracer shells, laser beams and missile exhaust trails filled the void. Colonel Schattler had yet to deploy our own starfighters - probably to maintain the element of surprise. If the enemy had seen us approaching, they didn't show it. The anti-starcraft defenses remained inactive on the side facing us.

"Intel suggests the hostages are being held in the second ring," Captain Wilson relayed.

"Makes sense," Julianna said. "Considering the cruise ship is docked there."

"Cut the chatter," Sergeant Reynolds, our squad leader, ordered. "Check your gear, ready your weapons and prepare to breach."

While the colonel oversaw the entire battalion, Captain Wilson oversaw Delta Company. I'd heard some of the other soldier refer to it as "dead" company, considering it consisted of undead soldiers. Twenty Rangers under the captain's command, with four sergeants acting as squad leaders.

The second ring of the space station neared and the *Daedalus* jolted as it slowed. It drifted toward the hull of the pirate base and then the maneuvering thrusters kicked in to bring it close enough.

"Latching complete," a voice announced over the intercom. "Commencing laser cutting."

I knew from talking to the other Rangers that the latching procedure involved powerful magnets surrounding an outer airlock of the *Daedalus* drawing the two ships together. Once close enough, the laser drills would pop out and begin drilling a hole in the target ship or station. They said the ideal place to drill was by an enemy airlock, because once we pulled away the inner airlock would close and the enemy ship would not lose hull integrity like it would if we drilled through an outer wall.

A zapping sound reverberated through the ship as the lasers engaged. There was no sound in space, true, but energy coils lay inside the ship and were loud.

All five companies in the seventh Ranger battalion stood ready, in separate holds so that if one were breached the others would survive. When the breaching completed, we would each leave our separate holds and funnel into the ship. The *Daedalus* did feature multiple outer airlocks on each side, allowing for up to two points of entry at a time, but today it was only one breach.

The problem with breaching was the enemy could create bottlenecks if they had enough time to prepare. Or if we breached at the wrong location.

For one reason or the other, they were ready for us.

"Enemy airlock breached, enemy airlock breached," the voice announced. The door to our compartment slid open and we activated our helmets, sealed them and headed into the hallway. Remaining sealed against vacuum and hazardous or noxious gases was standard protocol until the air was confirmed to be breathable.

Plus, it was always a good idea to wear a helmet when going into combat.

Two other companies had reached the breach ahead of us. We heard the zap of enemy laser fire meeting the crackle bam of our coilguns. No screams, yet, but the global battalion comms had devolved into a cacophony of voices updating the status at once.

"Enemy on both sides, I repeat, enemy on both...agh" the warning turned to static as the Ranger was hit.

"Grenade, grenade!" a voice shouted, though it was unclear where the grenade was. I wasn't even in the airlock leading to the enemy ship - there was no threat of a grenade here.

"All non-company commanders, switch to company comms," a gruff voice barked.

I obeyed and the noise faded the instant the channel switched. Our company captain, in this case Captain Wilson, would tell us of any global orders. That's how it was meant to work, anyway. Though if he fell our sergeant would join the global channel and if *he* fell then one of us would join the global channel to report the loss of the sergeant.

"Alpha and Charlie company are taking heavy fire," Captain Wilson said, calm as if he were reporting that it was raining, as we neared the seared door leading to the enemy station. "We're up next, Delta. Don't let me down."

"Halbert, you're up," Sergeant Reynolds ordered.

I groaned inwardly, though I knew showing fear or cowardice in front of the enemy was a good way to end up in the brig, or worse. Deserters ended up dead, one way or the other.

I stepped through the charred hole and then through the inner door which had been opened by an emergency manual release lever. I immediately stepped over a fellow Ranger, helmet retracted, which only happened when they were dead. The nanites in the body of a Ranger and in their suit would deactivate and retract into the dispenser on their back upon death. Then, if the dispenser were removed without proper codes, it would self-destruct. It was a fail-safe designed to keep Federation tech out of the hands of less-than-savory factions.

Lasers flashed above the heads of the remaining Rangers, while shrapnel lay in a heap on the floor, along with three more Rangers.

I raced to an open spot and ducked down behind a glowing pink portable energy barrier. They were designed to project a shield upward when the projector was deployed. They had a limited lifespan, of course, both in time and capacity. Too much damage would overwhelm the generator and cause it to fail, sometimes explosively. I opened my voice comm to speak to those around me. "How many are there?"

"A dozen on this side," the Ranger beside me said, pointing. "And watch from behind too, as there's stray lasers flying everywhere."

I nodded. My first combat mission and it was a practical ambush. Or just fortunate circumstance on the part of the enemy.

"These shields won't hold much longer," a second Ranger said, kneeling to the left of the first. "Did you bring one?"

"Of course."

"Be ready to deploy it in front of an existing shield when they start to fail. You'll see it flickering." He popped up and fired a flurry of bullets before ducking back down.

I lifted my coilgun and gradually peaked over the barrier. Technically I could see through the barrier, but it was distorted. The enemy had their own barriers set up, these a dark red.

I took aim and fired, knowing time was of the essence. Zap bam the coilgun fired, the electromagnetically accelerated shell slicing through the air at thousands of feet per second, instantaneously for the purposes of close quarters. It slammed into the barrier and shattered, its energy absorbed. My second shot went high, slamming into the ceiling and shattering, barely leaving a dent.

In the early days of space combat, I'd learned, the walls had been thinner, which resulted in a risk of high velocity rounds piercing the walls of space ships or stations. But as time went on, the walls and hulls of such places were vastly improved. Now they were typically mage-forged, their molecules bonded together so tight they could even absorb a railgun shell or two before shattering. Even interior floor, wall and ceiling plates would be forged of hardened alloys resistant to physical damage.

Enemy counter fire came as a torrent of red beams of light, slamming into our barriers. They were banking on overwhelming the generators of the barriers.

"Grenade!" someone shouted, I thought to my right. I ducked as a grenade came soaring and landed right in front of *my* barrier. It exploded and my barrier blinked out of existence, while the ones to my right and left flashed urgently, warning of their imminent demise.

There I crouched, exposed. I fumbled for my replacement shield generator but knew I would be too slow. *Stupid, stupid, why hadn't I pulled it out and had it ready?*

Berating myself could wait. I considered leaping to one side or the other, hiding behind one of the other shields. But something inside me *wanted* to fight, wanted to move forward and not cower behind a barricade.

So, in that moment, I decided to use physics against them. *Just like we practiced,* I said. I summoned a ball of gravitons in front of me. It swirled into existence, a ball of black nothingness to the common onlooker but a cluster of millions of tiny gravitons to my eyes. Then I expanded it, held tight in my mental grip, turning it into a swirling vertical disk, like a pitch-black axial fan spinning faster than the eye could see.

I walked forward, the spinning disk of gravity before me. The enemy laser fire predictably smashed into my shield and was absorbed. I felt the energy growing and dispersed excess energy into the air, warming it. I didn't want the graviton shield to grow too large, or it would start ripping at the walls of the station.

When I'd first demonstrated this ability before my Uncle Jason, he'd stood astounded, marveling at my prodigious command of gravity after just three short days. Captain Wilson had worn a feral grin, likely imagining the multiple uses for such a deadly ability

Behind me, my fellow Rangers were focusing on the opponents in the opposite direction, pouring all their firepower in that direction with no fear of being shot in the back now.

My gravity shield met the enemy energy barriers and barely hiccupped as it absorbed the energy and swallowed the generators whole. It wobbled as it increased in power and it took more of my concentration to maintain its shape. But then it passed the line where the barricades had been and absorbed the first of the pirates, turning them to mush and sucking them in much like it had my fellow recruits back in basic training.

The smart pirates turned and fled, while the stupid ones stood, continuing to fire, and died.

I continued on my path, following the curve of the hall wherever it would lead me. "Sir," I said over my company comm channel. "I've got them on the run on the right-most path."

"Yes, I can see that, Private," Captain Wilson said. "I'm sending the rest of Delta Company to follow you. The other companies will take the left path. Whoever finds the hostages first wins. And I like to win."

Wins what? I wondered but didn't ask.

With Delta Company at my back, including Captain Wilson and Julianna, we made our way down the right fork. We passed sealed doors along the way and checked each room as we passed. It wouldn't do to be hit from behind.

We'd lost two Rangers from Delta Company by my count, during the initial push. I hoped we wouldn't lose anymore. Periodic laser fire peppered the shield but could not pierce it. But I felt my power being taxed and the shield shrinking, so I had to release my hold on the shield and press against the wall like a normal soldier. I'd have to work on my stamina.

We pressed on, continuing to meet minimal resistance, and at last found ourselves at an airlock. "Halt here," Captain Wilson commanded. He fell silent for several long moments before speaking. "Command says this leads to the cruise ship. Scans show the hostages may still be on board. Let's move." He gestured for me to lead the way. "First and second squad onto the ship, third and fourth squad remain behind.

"I don't think I can summon another shield right now," I protested.

"Just do your best," he said in a terse tone suggesting he didn't have time for my protestations. And considering the circumstances and time being of the essence, he would be right to feel that way.

I carefully activated the door control. The door slid open with a hiss. I raised my rifle to my shoulder and stepped through the doorway.

Julianna rushed up next to me, rifle also held at the ready. "I've got you," she reassured me.

We encountered no traps or anything passing between the first door and the second. Beyond this door would either be a ship full of pirates or a ship full of cruise passengers. Hopefully more of the latter.

I pressed myself against the wall next to the door control while Julianna took up position opposite me. The other Rangers lined up on the wall behind one of us. When everyone was in position, I counted down with my fingers and then triggered the door control. It slid open with a hiss. I braced for laser fire to stream through the opening...

No laser fire came. I carefully peaked around the corner, expecting to see enemies lined up, weapons leveled at me, prepared for exactly that moment. But the corridor was clear and stretched into the distance for several feet before reaching a junction.

"Sir, did Command say where in the cruise ship those prisoners were?"

"Starboard side," he answered.

I envisioned the ship in my mind. The starboard side meant the right side, and because the cruise ship's front, or fore, was docked with the station, the starboard side meant left from our perspective. "Left at this junction up ahead, then," I said.

At said junction, we carefully pointed our weapons to the left and right. Captain Wilson left four Rangers to guard the corridor while the remaining seven of us, six plus Captain Wilson, headed left.

The sound of nervous chatter came from ahead, behind a pair of elaborate-looking doors. I deactivated my helmet and pressed my ear to the wood door. It must have cost a fortune to get real wood on this ship. From within, I could hear men and women, and maybe even some children, speaking. "Women and children, and men, sir," I reported. "No indication of pirates."

"Then what's keeping them in there?" he mused.

I looked down and saw a heavy metal chain tied through the handles of the door. "Looks like they were locked in." I moved aside so he could see it.

"Okay, break the chain," he ordered. "I'll notify Command." He paused for a long moment. "Shit, we're being jammed."

"Jammed?" I blurted. "But they're just pirates. How would they have jamming tech that can affect ours?"

"Something smells fishy," he agreed. "Break the lock, quick. We need to get back to the *Daedalus* before..."

An explosion rocked the cruise ship, almost sending me to the deck. I barely stayed upright and managed to withdraw my vibroblade. I held it to the metal and it screeched as my blade sliced through it, the razor-sharp mage-forged blade vibrating at hundreds of cycles per second. I flung open the doors.

The faces of dozens of cruise guests met me. Relief swelled up in the form of tears while they swarmed the doors, eager for freedom.

"Form an orderly line!" I shouted. "We're here to rescue you!"

"Where is Charlotte O'Hara and Dennis Rickman?" Captain Wilson bellowed, amplifying his voice to be heard above the din. He repeated himself, even louder this time.

Who are they? I wondered? But I didn't have time to ask. I had to forcefully shove several men back and order them into the line. I understood they were panicking, but they were causing more chaos.

A man and a woman, both barely twenty if that, approached. "I'm Charlotte," the blond girl said.

"And I'm Dennis," the dark-skinned boy said.

"Rachel. You take these two on ahead," Captain Wilson ordered.

"Yes, sir," I responded, trying and failing to keep the curiosity out of my tone. "May I ask, sir...," I began.

He sighed, agitated, but didn't deny my request. "They're extremely high-value targets. Their parents paid billions to ensure their safe return. It's the whole reason we were called in."

"Oh," I said, dumbstruck. Here I thought we'd been called in because it was what we did - helping people. But we only helped when they paid? That felt wrong to me. I opened my mouth to say more.

"Cut the chatter," he snapped. "Julianna can go with you. Get moving, now!" He shoved me toward the way we'd come.

Discouraged from asking further questions, I led the two twenty-somethings back. Why didn't we just stay with the rest of the group?

We'd made it to the airlock between the station and the cruise ship when the ship rocked again, this time sounding from the direction we'd come from. I immediately activated my comms. "Sir, are you all right?"

"It's an ambush," he shouted through the comms. "Pirates coming out of the woodwork." Indeed, I could hear laser and coilgun fire in the distance. "Get those two out of here. We're going to cover the retreat as best we can."

Out of instinct I turned, preparing to race back to the defense of my fellow Rangers. But I had orders, and people to protect. I led them through the airlock and we ran back toward the *Daedalus*. We made it back without incident, meeting up with the other four Ranger companies as we did. They all looked the worse for wear, armor scorched and their ranks looking thinner than before. But two companies went off to support Captain Wilson and the remains of Delta Company.

Twenty minutes later, Captain Wilson and the remainder arrived...without the hostages.

"What happened?" I asked. "Where are the hostages?"

"They didn't make it," he said. There was no remorse in his voice.

"They *all* died?" I asked, incredulous. Something didn't add up.

"As I said, it was an ambush. They hit us on all sides. The hostages went running in all directions and got caught in the cross-fire. None survived."

I sat there in shock. A part of my mind thought that had to be wrong. There must be another explanation. But the soldier in me knew not to question what he'd told us. My CO wouldn't lie to us, would he? I searched the faces of the other members of Delta Company, but they wore stern faces that could have passed for solemn expressions. Maybe I could question one of them later, alone.

The captain seemed to sense my reticence to accept his story, for he stepped up to me and asked, "Is there a problem, Private?"

"It's just that...sir...I find it a bit far-fetched that none of the hostages survived."

"Are you questioning the official narrative?" His eyes narrowed. "That can be construed as treason."

"No, of course not, sir," I hastily reassured him.

"Then drop it," he said. "That's an order."

The *Daedalus* shuddered as it detached from the cruise ship. The two hostages we *had* managed to rescue huddled under a blanket together on the bench.

In the distance, the battle seemed to have intensified, with *more* pirate ships joining the battle and two having attached to the other side of the cruise ship. Maybe what the Captain had said was true - maybe the pirates *had* killed them all. But something didn't seem right.

The *Daedalus* made the shift to shadow space without incident or pursuit, another oddity, and we made it back to base a few hours later.

I caught Julianna's arm before she made for her bunk. "Do you really buy that story?" I asked, searching her eyes.

She averted hers to the floor. "I talked to one of the others. You won't like it."

"*What?*" I demanded.

"They weren't killed, Rachel. They were abandoned."

"Abandoned? What do you mean?"

"I mean they were shoved back into the room we found them in and the doors were barred. Then, presumably, the pirates were cutting in from the outside and reclaiming them."

"But then what was the shooting we heard?" I asked.

"A cover for their story to make sense."

"Why would they do something like that?" I asked, sitting on my bunk, suddenly feeling weak.

Julianna shrugged. "I heard something about a black-market deal. The pirates sell the hostages and split the profits with Colonel Schattler. But you didn't hear that from me, okay?"

I clenched my fists, anger boiling up inside me. If my father heard about this, he would blow a gasket. The seventy-fifth Ranger battalion would be shut down that minute...and my identity would be revealed. I wilted. I had to keep quiet about this if I wanted to maintain my cover.

"Is that why he sent us on ahead? Because he knew I wouldn't go through with it?"

"And because the families of the two hostages we did rescue were paying more than what the pirates could get on the black-market for them." She shrugged. "It's just business."

I stared at my friend, horrified. "Just business? Innocent cruise passengers being sold into slavery is just business to you?"

"Relax, Rachel. They're being ransomed back to the families - they'll see home again. They're not going to become slaves."

"I presume only if their families pay," I snapped. "If they can't pay, what then?"

She shrugged. "I don't know. That's above my pay grade to care."

"And won't the ransomed hostages tell the truth? How they were abandoned by the Rangers?"

"Not if they want to actually see their families again," Julianna said. "From what I heard, they have to agree to never speak of it or their entire family will be murdered."

"That's brutal."

"Brutal and effective," Julianna confirmed.

I stared at my friend, aghast. "Julianna, what's happened to you? You were so..."

Her nonchalant face faded, replaced with a glare. "I was so what, Rachel? So sad? So alone? Well I'm not sad, or alone, anymore! This is my family now, and I'll do whatever I need to in order to protect it."

"I..." I wanted to say I quit, that I would give up the life of a Ranger in order to expose the corruption I'd witnessed. But something made me hesitate. Perhaps it was fear, perhaps it was something else, but I still believed I could do more good from the inside than I could from the outside. Maybe I could prevent a future atrocity like this from occurring. "I understand," I said at last. "I may not agree, but I understand."

"So, you'll keep quiet?" she asked.

"Yes," I confirmed.

My friend nodded, her expression transforming to a smile in an instant. "Good. Good night."

What if I'd answered "no?" I thought.

Chapter 22

"What's your status, Ghost One?" I heard the voice of Captain Wilson through the comm suite incorporated in my implant. It tapped into my auditory nerve to transmit the signal to my brain, making it sound like I heard the voice in the air around me. It sounded different than the inner monologue voice Jarvis used.

"Approaching the manor now," I said through the same sub-auditory network. I crouched low to the ground, illuminated only by the light of Brakel's two moons. My tight-fitting synth suit felt strange compared to the thicker armor worn by Rangers. I felt naked, though they'd assured me the suit would absorb energy just as well as ordinary armor and could even take a bullet or two. It was the perfect suit for stealth missions like this.

"Remember. Discretion is of paramount importance, Ghost One. No shots, no loud noises."

"Yes, sir," I responded. We'd gone over the plan several times. I fingered the hilt of the portable electro-staff at my belt. With one button, I could extend it to the length of a quarterstaff and electrify it, using it as a staff or a pseudo-sword to stun, or even kill, opponents in relative silence. The only other weapons I carried were an energy pistol and two daggers.

I reached the wall surrounding the manor. It was brick, reflecting the backward planet I found myself on. The residents of this planet called it "classic." They enjoyed living in the manner of those centuries earlier. They claimed it was a throwback to simpler times. It just made my job easier.

Using a grapple, I scaled the wall and crouched at the top. Here, there were guards. Two stood by the door to the manor, while two more stood outside the gates - the reason I hadn't chosen the frontal approach. I knelt there for several minutes, watching the patrols of the remaining guards, memorizing their patterns.

I still didn't know the identity of my target, but six months in the seventy-fifth Ranger battalion as a full-fledged Ranger had taught me *not* to question my superiors. I'd tried to push the cruise ship incident and the other morally gray actions to the back of my mind and forget them. I mostly succeeded - now they only haunted my nightmares.

At last, I made my move. I leaped to the ground soundlessly, then crouched low and raced toward the rear entrance to the manor. Only one guard here, and he never saw me coming. I slammed my electro-staff into his gut, set only to stun, and he grunted and fell over.

Opening the back door, I dragged the guard inside before the next patrol passed and quietly closed it. The passing guards would assume he'd gone inside to use the toilet...the first time around. I had until the same patrol passed twice - about ten minutes - before the alarm sounded and their awareness would be heightened.

I found myself in an old-style kitchen, complete with a brick stove containing a black cauldron over glowing embers. I noted the lack of electric lighting and felt grateful.

I peeked out through the door leading out of the kitchen but saw no one. To the back stairs, then. I crept up the stairs, cringing with each step, expecting a creak to emerge at any moment. Fortunately, no creaks came and I made it to the third story of the house unmolested, stopped not even by servants. The middle of the night proved a good time for assassins.

His room is on the far eastern side of the manor, I reminded myself. They'd at least told me the target was a male.

Two guards in front of a room at the far end of the hall on the third floor told me I had the correct room in sight. I settled on my plan of attack and withdrew my daggers. My memory flashed to hours spent practicing throwing such weapons since joining the Rangers. I steadied my breathing, cocked my right arm back first and let the first dagger fly, with the second arm already cocking back.

The first dagger caught the first guard in the throat. He gurgled and fell. Before the second guard could do more than gape, the second dagger took him in the throat. I *had* been authorized to kill where necessary.

Two minutes I reminded myself. Two minutes until the patrol passed by the back door and noticed the guard. I would have maybe ten seconds beyond that, accounting for the time it took to investigate.

I tried the door but it was locked, as expected. The last line of defense. It was an analog door, no access panels in sight. I placed a small explosive charge between the knob and the frame, then activated it and stared expectantly. A soft *pop* emerged, followed by a slight whiff of smoke, but the latch had been severed.

Pressing on the wood, I slipped inside. A parlor, like the kind I might see in a holo depicting a scene centuries earlier, when women wore big dresses and men smoked cigars, met me. Candles on the walls and a fire still going steady in the hearth illuminated the couches and chairs. A pair of double doors presumably led to the bedroom.

I stood silent for several long moments, listening for any sounds which would suggest waiting guards. Hearing nothing, I crept around the couch and made for the door. This door was unlocked, as it was his private sanctum.

Now to meet my target. I expected he was a dangerous opponent if I'd been sent to kill him. Probably a pirate overlord, infamous assassin or gang leader.

I slid both sides of the double door open and peered inside. No lights illuminated my target, but I switched on the night-vision option within my implant and spotted him, laying in his bed.

I had retrieved my daggers from the corpses of the two door guards, and I contemplated using them for this job. But I had been ordered to leave no evidence that could be traced back to the Rangers. Command didn't want any evidence left behind.

I withdrew my electro-staff again and extended it, avoiding activating the electric coils at first. Approaching the side of the bed, I held my breath. I hefted my staff and held my thumb over the activation switch. *Three, two, one.* Click, zap, the staff electrified.

My target stirred, rolling over and grumbling groggily. Alarms blared in the distance.

Before he could react, I swung the staff down, striking him in the head. No capturing today. He shuddered and screamed as several thousand volts coursed into his head, then fell still.

Conscious of the alarms, I made for the parlor. A window on the far east-facing wall became my target and I shattered it with a strike of my still-extended staff.

Alerted by the noise, guards on the ground below began firing coilguns. No old-fashioned weapons here - they meant business.

I ducked to avoid the shots and drew upon my power to first surround me with an anti-gravity field and then to summon a ball of gravity above me. I tied them together and lifted off the ground. I forced the gravity ball higher and ascended at unprecedented speed. Up, up I went, ascending thousands of feet into the air. Several seconds later I reached low orbit and activated my comm. "Ghost One ready for pickup," I said. "Mission accomplished."

"Acknowledged, Ghost One," Captain Wilson said. "Bringing the *Daedalus* in to extract."

The assault ship streaked through the dark of space and slowed next to me, the airlock opening. It had no need to fear being spotted by sensors from such a primitive planet. If we were under fire they might need to take more drastic action to pick me up while avoiding enemy fire.

Once aboard, Captain Wilson clapped me on the shoulder. "Good job, Private. The Federation is safer because of your actions."

"Sir, you still didn't tell me who the target was," I pointed out.

"No, I didn't," he agreed.

"Are you going to? Sir," I added after a pause.

"I suppose you've proven you'll do the job no matter what. Fine." He sighed and pulled out his datapad, then tapped on it a few times before holding it out to me. "Do you recognize this man?" On the display was a plump red-headed man with a big nose.

"No, sir," I said.

"His name is Gregor Valanski. He's the CEO of Valanski Industries." At my blank expression, he continued. "They're an energy provider popular in this sector."

"Why did he have to die?" I asked, an uneasy feeling battling against a pre-conceived conviction that this person had *deserved* to die. For something.

"His company is suspected of having ties to the Cult of Rae, a fanatic cult. It therefore became politically expedient to eliminate him."

"Politically expedient?" I repeated. "You couldn't just bring charges and investigate him?"

He shrugged. "Bureaucracy. An investigation would have taken months, perhaps years, while he tied it up in the court system. It was decided by the Colonel that we end the threat now and see where it leads us."

"That makes sense, sir," I responded. *Sort of.* It didn't sit completely well with me, being killed before proven guilty in a court of law. Assuming he had been guilty, I agreed something needed to be done and was equally frustrated at the lack of justice in the Federation at times.

"You've all earned some much-needed shore leave," he announced. That elicited cheers from the other Rangers.

I found Julianna. She smiled when she saw me. "Hey, partner. You run into any trouble?"

"Nothing I couldn't handle," I responded, doing my best to act as nonchalant as possible. "Let's see what kind of trouble we can get into during shore leave."

Chapter 23

Ah, shore leave. After six months as a full Ranger and months of training before that without much of a break, I couldn't wait. It was only a week, but Julianna and I intended to make the most of it.

Wearing my army fatigues I strolled down a crowded street in Junmai City on the planet of Hazeldein III. I marveled at the unique sights. Hazeldein III was known for its Shar'hai inspired culture, being a desert world and all. Junmai City, in fact, had been built along one of the largest rivers in the region, while desert surrounded it on all sides.

The virtual tour guide Jarvis had pulled up explained that ninety percent of the planet was desert or permafrost, mostly due to its closer proximity to its sun than normal planets in the "Goldilocks" zone. It's founding colonists had run into several challenges when first reaching the planet, but had persevered and become a popular tourist destination. The sand-skiffs were of particular interest to me, as they would take tourists out into the middle of the desert to see the giant sand-worms.

"Do you want to get a drink?" Julianna asked over the din. "Or go straight to the sand-skiff tour?"

"How about drinks during the sand-skiff tour?" I asked.

"Sounds..." she stopped. "What's that?" she gestured up ahead, where a large crowd had gathered.

As we neared, I realized they were surrounding someone. I stopped in my tracks, sweat breaking out and fear striking my Ranger heart. Images of the mob on Xaros III surrounding me and killing my friend flashed before my eyes. Their words drifted to my ears: "Undead go to Hell, undead go to Hell."

Julianna pushed through the crowd and I felt compelled to follow. I had to protect her and this time I had the means to.

Together we pushed through the encircling mob and broke free to the center. There they found a man and a woman clutching each other and casting nervous glances at the mob. No, not nervous. Terrified. Their gazes settled on me and Julianna and they stepped back.

I held up my hands. "No, wait, we mean you no harm." I had to shout over the shouting of the crowd.

They stopped backing up, possibly because it brought them closer to the crowd, but seemed a little calmer. "Who are you?" the man asked. He eyed our fatigues. "Soldiers?"

"Yes, and we're here to help," I blurted. How to help was the next question. We could grab them and push them through the crowd. Or we could try to reason with the crowd. Yeah, right. I couldn't exactly call in the cavalry like when I was previously in this position. And trying to fight, well, I could hurt innocent protesters. As if any of them yelling hateful comments were innocent.

"What do we do?" Julianna asked. She didn't know my history.

"Try to walk them out of here," I said. "Take my hand." I held out my hand for the man to take. Then, when he grabbed it, moved toward the boundary of the crowd.

The crowd wasn't having it, however. I'd taken one step into the crowd when someone shoved me in the chest, pushing me back.

"Get out of the way!" I shouted.

"Undead go to Hell," the crowd chanted back.

I tried again but this time two men shoved me back, one hand on each shoulder.

"We are Federation soldiers! Get out of our way!"

"Not with the undead!" one of the big men shouted.

I knew it was stupid, but on impulse I shouted, "*I am undead too!*"

The big man's eyes grew wide. He pointed right at me. "She's one of them! She's one of them!"

If anything, the chanting of the crowd intensified. No one had drawn a weapon yet, that I could see, but I tensed, wishing I had my own weapons. Of course, weapons were not allowed while on shore leave. That didn't mean I didn't have other weapons at my disposal. Could I fly them out?

I won't let them hurt this couple like they hurt me. I would defend them. But how to diffuse the situation?

"Captain Wilson," I said through the squad comms. "Do you copy?"

No answer.

"Delta Company, does anyone copy?"

No answer. Either we were too far from the ship, which was unlikely, or we were being jammed, which was also unlikely. But what other possibility was there. "*Daedalus*, do you copy?"

"Are we being jammed?" Julianna asked, as if she'd read my mind.

"Who would know we were here to jam us?"

"Someone who wants to hurt us?"

"Let me check." *Jarvis, are you able to tell if we are being jammed?*

One moment, miss, he responded. Seconds later, *I am detecting a directional jamming field in the region, yes. It appears to be focused on this location. We are unable to broadcast.*

Damn. How long does it take to set something like that up?

Based upon the wave signature, this is a commercial jamming field. Devices emitting this type of field are typically portable.

Then why can't my military-grade implant break through?

I do not have enough power to amplify at the correct wavelength to breach the jamming field.

Damn. Help wasn't coming from the outside, then. "We're definitely being jammed," I confirmed aloud.

Was it my imagination, or was the crowd closing in? Several protesters were holding mobile devices, recording the event. But with the jamming field, they couldn't broadcast.

"That's it," I said. "The jamming field. It's to stop *this* from being recorded in real time and to stop them from calling for help." *Not targeted at us, then.* That made me feel *slightly* better. It wasn't a trap for us.

"I have to get to high ground." I looked to Julianna. "Defend them no matter the cost. I'll fly up and call for help."

Julianna studied me. "Go. But you better come back."

"I promise." Gathering my strength, I covered my body with anti-gravitons and tossed a ball of gravitons high into the air. I shot after it and pushed it on. After a few hundred feet I heard chatter from the *Daedalus.* "*Daedalus,* this is Private Halbert, do you copy?"

A moment later, a voice responded. "Private Halbert, this is the Tactical Commander. Over."

"Private Severstein and I are surrounded by an anti-undead mob and there is jamming at our location. I flew above it to request support. Over."

"Standby, Private Halbert," came the response. Silence fell for several moments. Then the line crackled to life. "Captain Wilson has ordered the *Daedalus* to your location. ETA, three minutes."

"Acknowledged, Command. Private Halbert out." I closed the line and looked to the crowd below. Three minutes. We just had to survive for three minutes.

Releasing both the graviton ball and the anti-gravity field encompassing me, I free-fell toward the ground. When I was a few feet from the ground, I re-summoned the anti-gravity field and floated for a moment before releasing it and dropping to the ground next to Julianna and the two civilians. "Reinforcements are three minutes out."

"Good," my friend replied. "We just have to hold out."

The crowd, emboldened by my re-appearance or perhaps just fired up enough after several minutes of chanting, chose that moment to close in. The same two men who'd pushed me approached and got right in my face. "Whatcha gonna do, bitch?" the first man said, cracking his knuckles.

"Yeah, you gonna go feral and kill us all?" the second man mocked, poking me in the shoulder.

I snapped, grabbing his finger and twisting. I heard something snap and he cried out in pain. "You're about to find out," I growled, unable to stop myself. I would *not* be the victim this time.

Miss, I am detecting the jamming field has dissipated. We are receiving signals again.

Good. But why did it disappear? My gaze settled on several onlookers holding up their mobile devices. *The cameras. They're trying to paint us as monsters.* I stepped back, horrified, but the damage was already done.

The man held his broken finger up for the crowd to witness and screamed for our heads. The crowd surged forward from every direction.

"Protect these two!" I snapped to Julianna, gesturing to the civilians. "Minimum force!"

"That's gonna be hard to do!" Julianna grunted, shoving two women back. "There's too many of them to be gentle!"

Come on Daedalus, I thought. *How much longer?* I shoved the first man who'd approached me back, trying to be as gentle as possible, but two more took his place.

One man tried to go for my waist, tackling me to the ground. I elbowed him in the back and he dropped face-first to the ground. He didn't give up, however, for he grabbed my legs.

I kicked him in the chest, perhaps a little too hard, and he went flying into the crowd, bowling several people over.

"Monster!" the cries shouted. "Kill them for good!"

"Rachel!" Julianna shouted.

A glance behind showed her on her knees, with several people clinging to her. I turned and made to throw them off her, but at least one person jumped on my back. That was the last straw.

Growling with rage, I grabbed the arms of the person on my back and whipped them over my head. Then, still holding onto their arms, I swung them around and smacked several others in the crowd with the man's feet. I let go and he disappeared into the crowd.

A gust of wind sent my hair streaming in multiple directions and I looked up. There floated four gunships, weapons manned and aimed at the crowd. Above them floated the *Daedalus*. Captain Wilson's voice came from a speaker attached to one of the gunships. "Back away from them or you're all going to get hurt!"

No one seemed to heed his words, for I continued fending off assailants.

A pop sounded and a canister streaked into the crowd. Moments later, smoke drifted across the ground. No, not smoke, gas. Tear gas, as it turned out, for people started choking, coughing and, finally, dispersing.

"Monsters," one of the big men said, spitting blood on the ground. "You got lucky."

A *crack* sounded and the concrete at my feet chipped. I felt a sting on my leg.

You've been hit by a bullet fragment, miss, Jarvis informed me.

Damn it! I ignored the twinge of pain and summoned a ball of gravitons. I expanded it into a shield, much like I'd done on the pirate space station and several times since, and held it between me and where Jarvis projected the shot had come - a building a few blocks away, higher up.

Another crack came and the shield absorbed a bullet, causing a tiny surge of energy.

Seconds later, the machine gun on the side of one gunship opened and a stream of bullets sailed toward the origination point. A third shot never came.

I hesitantly let down my shield.

People lay on the concrete, trampled but moving, while most had run away to a safe distance. The police had arrived, setting up a perimeter, finally. It looked like they hadn't decided whether to form a perimeter to protect us from the mob or the mob from us.

One gunship landed and Captain Wilson hopped off and crossed the distance to us. "Private," he said tersely. "I understand you ran into a little trouble."

I saluted. "Yes, sir. These civilians," I gestured to the man and woman who only now were untangling from each other, "were being harassed by a mob. They'd surrounded them, sir, and were calling them nasty slurs related to their status as undead. We felt compelled to help. But then the communications were jammed and..."

Captain Wilson held up a hand. "I've heard enough for now. Come along - you'll be debriefed on the *Daedalus*." He turned and, without acknowledging the civilians, headed back toward the gunship.

I looked to the man and the woman. "You're safe now. Go straight home and lock your door."

"Thank you, miss," the man said. "But we're going to get the hell off this planet as soon as possible. It's unknown if there's anywhere safe, though. Maybe we'll go back to Galatia IV." They stumbled toward the police line.

I ran up to Julianna and grabbed her arm, bringing her to a halt. "Hey, are you okay?"

"We nearly died, Rachel, *again*. Almost killed by racist fucks who think they're superior to us. Maybe it's the name - wasn't that girl at that high school named Rachel, too?"

"Maybe," I hedged. "I don't recall her name."

"It doesn't matter. This shit has got to stop. Someone needs to show them that not only are we not inferior, we're *superior* to them."

"But then are we any better than they are?" I asked. "That won't bring peace."

"Don't you remember the saying, 'If you desire peace, prepare for war?' Peace won't come by us asking nicely." She shook off my hand and stormed off toward the gunship.

Casting one last glance at the hateful crowd, some of whom were still glaring in our direction, I followed.

Chapter 24

"We're being co-opted," Captain Wilson began, "for a joint operation with the FIA."

The announcement made me perk up and pay closer attention. We stood in the ready room as a holo-display popped up, displaying what looked to be a large compound.

"This is a facility owned, officially, at least, by the Brahui Corporation, on the planet Urkusk, near the border with the Commerce Sector. But the FIA has uncovered intel, at a high cost, I'm told, that it's a shell corporation for the Xanos Reapers."

I remembered that name from something my father or Isabelle had mentioned, but I couldn't tip my hand. Instead I raised my hand. "The Xanos Reapers, sir?"

"I was getting to it, Private. The Xanos Reapers are classified as a terrorist organization. They're believed to have ties with the Cult of Rae, which, before you ask, worship some ancient god of the Krai'kesh and work to do his 'will' in this galaxy. Bunch of hoo-ha if you ask me, but not any crazier than the other religions out there, I suppose."

Not wanting to argue the merits of religions, I kept my mouth shut and waited.

Captain Wilson raised an eyebrow. "Not going to take the bait. All right then, back to business. The Xanos Reapers are believed to have had a hand in designing the virus that hit Galatia IV. A sensitive topic for many of you, I suspect."

Nods came from my fellow Delta Company Rangers. I found myself nodding too. If we could find who was responsible for turning us into undead it would go a long way toward getting justice. While millions had been turned into undead, millions more remained dead, and the genocide deserved avenging.

"This is our first big lead and a hit on this facility could yield information on where the virus was manufactured. As this is a joint ops, Deputy Director Thorpe and other FIA field operatives will be joining us."

My heart leapt at that revelation. Deputy Director meant Isabelle. I wondered if Kimberly would be with her, too.

"The strike will begin at nineteen hundred tonight," he said, laying out the plans.

ISABELLE SAT ACROSS the aisle from me, wearing a black body-hugging synth suit with the helmet down. She didn't acknowledge me, other than winking when she'd first spotted me. Right now, she looked bored, not fidgeting or talking, eyes closed as if she were meditating. Next to her sat my other friend, Kimberly, looking more nervous and taking turns gawking at the Rangers and the interior of the *Daedalus*. Her gaze had passed over me numerous times, but if Isabelle had disclosed my identity to her she was doing a good job of hiding it.

Rachel, a voice, Isabelle's voice, I realized, came in my head. Not like comms, but like Jarvis. *Do you copy?*

Isabelle? I asked, incredulous. *How are you communicating through my implant like that?* My cousin hadn't moved, still with her eyes closed.

I2I, or Implant to Implant, communication. It uses a different communication network, which is more heavily encrypted. We can't be eavesdropped on.

Oh. Well, that's good. I paused. *How have you been? I saw your father a few months back - he helped me adjust to my new powers.*

Yes, I was briefed on your powers. I'm glad you survived, and that's quite an interesting power you have.

I'd rather have developed shifting, or magic, I grumbled.

Well, you're one of a kind, now. Just like your father.

How is my father, anyway?

He is well. There's been political pressure from the Senate, so he's been on a tour across the Federation for several months.

A tour? Talking about what?

Recruitment numbers are down, so he's talking about the importance of a strong military and talking up the benefits of joining the armed forces. It's hard though, when we're not actively at war, to get people riled up.

The Empire is still out there, I pointed out. *They're still a threat. And this Cult of Rae and their lackeys are a threat, right?*

The war with the Empire is a cold war, my cousin pointed out. *And wars on terror don't engender the same level of fervor because there's no clear target. Hence your father going out talking about the coming threat of the Krai'kesh and our need for constant vigilance.*

I couldn't resist rolling my eyes. *The same Krai'kesh that have been "coming" for two thousand years.* I tried to put a sarcastic emphasis on coming, and hoped it translated as well through the implant.

Yes, which explains the push-back he's received not only from some Senators but from some of the people he speaks to. You can only cry that the sky is falling so many times before people become deaf to it.

Is Kimberly doing well? I asked, changing the subject. *Did you tell her about me?*

She's doing well, learning a lot and she's been through a lot. I don't have time to recount it all, but we almost lost her a couple missions ago. She was instrumental in getting us this intel, though. As for her knowing your identity, that's above her clearance level. The fewer people who know your identity, the less risk there is to you.

A feeling of melancholy washed over me. Sadness that my long-time friend wouldn't recognize me in a disguise. Logically, I knew that was the point, but emotionally it made me feel lonelier. I cleared my proverbial mental throat and responded. *Yes, that's probably for the best. You have what, a dozen agents with you?*

Two dozen, all from the local FIA office. I like to travel light, she offered as way of explanation. *Hence I didn't lug an FIA strike team from Tar Ebon with me. And maybe I wanted to see you again.*

That made me smile, which would look odd to outside observers, but I didn't care. *The Rangers won't let you down.*

I'm counting on that.

"Three minutes till reversion to real space," the Tactical Commander announced. "All passengers, strap in for rapid acceleration. Crew, man battle stations."

I pulled the straps over my shoulders and clicked them together to form a chest harness. They were uncomfortable, so I avoided wearing them until necessary.

The three minutes passed quick, then a jolt and verbal confirmation from the Tactical Commander confirmed our emergence from shadow space into real space.

See you on the ground, my cousin said, then she grabbed Kimberly's arm and disappeared in a cloud of shadowy smoke.

That wasn't part of the plan, I thought. Though Captain Wilson had only told them their part of the attack plan - he probably wasn't privy to the FIA's plans. The half dozen FIA agents in our compartment didn't seem surprised at the disappearance of their Deputy Director, so I assumed it *was* part of the plan.

A second jolt rocked the *Daedalus* and I was slammed back in my seat as the ship rapidly accelerated. Normally the inertial dampeners would stop the G-forces, but I'd learned there were times when the ship accelerated quickly, going from a velocity of zero to high max speed, that the dampeners would be temporarily overwhelmed. If we hadn't been strapped in I would have been hurled about like a rag doll, likely causing damage to me or others. Even using anti-gravity in a situation like that could be dangerous, as then the rear of the ship would slam into me while I floated with no velocity. To solve that, I could summon a gravity ball, perhaps attaching it to a point in the front, and have it drag me along at the same velocity as the accelerating ship.

"Entering atmosphere," the Tactical Commander announced a few minutes later. The ship rattled as it went, then the ride smoothed out. "Nearing the facility. Gunships, launch!"

The display of the outside of the ship showed four gunships streaming toward the facility we'd seen on the holo-map.

Anti-aircraft fire commenced, with shells hurtling skyward and exploding below and around the gunships and the *Daedalus*. Fortunately, the shields shimmered, absorbing the shrapnel released by the explosions. One gunship was hit and started leaning to one side but stabilized and continued on its path.

No sooner had the anti-aircraft fire begun than it stopped. Smoke rose from the locations of the guns. *That must be Isabelle's work.*

The *Daedalus* sailed toward the fortress, which had been built into the side of a mountain. The gunships were already in position, pouring lasers and bullets toward unseen targets.

At last our ship took position overhead. "Rangers and agents to the launch bay," the Tactical Commander announced.

I unstrapped and followed the rest to the launch bay. There we lined up and grabbed our parachutes. Donning my parachute, I followed the other Rangers and FIA agents and leapt out of the ship. Pulling the string, my parachute opened and I sailed down to the surface.

Enemies ran here and there, shooting up at the descending soldiers while we returned fire.

I spotted Isabelle below. She was swirling among a cluster of enemies, alternating between slashing with her blade and firing her pistol, disappearing in puffs of shadowy smoke, only to reappear moments later behind one enemy or another.

I tucked and rolled to absorb the impact and then raced to the edge of the building, choosing my first target and firing.

There were a lot of enemies, but we had the high ground, the element of surprise and gunships as fire support. The enemy was falling back to their inner sanctum.

Once the courtyard was clear, I descended and approached Isabelle, who stood with her arms crossed. "It's about time you grunts arrived."

"You could go on without us, ma'am," I said.

"Yes, but where's the fun in that?" She tossed me a mischievous grin, then sobered. "Plus, there is an anti-magic field in place, preventing me from shifting beyond those doors." She nodded toward the front doors of the building.

"Oh, so you lose some of your defensive ability," I observed.

"More than a little, yes. I can't turn myself partly transparent to avoid projectiles, can't shift to move quickly, can't swap out weapons easily."

"So, you're like a normal soldier?"

She groaned. "Yes, I'm a normal soldier who's been fighting for two thousand years," she said sarcastically.

I chuckled. "I should go, before someone notices us talking." It wouldn't do for Captain Wilson to see me talking to the Deputy

Director of the FIA and either chew me out or wonder why I was talking to her and ask about the content of our conversation.

Isabelle, taking that as her cue, strode toward the door to the inner facility. Her two dozen agents, which had been reduced by a handful, along with the remaining seventy-fifth battalion Rangers, followed. The corpses of our enemies littered the ground.

Kimberly sprinted across the field to catch up with her trainer. She wiped her mouth, and looked paler than usual, suggesting she'd been throwing up. Had this been her first mass combat situation? She didn't spare a glance for me, which forestalled me from approaching her to ask what was wrong.

A grenade shattered the glass door and myself, Isabelle and the other Rangers led the way inside. A glance back showed Kimberly remaining behind with the FIA agents. They followed at a safe distance.

The moment I passed through the shattered doorway, I felt *something* change. I could still feel the bundle of my power but it felt stronger somehow. Would the anti-magic field affect me the same as it did Isabelle? I felt a temptation to test whether I could still use my power, but there was no time to stop.

A few security forces fired at us, but fell back or died as a hailstorm of lasers and bullets hurled back at them.

Inside the fortress, it spread into a labyrinth of corridors stretching in seemingly every direction. "Does anyone have a map?" I asked through the squad comms, part sarcastically, part seriously.

"One of our agents sent what we believe was a complete map but it's turning out to not be accurate," Isabelle said as she led us to a dead-end. "They must have planted false data for her to find."

"Is the agent still alive?" I asked.

"Sadly, no. She was killed shortly after providing this intel."

"Stop pestering the Deputy Director," Captain Wilson said over the comm.

"Yes, sir," I responded, holding back a sarcastic remark.

"Should we spread out?" Julianna asked as we passed through a blast door into a new corridor, giving me a wink. She had my back. The corridor struck me as odd, for it had no doors along it, while a door at the far end sat closed.

"No. That could be what they want. I think this could be a shifting maze. If I had my powers, I could..." a roar interrupted my answer.

The door at our rear slid shut, almost slicing off the legs of one Ranger before he could leap out of the way. Half our group, including Kimberly, stood on the other side of the door.

The comms erupted with chatter, with the sergeants reporting what had happened. "The door won't open," one Ranger said, trying the door controls. "Should we try to shoot them?"

"Press your glove to the console, see if your implant can hack it," a sergeant ordered.

The Ranger did, but then stiffened as a *zap* sound filled the air. He crumpled to the ground. "Booby-trapped," the sergeant said, cursing.

"I have a feeling this was intentional," Isabelle remarked in a cool, calm tone. She turned her gaze to the far door. "And I fear this wasn't the only surprise awaiting us."

Her fear was justified a moment later as the door at the far end of the corridor slid up, revealing half a dozen or more undead. Only, they weren't the conscious undead like me. No, the skin missing from their faces, one missing an eye and another missing the skin from his arm, showing bone at one end, suggested these were the mindless variety.

The lead undead let out a feral roar and ran, not lumbered, toward us.

"Open fire!" Isabelle shouted, needlessly, for the team had already begun firing. Bullets tore through the flesh of the feral undead while lasers burned into them.

The lead monster fell, but the others kept on, showing no concern for their fallen comrade. They would be on us in seconds, despite the length of the corridor.

"Grenade!" one Ranger called, tossing a grenade in the path of the charging onslaught. It exploded seconds later, sending shrapnel slashing into the walking corpses, with minimal effect.

"We do this the hard way, then," Isabelle said, shouldering her rifle and withdrawing two swords from the scabbards on her back. They gleamed in the bright light of the corridor. She stood at the fore of the enemy assault, fearless in the face of possible death. Had she forgotten her diminished power in this place?

The first foe reached Isabelle and found themselves decapitated by a blurring casual swipe of her blade. The second blade thrust through the chest of the second enemy.

Possessing only a rifle and daggers, I chose to try to fire past my cousin. I pulled the trigger and electro-magnetically propelled bullets streaked through the air and slammed into the reanimated enemies further down the hall.

More of the enemies were running through the doorway. I estimated a few dozen. Who knew how many of the mindless creatures lay in the facility? It was clear our foe had laid a trap for us, using the monsters as their cannon fodder to rebuff our attack. Or were they trying to buy time for reinforcements to arrive?

Our backs were pressed against the wall, or door, in this case. We had nowhere to run. It was fight or die.

Isabelle stabbed another undead with both blades at once, kicking him back into his comrades, buying a moment of breathing room. Another grenade sailed toward the rear of the enemy column and sent a few more toppling to the ground, though they got up moments later.

"Rachel, does your power work in here?" my cousin shouted through the comm to be heard over the din.

"Let me try!" I said into my comm. Stepping back to let another Ranger take my place, I closed my eyes and envisioned summoning a graviton ball. As I reopened my eyes, the orb appeared as commanded, though it seemed darker than I remembered. "I can do it!"

"Good," she replied grimly. "Give them hell."

I moved the ball ahead of Isabelle and strengthened it. I felt air move past my face as the orb started to emit ever-stronger gravitational pulses. I poured more power into it, willing it to become a full-blown singularity.

I heard gasps as the singularity flared to life, becoming visible to people other than me. It was likely the first time many of them had seen me use my powers for anything other than flying, which would have seemed magical because they couldn't see the gravitational anomaly I followed.

Seizing the singularity in my mind's eye, I pushed the whirlpool of gravitons forward. The first enemy it touched turned to multi-colored mush and swirled around like water being sucked into a narrow drain. I felt it growing in strength, threatening to expand beyond its current diameter, and pushed my mind more firmly around it, forcing it to retain its current dimensions. Within seconds, the singularity returned to its customary pure black color and I felt more tired than I had a moment before.

I shoved the miniature black hole forward and swallowed up three more enemies in rapid succession, which almost caused me to fall to my knees as I grappled with the rapid increase in power contained within the singularity. But I held on, knowing if I lost control of the singularity and it continued absorbing mass or energy it could grow ever-larger until it swallowed the planet. I was the only power standing between my creation and possible disaster.

Moving more cautiously with the whirlpool of death, I crushed two more and finally it was at the far door. *Here goes nothing*, I thought, shoving the whirlpool toward the door. No sooner had the inky darkness touched the metal of the frame than the entire doorway twisted and ripped from the walls with an ear-wrenching screech. In the aftermath, the walls of the corridor framed empty space.

With that last exertion, I knew I had to collapse the black hole in on itself now or I wouldn't have enough power to. Summoning the last of my strength, I *pushed* on the edges of the singularity like one might push flattened dough, condensing the energy with the expectation that it would grow unstable and, devoid of new sources of energy, collapse in on itself.

At first, it didn't seem my action would work. I gritted my teeth as I railed mentally against the power of my creation. But I pushed once, twice, three times and finally, after four agonizing seconds, the black hole wobbled and then winked out of existence, leaving only stunned silence.

"Amazing," Isabelle said in an admiring tone. "Let's press forward. Did anyone get that bloody door open yet?" she asked through the channel.

"Negative," a voice replied. "We're bringing up a tech crew, but it might still be booby-trapped, so we're not taking any chances."

"Fine. Make yourselves useful, though, and look around for any points of interest. If you can pinpoint the nullification generator, I would be most appreciative. Once it's destroyed I can get everyone out quickly."

"Yes, ma'am," the man on the other end replied.

A few straggling undead charged through the opening my power had created, but they were cut down by concentrated fire. Now that the element of surprise had been lost, they had no chance to cross the distance.

Isabelle led us down the corridor, stepping over the unmoving corpses of our enemies, to a junction. "Which way?" she mused aloud to herself.

"Let me try something. Ma'am," I amended a second later. I had to remember my cover identity and not talk so familiarly to her.

She turned and raised an eyebrow at me. "Go ahead."

I closed my eyes and cast out my senses. If my hypothesis was correct, I could pinpoint...there. I raised my arm and pointed left, toward the direction I felt the nullification generator, which cast out waves of gravity. "The generator is that way."

"Are you certain?" she asked.

"Yes. I can feel the gravitons pulsing off it."

"Gravitons? What made you think to try to sense it?"

"I felt my power grow stronger when I entered the building, which coincided with the magic nullification field. I theorized that the magic nullification field either uses gravitons to suppress magic, and your power, or, at the very least, this particular model is doing so."

She inclined her head. "I'm impressed, Private. Left it is."

Julianna punched me on the shoulder. "Show off."

"Shut up," I said, attempting to sound hurt.

Isabelle spoke through the squadron comms as she walked. "Captain Wilson, we believe we've found the generator."

"Good, because enemy reinforcements are inbound. I'm sorry, but I'm pulling the remaining troops out to mount a defense."

"How long can you hold them?"

"I've launched our fighters, and our gunships are moving to intercept also, but the *Daedalus* wasn't meant for prolonged fights, and the enemy has three squadrons and three corvettes moving in."

They'll be outnumbered, I thought. The *Daedalus* was only about as big as a corvette, which made it maneuverable but also no match for larger, or more numerous, capital ships.

"Do your best, and if you have to leave, do so."

"We're not going to leave you behind, Ma'am. And we don't leave our soldiers behind."

"That's an order, Captain Wilson," Isabelle snapped. "If it's the *Daedalus'* life and the lives of her crew on the line, get to safety. We'll find our own way to safety."

"Fine," my CO said, not sounding pleased.

The left corridor at the junction wound its way deeper into the mountain, seeming to curve as it went. Here, doors lined the corridor infrequently, which meant our team had to split up and clear the rooms as we went, slowing things down. But better to do that than find enemies at our rear.

Most of the rooms were sleeping quarters, and vacant, with possessions remaining. Some looked like labs, but were cleared out. In a few rooms, we found men and women dressed like scientists. Isabelle ordered them to be brought along but insisted they wear stun cuffs.

At last we reached another junction. I pointed to the right, for I could now feel the residual energy emitted by the magic nullification generator radiating from that direction clearly.

Isabelle turned the corner and jumped back immediately. In front of her, rapid bursts of laser fire lit up the hallway, striking the walls and sizzling in the distance.

"Two laser turrets," she reported. "Idiot," she said, seemingly to herself. Everyone knew it was standard procedure to look before turning a corner. It felt odd to see her slip up. Being without her powers must be getting to her finally.

"I got something for it, ma'am," one of my fellow Rangers offered, stepping forward with an RPG launcher.

Isabelle gestured. "Be my guest."

The Ranger poked his RPG launcher around the corner while swiveling the screen to see what the tip of the weapon was aiming at. He pulled the trigger and a grenade sailed through the air, landing between the two turrets. The grenade exploded moments later, disabling them both.

Isabelle swept around the corner, pistols spitting bullets to confirm the operators of the turrets were well and truly dead. The blast door behind them remained closed.

"Rachel, do your thing on this door," she said. "We don't have time for explosives."

I approached and touched my hand to the metal. Then I summoned a ball of gravitons and expanded it to singularity strength in the space of a moment. Only this time, I made it vertical instead of horizontal. It consumed the door and started to consume the walls, following a circular pattern.

Laser fire from people in the room faded into the singularity.

I stepped to the side and, maintaining my control on the baby singularity, prepared to close it. "I'm collapsing it in three, two, one," I said, as way of warning.

The instant the singularity collapsed into a pinprick of darkness Isabelle moved in, firing again. By the time I followed her inside, two guards were dead and three technicians had hands up in surrender. One hadn't surrendered, however, and was typing furiously on the console. A trash can icon with files flying into it on the holo-display made it clear what he was trying to do.

Isabelle was having none of it, however, and a bullet to the head stopped the technician. She then approached the console and canceled the deletion. "Somebody cuff those three," she waived vaguely at the techs who'd surrendered. She produced a storage drive and stuck it into an open port on the computer system. The holo-display switched from trashing files to copying them to

Isabelle's storage drive. "Rachel, find a way to turn that nullification field off."

While the other Rangers secured the new prisoners, I approached an empty terminal. While I appreciated being given an important job, I worried her over-reliance on me might tip off my true identity. I *did* have the same name in my pseudonym as my real name. Then again, Rachel was a popular name.

I searched through the menu options until I found a control for the nullification field. Nothing indicated that it was anything more than what it was called. Could it be that *all* nullification fields blocked magic by emitting gravitons? I'd have to ask my Uncle Jason about it next time I saw him. Assuming we made it out of here. I hadn't heard that the *Daedalus* had retreated yet, but I knew it could be any minute. I switched off the field and immediately felt my power grow weaker - back to normal, rather. "It's off," I said.

Isabelle didn't answer, her eyes focusing on something displayed on the holo-display. Project Necromancy. And the icon beneath it, the symbol of the United Federation of Planets.

I stepped up beside her. "What is Project Necromancy? It has a Federation logo."

"It's nothing," she said, hurriedly closing the file. She wouldn't meet my eyes.

My eyes narrowed. "I don't believe you. What's Project Necromancy?"

"We don't have time to discuss it," she said, still not meeting my eyes. "The field is down, I can shift us all out of here. Gather up!" she ordered. She looked at me, leaned close and whispered, "We can discuss it later."

"Damn right we will," I whispered back. While I didn't know the contents of the file, the name sounded suspiciously like what happened to Galatia IV - resurrection of the dead.

Everyone gathered in the room and then we shifted.

WE'D MADE IT TO THE *Daedalus* just in time to make for the void and, in this case comfort, of space, with enemy forces in close pursuit. Fortunately, we'd only lost four fighters and one gunship. How the enemy had been able to mount such a large defense on a Federation-controlled planet was a question I had, but the burning question about what Project Necromancy consisted of superseded it.

Following the debriefing, I stopped in the hallway. *Jarvis, call Isabelle.*

One moment, Jarvis replied.

Yes, Rachel? Isabelle responded a few moments later.

We need to talk, I said, thankful that emotion was hard to convey through implants. I was barely keeping my anger in check.

Meet me at my quarters, she said before closing the line.

I stormed to her quarters and knocked, heedless of who might see. The hallway was empty, however.

The door slid open. "Come in," Isabelle said in a neutral tone.

I stormed in, eyes seeking out my cousin, who sat behind the desk. She'd been given Captain Wilson's office temporarily by virtue of her rank. I waited until the door slid shut behind me to speak. "Do you have a moment?" I wanted to shout my question again, but figured that wouldn't be productive. Despite my real identity, she was still my elder.

"Please, sit down," she said, gesturing to a chair in front of the desk.

I sat. An awkward silence settled over the room. "You can't tell me that project is nothing."

My cousin sighed. "No, it's not nothing."

"Then what is it?" I clenched my fists.

"What I'm about to tell you is top secret information, Rachel. If you were actually a private you would have been sent to the brig for asking me repeatedly or been told it's above your clearance level."

"But I'm not," I said, gritting my teeth.

"No, you're not, which is why we're talking. But what I'm saying is, this information cannot leave this room. Can you agree to that?"

I grudgingly nodded.

"Good. Project Necromancy was a top-secret project to study the exact same thing the Xanos Reapers ended up engineering through the shell corporation Kimberly's father worked for. Only...it was established over twenty years ago."

"You're saying the Federation knew about this virus *twenty years ago*?" I asked, incredulous.

"Not just knew about it...the Federation research department developed it."

"So...Galatia IV was an inside job?" Rage built inside me.

My cousin held up her hand and shook it. "No, the research was lost when Icarus Station was destroyed. We thought that was the end of it. But we were..."

"Wait," I interrupted. "Did you say Icarus Station? As in the Icarus Station my mother was in command of?"

Isabelle nodded sadly. "You wanted the truth. Yes, it is one and the same."

"That was the secret she died protecting," I said, realization dawning. "My father said she died protecting secrets that could never be allowed to fall into the wrong hands."

"It was one of the secrets," Isabelle agreed. "Every project on Icarus Station was top secret. It was easier to ensure secrecy that way, rather than having separate projects on different stations and risk interception of staff or materials while in transit between teams."

I blinked back tears. "If the station was destroyed, how did Project Necromancy make it into the hands of the Xanos Reapers?"

"That's what I've been trying to determine. We thought this secret had been buried with…" she stopped.

"With my mother in her grave," I finished, bitterness creeping into my voice. "And she died for nothing, since the secret got out anyway."

"She did *not* die for nothing," Isabelle said, heat in her voice. "Her death delayed the virus being unleashed by evil parties for almost twenty years, and several other projects being developed on that station remain buried. Her death was not in vain."

I didn't see it that way. Anger burned within me. Anger at my father for not telling me the truth. Anger that he allowed my mother to be put in such a position where she sacrificed her life for the Federation's secrets. Anger that the Federation had even been researching the virus which ended up killing or ruining the lives of millions. I couldn't speak. "Did my father know?" I had to ask - had to know.

Isabelle closed her eyes for a moment. "Yes. No top-secret projects are withheld from the supreme commander."

"Or you," I said out of spite. "That's why you were worried when that popped up on the holo, wasn't it? It proves the Xanos Reapers used the *Federation's* research to engineer the virus."

Isabelle's silence was confirmation enough. "I didn't know positively until today," she said so quietly I almost didn't hear her. "I'm sorry. It was for the greater good." The armor she wore all the time was torn away as the shame of what the Federation had authorized overwhelmed her.

"Greater good," I mocked, snorting. "Tell that to the families of the millions dead and to those left undead, hated and ostracized by society." Without waiting for her response, I stood up, slammed the door control so hard the glass cracked, and left.

Chapter 25

Three weeks after the assault on the Xanos Reapers facility and I was still brooding about what felt like a betrayal. I tried to shove it aside - temporarily - as Captain Wilson spoke once again in the briefing room of the *Daedalus*.

"Because of intel received on Urkusk, we now know the location of a secret base where the Xanos Reapers are continuing production of the virus."

That caused gasps from both the living and undead Rangers. Even my eyes widened with surprise. They had the research, but for them to continue producing the virus, that was bad.

"The good news is the virus is not *yet* complete. But time is of the essence."

An image appeared, this time of a giant asteroid floating amid a variety of smaller asteroids. "The complicating factor is this. The base is located deep within an asteroid. Our probes revealed several other nearby asteroids which look like they are watch posts or house defensive platforms and fighters. The tacticians with the Navy suspect the entire cluster will come alive at the first sight of Federation ships. The asteroid also features an immensely powerful shield, which would keep our fleet busy for hours bombarding it. Long enough for the Reapers to call for reinforcements or escape."

A video replaced the image. It showed a pirate ship shifting in at the edge of the asteroid field and approaching the base without incident. "There is a lot of activity in and out of this asteroid. The plan is to infiltrate the facility and sabotage their defensive capabilities ahead of the main fleet.

"To accomplish this, the *Daedalus* will be transformed into a replica of a pirate ship. Everything from the paint on our hull to our transponder's engine signatures will be modified to be authentic. This should allow us to pass through their defenses and get aboard the asteroid. Once there, we will infiltrate the base and disable the shield generator. Then we exfiltrate and call in the fleet. With its shields down, a series of bunker-buster nukes will be fired into the crust of the asteroid and crack it in two. The heat and radiation from the nuclear blasts will obliterate the virus."

I shuddered. That was a lot of force to bring to bear on the asteroid. Time would be of the essence as we hurried to escape before the nukes launched. No one asked the obvious question.

After the briefing, Julianna found me cleaning my rifle. "Hey," she said, sitting across from me at the table.

"Hey," I said, not looking up from my work.

"You haven't been yourself lately," she began. "Ever since the last mission."

I wanted to tell her. Wanted to spill the beans about what I'd found out - what Isabelle had told me. But I couldn't. It was information a grunt like me wouldn't have, Ranger or not. My need for secrecy, to maintain my cover identity, overwhelmed my anger. "We almost got caught in a trap," I hedged, thinking fast. "I don't want to see that happen again."

"You think the Federation would nuke its own people?"

"If it's for the greater good, yeah," I said, mimicking the pair of words my father and cousin were fond of using. "What are the lives of a few Rangers compared to how many millions or billions who will die if the virus makes it off that asteroid intact? Imagine it being released on Tar Ebon."

"It would be an apocalyptic event," she agreed. "There'd be no stopping it."

"At least then they'd know our pain," I grumbled. Maybe a few billion more undead would help even the cosmic scales and end the ostracizing I'd witnessed thus far.

My friend lowered her voice. "Some of the others were talking about getting back at the living," Julianna said.

My eyes narrowed. "Getting back how?" That was dangerous talk. Treasonous talk.

"Something big, that's all I know."

"Who is talking about it?"

She hesitated, as if realizing she'd said too much.

"I won't tell," I promised.

"Captain Wilson, Colonel Schattler."

My eyebrows raised in surprise. "All the way from the top?"

"It sounds like it goes beyond them. They're just one cog in the wheel, but undead inside and outside the military are angry at the mistreatment. They want action."

"Does this movement have a name?"

"They call themselves the Dread Legion."

"Sounds dreadfully ominous," I said, smirking.

"Shut up. I'm serious."

"Why haven't I heard about it?"

"You've been holed in your bunk for the past three weeks," she pointed out. "When you're not training. Nobody's had the chance to speak to you."

"Oh. Developments are happening that quick?"

"Well, no," she began, hesitant again. "I've known about it for months. But we've only recently started reaching outside of the inner circle."

My friend was in an "inner circle" and hadn't told me anything about it? I felt a twinge of anger that she hadn't shared the information with me. But then again, I hadn't told *her* about my true heritage in all this time either.

"So, are you in?"

"Do I have to give an answer right now?" The truth was I wanted to say no, but was afraid of retaliation. If I wasn't with them, would they consider me their enemy?

"Soon," she said, unhelpfully.

"Let me think on it," I replied, buying time.

I SAT ABOARD THE *Dread Stallion,* the cover name for the *Daedalus,* as it shifted out of shadow space. On the display, the asteroid field neared.

Not being near the bridge, I couldn't hear what communications were transpiring. But I imagined the Xanos Reapers questioning the bridge, asking for confirmation codes or their transponder signal and business in the region before they blew us away.

Things must have gone according to plan, because the ship didn't take evasive action and no calls to prepare for shift came. Instead the ship remained on course for the large asteroid.

I tugged at my new uniform. We'd ditched any trace of advanced Federation armor in favor of crude armor true pirates would use. My own uniform consisted of an ill-fitting tan tunic beneath a breastplate. Armor plating covered my wrists, forearm, the back of my hands, thighs, knees, ankles and groin, but it was disjointed and not formed of a single piece like Federation armor was. It was uncomfortable and left me feeling extra vulnerable.

Fortunately for me, I had my gravity manipulation powers to fall back on in lieu of armor. But as I'd found out, using my power offensively, like to suck people into the singularity, drained my energy faster than using it defensively to absorb lasers or projectiles.

Twenty minutes after shifting into the system, the asteroid base loomed ahead. Dozens of defense batteries bristled along the surface of the asteroid. Two fighters streaked toward us and took up escort formation. I harbored no doubt they would turn on our ship in an instant if given a reason. Pirates weren't given a cutthroat reputation for no reason.

A few minutes later, the *Dread Stallion* touched down in the massive landing bay and a *clank* suggested the landing clamps locking into place. If they didn't want us to leave, we would need to cut the landing clamps in order to get out. A look at the external displays showed three other corvettes similar in size to our ship, multiple transport ships and freighters and dozens of starfighters. They weren't messing around when it came to security.

"All right team," Lieutenant Fanshawe said entering the ready-room. "Listen up. Remember the plan and your backstories. You all have your targets. Use your encrypted squad channel to communicate once you're in position, then await orders."

Lieutenant Juliet Fanshawe was Captain Wilson's living stand-in for this mission. He was with the fleet and the rest of the Seventy-Fifth, since only two companies had been requisitioned for this mission. It wouldn't do for a corvette to be housing more than one hundred pirates - that would raise suspicion. And Captain Wilson claimed his face was widely circulated, hence he deferred to the lieutenant.

The rear door to the ship opened and the ramp lowered. A well-dressed man in a suit stood there, with two dozen guards pointing their weapons toward us.

The lieutenant strode calmly down the ramp while the rest of us prepared to disembark with crates and other containers. Our official story was that we were smugglers. The cover story also explained why we were only allowed to wear two side-arms per person - smugglers didn't often use heavy weapons.

"We have several crates of cargo," the lieutenant began. "Food, mechanical and medical supplies."

The man in the suit bowed. "Excellent. Mister Helinski will be pleased." He held out a hand. "I just need a copy of your manifest so I may validate it against our records."

A lump formed in my throat. This wasn't part of the plan. Advanced validation of manifests among pirates and smugglers? Who would have thought? Well, someone should have, because it seemed we were about to be caught. I fingered the hilt of my pistol, shifting slightly to ensure I had a clear line of sight of my soon-to-be foes.

"Of course," Lieutenant Fanshawe said smoothly, offering a datapad.

The man in the suit studied the data on the pad, then tapped into his own pad. He pursed his lips.

I firmly grasped the hilt of my pistol this time, preparing to draw and already picking a target - a big man with bushy eyebrows standing next to the suited man. He looked like he would be dangerous in a firefight.

At last the suited man smiled and returned the datapad to the lieutenant. "Everything looks to be in order. Please proceed to these areas with your loads." He produced a data chip and handed it over.

I released the grip I'd had on my pistol and relaxed my muscles slightly. Then I bent over and picked up two crates of medical supplies with the ease of my undead strength.

The plan called for separate groups of our team to reach key areas on the asteroid base, then, when the signal was given, strike in unison. Acting too early and giving advance warning to the enemy could be disastrous and could foil the Federation Navy's attack plan entirely.

My area was the shield generator, which, according to intel, was located near the laboratory. Assuming that was correct, I would drop my supplies, which secretly contained rifles and heavy weapons, and my team would make for the shield generator when the signal was given. It was a bit of a flimsy plan, but under no circumstances could the virus be allowed to leave the asteroid. I imagined the Federation setting up a blockade and losing dozens of ships as the Xanos Reapers chose this proverbial hill to die on. Even with a blockade, all it took was one ship to get out and it could spread like wildfire across the Federation.

Julianna, myself and four other Rangers were assigned to the first group. The second group of six Rangers would make for the weapons control center, with their crates containing mechanical parts. The third group carrying foodstuffs would make for the communication center in order to signal the fleet. The thick asteroid would not permit long distance communication with just our implants or even with the *Daedalus*. Only using the external array would work.

The final group, consisting of two dozen Rangers, would remain with the lieutenant and prepare to wreak havoc in the hangar bay once the chaos began. The *Daedalus* had been stripped of its gunships and fighter complements for this mission, but it still had its external weapons. The landing clamps would still need to be dealt with before we could exfiltrate.

The three remote groups departed the corvette-disguised-as-a-freighter and split in separate directions.

Crew members we passed paid us no mind as we moved through the cavernous tunnels.

I reached out with my power as I walked. Below our feet, gravity waves pulsed out, keeping people and objects on the ground as if they were on a planet the size of Tar Ebon.

We reached the medical section, a facility within a cavern of the asteroid. Security, if you could call it that, waved us through and grunted out directions to where to bring the supplies. According to the schematics, the shield generator was beyond the medical facility. There should be a door on the far side of the warehouse.

Once inside the facility, we saw more evidence of security surrounding one particular door at the far end of the hallway and signs proclaiming "restricted" with pictures of vials and a skull and crossbones. *That must be where they're developing the virus.*

Miss, I'm detecting a magic nullification field approximately one hundred and twenty yards ahead.

Makes sense. One mage getting in there could set fire to the whole place. And the normal guards wouldn't be able to stop them easily.

Jarvis didn't reply. He seemed to have learned when I was talking to myself or talking to him and kept quiet most days. If there was an analytical question, he was always ready with answers, but he lacked personality. Maybe one day I'd get around to improving his programming.

We took a right, as directed, and reached the medical supply warehouse. I set down my two crates and stretched, looking around. Dozens of piles filled the warehouse, while hover-lifts and workers moved this way and that. A large door at the far end of the warehouse caught my eye. *The door to the shield generator, as expected.*

Julianna and the other four Rangers looked toward me, each having dropped their load as well. "Now we wait," I said. "Command, this is med team. We are in place."

"Acknowledged, med team," the lieutenant said. "Stand by for signal and maintain radio silence."

I clicked in response, then sighed.

"You know it'll look suspicious if we sit here for too long," Julianna pointed out.

"Start opening the crates and unload...slowly," I said. "Then we hope the other teams do their jobs fast." *Hurry*, I thought.

I'd unloaded my crate down to the layer of medications above my rifle and unloaded the other crate entirely. The comms team had checked in, but the weapons control team hadn't yet. We couldn't go much slower.

"Weapons team compromised!" a male voice shouted through the comms. "We are pinned down and unable to reach the target."

Shit, I thought, remembering the saying about the best laid plans of mice and men. Well, we were the mice about to be squashed if we didn't move. I swiveled my head from side-to-side, but the workers had disappeared. "They're on to us." I activated my comm. "Lieutenant, I think we've been made. Recommend we move now."

"Comms and med teams, you are a go. If either team is able, make for the weapons center on your way out."

I reached into my crate and withdrew my rifle, grenades, utility belt, a pack of heavy explosives and my electro-staff. I checked my rifle and turned the safety off. Locked and loaded.

The others had just dug their weapons out when red alarms along the walls lit up, sirens sounded and the door at the far end of the warehouse burst open. A dozen or more warehouse workers with pistols rushed in.

I fired a burst in their direction and then dove for cover behind a crate. The others did the same.

Laser fire burned into the metal crates and flashed overhead, searing the air.

I whipped out a grenade, armed it and tossed it toward our enemies, who dove for cover. The explosion took out two or three of them.

A laser slammed into the crate next to my shoulder. "They're behind us!" Julianna warned.

Three Rangers swiveled to face the newcomers, while me and the other two continued firing at the first group of pirates. We couldn't keep this up for long. We would run out of ammo.

I must do something, I thought. But what could I do? Summon a singularity and send it toward them? Swallowing that many bodies would probably knock me unconscious.

Create a shield to absorb their shots? Yes, but I couldn't make a shield completely around us and hold it for long, and they could just wait us out, which would mean the mission failed.

Wait, I thought. The anti-gravity generator on the asteroid. It still pulsed, like a distant heartbeat. What if I could somehow turn it off, even temporarily? "I'm going to try something!" I shouted. "Cover me!"

I closed my eyes and reached out toward the source of the gravity. Down, down and to the left. Like waves in the ocean pounding the beach. I rode the waves with my mind's eye, like surfing on an ocean of pure darkness. Down my mind spiraled until I reached the dark heart of the asteroid.

"All Rangers, activate mag-boots," I ordered through the comm channel. "I'm about to do something crazy." I activated my own mag-boots. Without waiting for a response, I *twisted* the gravity source and...there...I changed it from emitting gravity to emitting anti-gravity.

The effect came near-instantly, as I felt a repulsion negated only by the power of magnetism present in my boots. The enemy, not having heard our words, rose into the air, arms flapping, weapons floating from their startled grips.

In that moment, they became like fish in a floating barrel. I fired at first one target and then another and another. The velocity of the bullets overcame the lack of gravity so they flew straight. My comrades joined in and within a minute dozens of corpses floated to the roof of the cavern.

"Quick, to the shield generator," I ordered.

"Are you going to reverse whatever it was you did?" Julianna said. "Or are we just going to keep walking like this?" She demonstrated by deactivating one boot and lifted her leg, then took a step and reactivated it. She repeated the step with the second foot.

I grunted. I hadn't thought that far ahead. "We don't have time for me to re-enable. And we don't know how many more enemies are still out there, floating around. If I reverse the effect it would put us back at square one."

The matter settled, we made for the far door. Once we got the system down - deactivate, step, activate, repeat with second foot - we seemed to make almost normal progress.

Blood floated toward the ceiling from the corpses. Unlike zero gravity, this was anti-gravity, so we were essentially stuck to the ceiling looking toward the floor. It wasn't a powerful anti-gravity field because it fought the natural gravity produced by the mass of the asteroid, but it still meant everything eventually floated to the ceiling if it was heavy enough. Looking back, even the crates were rising a bit more off the ground every moment.

We passed through the door which would lead us to the shield generator and found ourselves in a long hallway. Several enemy guards were pinned to the ceiling or had grabbed on to door handles, outcroppings or anything to keep them on the floor. Some with mag-boots had been clever enough to clamp to the walls, so they stood on the side.

But still, the disorientation of their awkward positions made them easy pickings for our team. We cut through them, leaving none alive. God knew they wouldn't show us any mercy, given the chance.

"Comms team is in position," a voice said through the squad channel.

"Signal the fleet," the lieutenant ordered.

The door at the far end of the hall opened without incident and there stood the shield generator. It was a large rotating cylinder with thick cables running toward the roof of the asteroid at various points. I presumed those went to the shield generator emitters, which would send the energy field to emitters on the other side of the asteroid, creating a blanket around the enemy base. But there was only one generator, and we were going to blow it to hell.

Surprisingly, few guards floated in the shield generator room. A few lab techs looked to be floating in a control room, but we didn't bother with them. We didn't want to shut the generator down temporarily.

"Spread out evenly around the base. Place your charges but do not arm until I give the command," I said. "Lieutenant, this is shield team. We are moving into position around the shield generator at this time."

"Good, shield team. Whatever you did to reverse the gravity sent pirates into disarray. Once you're done, get your asses to the weapon control center to support comms team."

"Have we had any more contact from weapons team?"

"Negative," her voice sounded grim. "The mission comes first. Without those weapons down our navy stands to take heavy losses on their attack runs."

"Understood. Team One out," I said, closing the channel.

The six of us spread out and placed charges around the shield generator. "Set for two minutes," I ordered, setting my own charge for two minutes. My finger hovered over the arm button. "On my mark. Mark." *Beep*, the charge was armed.

We clumped our way back the way we'd come and were halfway down the hall when the charges detonated. A sickening screech of metal accompanied the shield generator falling apart. Mission accomplished.

Using the map as an overlay in my mind's eye, I led our team toward the weapons sector. The third team was already engaged with the enemy. These foes were better prepared and had clamped themselves to the floor.

"Need some help?" I asked as we clumped up behind the third team. They were missing one Ranger.

"Yeah, they've fortified the control center and countered your tactic," the squad leader replied. "Got any more tricks up your sleeve?"

"The fleet has shifted in-system," the lieutenant said. "They've engaged the enemy fleet but bombers are delayed until weapons are confirmed disabled. What's your status, teams?"

"The enemy is entrenched," I said, summarizing what the squad leader of team three had said. "But I'm going to try to dig them out."

"Do it quick, Private."

"Yes, ma'am," I said, scrambling to think of something. *What if I fly past them,* I thought. *I could use a graviton ball to zoom past and shoot as I went. But I'd be exposed. I'd need a shield of gravitons around me to protect me. But then I wouldn't be able to shoot out. What if...*I had it.

"What's your plan?" Julianna said from next to me. "I know that look in your eyes."

"Time dilation," I said.

Her brows furrowed. "How?"

"Well, my...," I cut off. I'd almost said "my father." "...My research has shown that intense sources of gravity can cause time dilation to outside observers. Whatever is caught in the gravitational field moves more slowly compared to an observer outside said field."

"So?"

"I'm going to slow our enemies down. Get ready for gravity to disappear," I said through the squad channel.

"You mean go back to its original intensity?" the lieutenant asked.

"No. It'll drop to only the asteroid's natural gravity, which is minimal. Recommend maintaining mag-boot contact. Team One out." It was time.

I closed my eyes and found the gravity generator again. I inverted it, restoring it emitting gravitons. Then I summoned a wall around the gravity generator and, as the pressure built in my mind, formed a funnel streaking from the invisible enclosure toward the room we had just entered. The gravitational waves, acting like water in that they wanted to take the path of least resistance, traveled through the funnel like water in a pipe. The edge of the funnel lay a few feet in front of the foremost Rangers, meaning only our enemies would be affected by the gravitational field.

I opened my eyes. The enemy noticed the effects immediately. They moved sluggish and their arms lowered despite their efforts to pull them up. Time to turn up the power. I channeled all my power, leaving only a little in reserve, toward the gravity generator. The inclusion of my power super-infused the generator and as a result the waves came stronger and more frequently. The tidal force being generated by it increased and our enemies continued to slow.

Maintaining my shield around the gravity generator, I walked forward. "Wait here," I announced aloud. Once I was within the bounds of the gravity field the pirates ceased being slow and seemed to move at my speed. And they were struggling to bring their weapons to bear upon me. I didn't have much time. A glance behind me showed Julianna seeming to breathe faster. The time dilation field was affecting me.

I released my mag boots and at the same time surrounded myself with just enough anti-gravitons to negate the effect of the intense gravitational field. It worked, the enemy slowed to a crawl. Bringing my rifle up to my shoulder, I walked among them. Where they could barely bring their weapons to aim toward my knees, I was fully capable of shooting them in the chest or head, and I took advantage of it. Bang, bang, bang. The enemies died without firing a shot at me.

Exhausted, I released the containment field and anti-graviton field. Gravity returned to "normal," or what it had been when we first arrived on the asteroid, in a flash. I bent over, head pounding as if someone had taken a jackhammer to it.

Julianna and the other Rangers passed me, laying out every spare explosive we had.

"Where did the weapons team go?" I asked. "What happened to them?"

"We found them when we were on our way from the other direction," the squad leader of Team Three said. "They were ambushed from both directions before they'd even had a chance to set their crates down."

"Hmmm," I said, wondering how they'd been made.

Minutes later the weapons control center exploded. The pirates were now toothless, defenseless and unable to call for help. "Team One and Three headed back to the hangar," I reported.

"...Teams...hurry...nukes...inbound..." the lieutenant's voice came through as static.

My mind seized on one word, ignoring the static that hadn't been present before: "nukes." "Lieutenant, say again."

"Nukes...inbound...detonation...imminent." Through the crackle of the static I made out the words. "Leaving..." her words cut off as the asteroid shook. The first nuke must have hit.

No, I thought. By instinct, I closed my eyes and drew upon the last reserves of my power. I shrouded myself in gravitons and formed a singularity above my head. Opening my eyes, I sought out Julianna. "Julianna! Take my hand!" I reached out to her, several meters away.

The next detonation hit before she'd taken more than a step. I watched in horror as a wave of immense heat and energy surged through the cavern, turning Julianna to ash. I screamed, both in rage at her death and in pain, as the heat slammed into my gravitational shield and funneled toward the singularity. Fed new energy independent from me, the singularity stabilized and no longer leached off me. A third detonation washed over me but this time I barely felt it, whether because I was numb at the death of my friend or because the singularity had grown too strong, I wasn't sure.

A fourth detonation occurred farther in the asteroid, but it caused chunks of rock and debris to hurtle toward me. They were no match for the power of the singularity I'd given birth to, however. I stood at the eye of a detritus hurricane, anger burning deep inside.

When the debris cleared, a huge hole in the top of the asteroid gaped above me. Shoving the singularity straight up, I soared toward empty space. With the asteroid broken, there was no need for an anti-gravity field around me to allow me to follow behind the singularity.

There I floated, eyes searching the vacuum. I sought the source of the nukes. Through the asteroid field I spotted a cluster of ships. I turned the singularity in that direction and shot straight toward the fleet.

The first asteroid the singularity met collapsed as rock met the event horizon. I passed through empty space a moment later. The same phenomenon happened with all the asteroids between me and the target of my ire.

I emerged from the asteroid field traveling incredibly fast. I willed the singularity onward with single-minded purpose. Gone was the innocent girl from Galatia IV. In her place was an undead killing machine Hellbent on avenging her friend's death. *You didn't die in vain, Julianna*, I thought.

The Federation fleet, seeing me coming now, or at least detecting the singularity, began firing. A starfighter flashed past me and swiveled around to face me. It fired a stream of bullets at me, but I held up a hand and the bullets flowed instead toward the singularity. Then I clenched my fist and caught the fighter in the grip of the gravity-well too. It spun out of control until moments later the black hole tore it apart.

Weariness had fled, replaced by rage. The fighter being swallowed into the black hole fueled my rage and made me hunger for more. I imagined if I could see my face in that moment I would have feared what I saw. In retrospect, my feelings were mirroring the singularity. It had taken on a life of its own - not sentience per se, but a chaotic hunger that spoke to the basest nature of my virus-infused body. It brought to the surface the primal urges I'd have felt if I hadn't had the treatment to "cure" me.

I picked up speed as I soared toward the first capital ship. A frigate, by the looks of it. Growling, though there was no sound in space so it only resulted in the rumbling sensation in my throat, I aimed straight toward the front of the ship. The black hole touched the silver metal of the frigate and *twisted* it, swallowing it faster than my eye could follow. Fragments of hull, electronic equipment, bodies, all swirled and disappeared into the whirlpool of death and destruction crashing into their midst. Before I knew it I was through, and a glance behind me showed a bisected ship with the entire middle of it missing. Bodies spilled into space. *The ones swallowed up were the lucky ones - it was probably painless for them.*

Not losing momentum, I arced toward the second ship, a cruiser. It continued to fire at me. I saw what looked like a nuke flaring toward me - it was larger than the other missiles - but it flew into the singularity and died without even flare of light or heat escaping. Next, the ship tried to evade, turning, but it didn't deter me. I hit at an angle and cut diagonally through it, leaving a gutted hulk behind. I stopped, floating in the void, feeling near infinite power.

Fighters streaked through the void but not toward me, this time. They fled to their capital ships and, one by one, the remaining ships shifted into shadow space.

Without enemies in sight, I deflated, my anger cooling in the icy void of space. The reality of what I'd done washed over me in waves, bringing on a feeling of nausea. If I'd eaten anything recently,

I might have thrown it up. *What have I done?* No. What had they *made* me do? The Federation, firing into the asteroid. If I hadn't had my powers, I would have been vaporized like...like Julianna. I had to think her name. I couldn't let her memory fade. Had the Federation known we were in there? Had they intentionally sought to eliminate us?

I lost track of time, floating there alone in the soundless depth of space. A living human would have long been dead, which made me thankful for the lack of a need to breath. Still, without the anger burning deep inside I felt weak. The nearest planet was millions of lightyears away in an unknown direction and there was no way I could maintain a gravity ball long enough to reach habitation before I died from thirst or hunger. I thought about going back to the wreckage of the asteroid to check for an alcove with supplies, but I was certain the nukes had irradiated the entire area.

Jarvis, how long can I last out here?

The virus and nanites are insulating your body. But thirst will cause severe dehydration and organ shut down within thirty-six hours.

Far longer than it would take to reach a planet, right?

Correct, he said, confirming my fears.

And how much radiation can I take?

You've already received a severe dose from the nuclear detonations, but the nanites and virus repaired the damage. Prolonged presence in a radiation source of that magnitude will overwhelm the healing capability of your body within three hours, twenty-four minutes and ten seconds.

Thanks for the precision estimate on how long it would take for me to die, I said sarcastically.

Of course, miss.

That was sarcasm.

Ah. I will make note of this experience to improve my personality matrix.

Well, do you have any suggestions for how I can not die?

At this point, unless a third-party intervenes, any attempt at survival will ultimately end in failure.

I closed my eyes. What were the odds of that happening?

Time lost meaning as I floated, watching the asteroids stream through the void. For a time I lapsed into sleep, I think, because I jolted awake as a light flared though my eyelids.

My eyes snapped open to the sight of a ship shining a spotlight on me. It appeared to be an assault transport. In the distance, a corvette that reminded me of the *Daedalus* floated. Fear surged in me, followed by tensing of my muscles as I prepared to summon my power and defend myself.

My comm crackled. "Rachel, come in. Private Halbert, do you copy?" It sounded like Captain Wilson's voice.

"Captain?" I asked, even my sub-vocal voice sounding weak.

"You got it, Private. We came as soon as the fleet came back two ships short and the *Daedalus* didn't."

"They...killed...everyone," I said, struggling to string my words together.

"All right, we're opening the outer airlock. Can you reach it?"

"Yes." Suiting action to words, I gathered what felt like the last of my strength and summoned a small graviton ball which I followed into the open airlock. I released my power and slumped to the floor.

The outer door closed and the room pressurized. When the inner door opened Captain Wilson stood there, arms crossed.

I stumbled to my feet and he took my hand and helped me out.

"Get her some water and some food," he called out.

Moments later, two Rangers showed up with the requested sustenance.

The captain directed me to a bench. "Eat, drink and get your bearings. Then tell me what the hell happened out there."

I nodded and did as he directed. When I was ready, I started talking, meeting his questioning gaze. "Sir, we had completed the mission and were on our way back to the *Daedalus* when the Federation fleet fired on the base with nuclear warheads." I paused for effect, but he didn't react, just watched me with his usual dispassionate calm. "My entire team...they were vaporized after the second blast. I used my power to survive."

"And then you went after the fleet," he finished. "Private...what the reports said you did...you killed hundreds of crew members. You're lucky no one knew it was you or MPs would be here to take you into custody." He pointed out the viewport toward the shattered hulks of the ships I'd destroyed

"Wait," I said. "No one knows it was me?"

Captain Wilson shook his head. "Few people know about your power, and none in command of that fleet. So...I kept my mouth shut until I had all the facts."

"And now that you have the facts?"

"We've been betrayed," he said. "Sounds like the Federation wanted some undead Rangers out of commission...permanently. It's what we've feared would happen for a while now."

"Yes." The memory of my conversation with Julianna returned in a flash. "Julianna told me about your group. I want in," I said firmly.

The captain watched me for a long moment, whether for signs of hesitation or doubt I don't know, but he finally nodded. "You're in. And now it's time to get revenge."

Chapter 26

A day after the incident at the asteroid base and the account of the attack was nowhere to be found. I'd clicked through every holo-news station and no one was talking about it. Instead, most of the "top stories" were about a delegation of important Federation officials traveling around lobbying for support for one thing or another, a video of a cat dancing to a specific song and rumors of a trillionaire and his wife divorcing and splitting their estate.

The ship I sat on, the *Gamut*, wasn't the same as the *Daedalus*. It was structurally the same, but it lacked my team. Julianna. There were more undead here, with most of the crew being like me, which was a change from the *Daedalus*. Many of those lost on the asteroid base were living, and those who hadn't gone on the mission had transferred out.

Captain Wilson walked in as the news anchors began talking about the "important" Federation officials. I half-wondered if my father would be among them. "Display, off," he ordered and the holo blinked out of existence.

I met his stern gaze and swallowed a snappy comeback. "Sir?"

"It's time."

"Already?" It had been a day since I'd been rescued. My belly was full and I'd slept for twelve hours straight, but this soon?

"Strike while the iron is hot," he said. "Our targets are going to be on the opportune planet in a week. The plan's already in motion."

"Can you tell me what the plan is?"

"Come with me, and I will."

I nodded, stood up and followed the man. He led me to Colonel Schattler's quarters and, not waiting for an answer to his knock, opened the door and entered. "Sir, she's here."

The colonel looked up and smiled, the first time I think I'd seen him offer a genuine smile. "Private, thank you for coming."

Not that I'd had a choice. "Of course, sir." I stood there, waiting.

"Please, sit down." He gestured to a pair of chairs.

I took the one on the left, while Captain Wilson sat in the other.

"Tea?" the colonel asked, lifting an antique porcelain teapot and pointing to a pair of antique matching tea cups.

"No, thank you, sir. I'm still recovering from yesterday."

"Of course." He cleared his throat. "What has Captain Wilson told you so far?"

"Very little," I said carefully. I didn't want to share that Julianna had given me information before our mission.

"Well, the captain and I are part of a coalition of undead across the Federation who are dissatisfied with the new status quo imposed upon us by society and the inaction on the part of the Federation government to protect our kind."

The Dread Legion, I thought. "What's the name of this coalition?"

"We call ourselves the Dread Legion, because of how society dreads our existence and because we are everywhere, now."

"And what is it your group wants?" I asked, cautiously.

"We want society to finally realize our power," he said. "*We* are the next evolution of humankind and we deserve to have a place of honor within the Federation." His face took on a feral expression. "And if they won't honor us, we'll teach them to fear us."

I found myself nodding. Twice I'd found myself attacked by the living, with the first almost resulting in my death. Change and acceptance wouldn't come through peace.

"Do you want in?" he asked.

The memory of Julianna being vaporized before my eyes rose up. "Tell me one thing, sir. Why did they attack the asteroid with us still in there?"

The colonel didn't break eye contact. "They knew you were there. But the 'why' died with the commander of that cruiser you destroyed. My guess is secret orders to ensure you didn't survive."

"Me? Why me?"

He raised an eyebrow. "Word's gotten around about the Ranger who can control gravity. You're one of a kind. So, my guess is when word got around that you were going to be on that mission someone saw an opportunity to get rid of you."

"You think a Cultist within the navy?"

He shrugged. "Could be. Or just the Federation wanting to destroy aberrations."

"I'm in," I said with determination.

His smile returned, wider than before. "Excellent. Welcome to the Dread Legion."

AS IT TURNED OUT, THE Dread Legion had agents throughout the Federation. They were mostly undead with some living sympathizers, or in some cases supplicants, allied with them. They held positions in all walks of life, from lowly privates to colonels and higher in the military and from custodians to CEOs in the corporate world. And they were all pissed at the Federation's handling of the undead crisis.

And so there I was, a day after speaking with the colonel, sitting in a briefing room aboard the *Gamut* as we plotted treason. Well, we didn't call it treason - we called it avenging the dead. Perhaps it made us feel better about what we had to do.

"A delegation of high-ranking officials, both from the military and political ranks, will be speaking on the supposed threat of the Krai'kesh. They're hoping to garner support for one military project or another. The reason they're there doesn't matter. What matters is, the whole Federation will take notice when we kill them."

Six months ago, hell, six days ago, I would have gasped at those words. But now? Numbness washed over me, dulling my feelings. No one took notice when Orin was killed by an angry mob. No one batted an eye when Julianna and my entire team was murdered in cold blood by the Federation. Why should I care if a few overpaid blow-hards died?

"Here's the plan..." he began.

Chapter 27

The planet Galywix II was not a populous planet by galactic standards, but today it felt as if all ten point two billion people had turned out to its capital, Liberty City, for the festivities. I squeezed between a young couple, dodged half a dozen children racing underfoot and barely evaded an old man who'd walked in my path as I made my way toward my designated high-rise.

Two days earlier, the dozens of Dread Legion agents and I had landed on Galywix II, courtesy of customs officials belonging to a group called the Sons of Liberty, a freedom-fighter organization. I supposed that's what the Dread Legion was, since we were fighting for the freedom of the undead.

Once we'd made landfall, Captain Wilson had gone over the plans while Colonel Schattler had looked on. He'd designated all the buildings and given us tours of them. He'd marked out every piece of the plan and what role each member would play. Then he'd gone over the plan twice more, making for a long day.

I learned the Dread Legion had picked Galywix II because of its smaller size and its fervently loyal Federation population. The thought was security forces would be lulled into a false sense of security, giving us an opening. An attack like this would never have success on Tar Ebon or any tier one world with surveillance and security everywhere. But here, on a planet that technology-wise reminded me of my home world, there was far less police presence and the Shadow Watch Guard had only arrived the day before.

I rubbed the handle of the leather case in my hand with my thumb. I would be the weapon of their demise.

I'd offered to use my powers during the attack, but the colonel and his shadowy associates had vetoed that. They argued it would immediately make clear who was responsible and paint a target on my back. They said they wanted to pin this on the Cult of Rae, though how that would gain more respect for the undead was something I hadn't understood, until I overheard the captain telling several agitators to shout expletives against the undead during the time leading up to the attack. Whether there actually *were* any undead among the dignitaries was irrelevant - all that mattered is public perception that hatred of undead had caused the heinous attack. Thus, the living would rally around the undead.

I approached the Galactic Hotel and the doorman nodded to me as he swung the door open. Another Son of Liberty, his father had been wrongfully imprisoned on Delgin V, the prison planet, and he wanted revenge. He held out a room key, which I swiped. "Straight to the elevator," he whispered as I passed. "The way is clear."

I nodded without responding to him and made for the elevator. I wasn't alone, but the young couple with three children paid me no mind. I punched the number four button and rode the way in silence, ignoring the blatant looks from the family. I wanted to shout at them - to ask if they'd never seen my kind or something - but I wanted to be as unremarkable as possible. *Blend in*, I reminded myself. A lot was riding on me.

Once on the fourth floor, I found the room, swiped the key card and entered. I breathed in the infuriatingly clean scent that accompanied seemingly every upscale hotel, then set to work. Tossing the leather case on the bed, I opened the latch and withdrew the first piece of my sniper rifle. I set about assembling it at a leisurely pace - I had at least fifteen minutes before my target came on stage.

Captain Wilson hadn't told me who my target was, yet. He explained it was need-to-know and to be ready for the first speaker. A stolen pamphlet showed the first speaker's name as Xavier Clement, and a query by Jarvis revealed the man to be a philanthropic billionaire. But why keep that a secret from me?

I placed my rifle on the bed minutes later and took out my binoculars. Then, at the window, I determined the range from my window to the place directly behind the podium. Captain Wilson had stressed the importance of a head or heart shot. "One shot, one kill," had been his words, which I'd laughed at. He acted as if I hadn't been trained as a Ranger.

Would I still be a Ranger, after this day? After I killed this man? Could I go back to serving the Federation that so clearly wanted me dead? A blasphemous thought arose, telling me I should go to my father and explain things. *Let him open an investigation*, the proverbial angel on my shoulder whispered. *There doesn't need to be bloodshed.*

"Yes, there does," I said before I realized I was talking to myself. I shook my head. Now was *not* the time to start going insane. "Ghost Ranger in position," I said into the encrypted handheld radio I'd been given. Captain Wilson explained not everyone had implants and there was no way to be sure they were one-hundred percent secure. Instead two-way radios using special encryption were being employed. I had my doubts about these being secure, but it wouldn't matter in a few minutes.

I watched the swaying of the crowd for several minutes before movement behind the stage caught my eye. It was time. The crowd started cheering, though I heard fragments of the protests staged by my fellow agents. "Undead go home!" and "Undead stay dead!" were among them. Right on time.

"Ghost Ranger, prepare to take the shot on my mark."

"Yes, sir." I lifted the window and shouldered my rifle. There would be no tip sticking out to give me away today. But I'd have to waste no time getting to the extraction point after I fired.

A man, looking to be in his middle-years, with combed over black hair and a shiny smile stepped up on stage. I followed him with my rifle, sighting in on his head as he came to stop behind the podium.

"That's Xavier," Captain Wilson said through the radio.

I nodded, which caused the scope to drift up for a moment. A flash of black behind Xavier caught my eye. I moved the rifle up slightly and froze. A Shadow Watch Guard stood in one corner of the stage, rifle held at ease, head swiveling this way and that. Zooming out, I got a view of the entire stage and found a Guard in each corner and one directly behind Xavier. Something wasn't right. Only high-ranking government or military officials got Shadow Watch Guard details, and this man was neither. I refocused on his face as he began to speak.

"My fellow citizens," he began. "I apologize for the subterfuge, but I did not want to detract from today's guests and the enthusiasm built up for this stop on the tour." He smiled. "At least until now." He touched a hand to his face and it *changed*, re-arranging itself until...I gasped. The face of my father smiled out at the crowd.

The crowd went wild, cheering and screaming even more than before. They hadn't expected the Supreme Commander of the Federation to be there to speak to them.

I stared in shock, arm shaking. They wanted me to shoot my father?

"Ghost Ranger, take the shot," Captain Wilson ordered.

I froze, finger on the trigger. All the rage I'd felt toward the Federation melted away as my father became the face of said entity. Memories of growing up, of sitting on his lap reading stories, of him seeing me off to my first dance and so many other experiences bubbled to the surface, threatening to overwhelm me. A tear slid down my cheek.

"Ghost Ranger, take the shot," Captain Wilson ordered again.

"No." The word surprised me. I'd committed, I'd said yes. Was I really going to back out now?

"Take. The. Shot." Wilson's words were deliberate yet forceful.

"I can't," I said.

"You said you wanted to avenge your friends. You said you want equal rights for the undead. *This* is how you get them. This is the shot that starts a revolution, Rachel! Fire the shot!"

I didn't want to, but I had to explain. "He's my father."

"We know," a second voice cut in. Colonel Schattler. "Why do you think we chose you for this mission, Rachel? Did you really think your flimsy disguise could keep you hidden from us? You didn't even change your name."

I'd been assured the disguise was air-tight. But that didn't matter now. My father's life hung in the balance. "I won't do it."

The colonel tutted. "Still a silly girl at heart, I see. No matter, we prepared for this eventuality. Captain, proceed."

Fear clenched my throat as I realized the implication. He'd said he would be at a high vantage point to oversee the operation. Now I realized he was also in a position to take the shot in case I refused.

Unable to call for help in time, I did the only thing I could. *Bang.* My bullet sliced through the air faster than even my eye could track and slammed into the wooden podium at my father's feet. *Come on,* I thought, lowering the rifle and waiting for the second bang. Would my warning be enough?

My father looked down at the cracked wood, then up, seemingly straight in my direction.

A flash caught my eye from atop the building across from me. The bullet soared toward my father from where Captain Wilson had been hiding as the crack reverberated through the air. The projectile streaked toward my father and passed *through* him as he blurred. The wood behind him cracked as the bullet impacted. *There's his famous time-bending powers,* I thought. With my warning, he'd been able to slow time around himself long enough to dodge the bullet, making it seem to me, an outside observer, that it had passed through his blurring body.

Within a heartbeat five armored Shadow Watch Guards swarmed my father, huddling over him, while at least a dozen more surged from behind the stage, rifles raised and pointed in every direction.

"All teams, evac now!" Captain Wilson snapped through the radio. "And Rachel...you'll pay for this." The line went dead and the radio grew hot. I tossed it toward the bed and it exploded mid-air. A fail-safe to ensure the investigators couldn't trace it back.

I stood there, dumbfounded. What to do now? If I evacuated through the planned route, the Dread Legion members would try their best to kill me. But if I stayed? I watched dozens of security forces lead by black-clad Shadow Watch Guards swarm my hotel and the one across the way. Meanwhile, the familiar roar of gunship engines heralded air support. Would they hesitate to fire missiles into my room, no questions asked? I made for the door of my room, not wanting to find out.

I'd made it halfway to the door when a shadowy mist appeared, causing me to stop. It formed into the shape of a human a heartbeat later and there stood Isabelle in her synth-suit, helmet down. Her weapons sat at her side and she had her arms crossed. "You really stepped in it this time, cousin," she said.

"Isabelle. How...?" How had she known where I was? How had she even known it was me? But I couldn't get the words out.

"I figured whoever made that shot was either a shitty sniper or someone who cared about my uncle." She held out her hand. "Take my hand. We have to get out of here before those muscle-bound hotheads show up to shoot first and ask questions later."

"But I just...I just tried to kill my father," I said.

"But you *didn't*. See the distinction?" She sighed. "Listen, take my hand and we'll get out of here, then everything will be explained. Deal?"

In the distance, I could hear the crash of doors being broken into on my floor. It would be a matter of seconds before they reached my room. Stepping forward, I clasped her hand.

"Good choice. Hang on!" The world turned to shadow as we shifted.

Chapter 28

The gray of the shadow realm gave way to color as Isabelle returned us to reality. We stood in a hallway in a military facility.

"Clevis Base. The closest Army base on Galywix II." Isabelle explained as she strode away with barely a glance. "Come. Your father is this way. My mother got him out." She made no move to restrain me with stun cuffs, which I was sure she could have summoned with a gesture. But why hadn't she shifted us directly to my father?

I followed, nerves of steel melting beneath the heat of the memory of what I'd done. I'd almost killed my father. If he hadn't revealed himself before I fired...if I had chosen not to aim at the ground.... I was no longer a school girl. I would face my punishment, whatever it might be. That was the reason for the walk - to frighten me - or at least to give me time to dwell on what awaited me.

We passed through a pair of blast doors, guarded by half a dozen Shadow Watch Guards that I could see and another half dozen camouflaged inside the room, their signatures visible to my enhanced eyes. I wondered if any were Terrence or the others. That would only magnify my shame.

My father stood at the table, reviewing a holographic representation of the venue he'd just been speaking at. My aunt stood across from him - I recognized her from the holos - and studied me as I entered, face impassive.

Isabelle cleared her throat. "Here she is." I sensed irritation in her voice, though whether toward me or toward my father, for making her his errand girl, I couldn't tell.

My father turned and met Isabelle's gaze. "Thank you, Isabelle. You may go. All of you may go." His last comment was directed at the guards around the room.

"But..." Isabelle began, even as the cloaked guards streamed out of the room. Her mother had not moved.

"Please," my father said, voice softening a bit.

Isabelle stood there for a few awkward moments, as if deciding whether to argue or leave. At last she sighed and turned to leave. She met my gaze as she passed and for a moment I thought I saw sadness resting there before her mask slipped back into place. "Good luck," she whispered, sounding as if she were saying good luck before the guillotine blade fell.

My father spent several long seconds staring at me after the blast doors had shut. "Are you alright?" he asked at last, face and eyes softening. He made no move to embrace me, though. My aunt raised an eyebrow but her face showed no sign of warming.

I cleared my throat, buying time to process the lack of screaming. Not that my father had ever been one to scream often, but if there was one time when screaming would have been appropriate, it was in that instant. Why wasn't he shouting? "I'm not hurt," I replied cautiously, hedging my response and bracing for the outburst.

My father nodded. "Good. I hoped Isabelle would get to you before any overzealous guards reached your room and took justice into their own hands."

I would have deserved it, I thought. Instead I said, "Instead I face your judgment?" I focused my gaze on my aunt. "Or yours?"

My father shook his head. "No. You face no judgment today, Rachel. In fact..." he hesitated and, for a moment, looked unsure of himself, "...we want to apologize to you."

My head snapped back as if I'd been sucker-punched and I took a step back. My gut dropped and my mouth opened in shock. *They wanted to apologize to *me*?* "Why?" I managed despite the shock. "I just conspired to commit treason against the Federation!"

He cleared his throat and looked back to my aunt for a moment. "Do you want to tell her?"

My aunt shrugged. "I can." She made no move to tell me anything, however.

"No, it's my responsibility," he said. He turned to me and straightened his back. "Rachel, I'm sorry. We used your affliction to infiltrate the Dread Legion."

"Used me?" I asked, not understanding. "I joined of my own free will."

"Yes, but we intentionally placed you in a position where you would want to join them. We encouraged anti-undead sentiment against you and backed you into a corner," he held up a hand to forestall me, for my mouth had opened. "Then we tapped into your implant to collect visual and auditory information while you were within the Dread Legion."

I stood there, silent as the night for several moments, as my mind tried to process what my father was telling me. He had turned people against me intentionally? And then spied on me? I felt my face warming, a remarkable feat considering I had no warm blood in my body, and felt anger rising. "You...you really did use me," I said at last, straining to keep from shouting. Here I had been worried my father would be shouting at me, but now I knew the truth. "You humiliated me, then you violated me...my private space. And for what?" I stood, waiting an answer, eyes flicking between my father and aunt. "Why?"

It was my aunt's turn to speak this time. "We had credible intelligence that Octavius and his organization was a threat to the Federation. We'd been watching him for years, even before he called it the Dread Legion. The threat level spiked when he was infected and rose from the dead. He used his newfound abilities to gather like-minded individuals to him and his anti-Federation sentiments only grew."

"Why didn't you just take him out?" I asked.

"The Federation isn't a dictatorship," Bridgette explained. "If I'd had my way, I would have ended him in the night, but that isn't the way of truth and justice."

"We needed evidence," my father said. "Killing him without a trial and evidence could have backfired on us."

"So you turned me into a living surveillance camera?" I snapped, hands clenched into fists.

"We tried other agents," Bridgette cut in. "Three died, whether through accidents or because Octavius was on to them, we don't know. Two weren't even contacted. His paranoia only grew after his death and he didn't seem to trust anyone living any longer. You were our only option."

"There are millions of undead in the galaxy now," I said. "Why couldn't you have used one of them?"

"None of those millions had the background necessary to interest Octavius, which we intentionally leaked. Nor did they have the motivation. Your motivation was genuine enough to fool Octavius."

"It *was* genuine," I said. "Because you almost killed me, several times!"

"We were not responsible for the firing on the asteroid base, I assure you of that. The after-action report revealed Octavius briefed the commander of the cruiser and told him only hostiles remained."

I deflated a little. "I killed all those people because of an accident?"

"No. Octavius killed all those people, using you as a weapon."

"He only used the weapon *you* gave him," I snapped, anger returning to full strength.

"Regardless, you had the jaded spirit and undead disposition Octavius was looking for. You were the perfect candidate."

"Were you intending to save me? After the asteroid explosion. Or were you going to let me die?"

"We had high confidence you would not die. You're tougher than you know."

I rolled my eyes. "That's comforting. You sent me out like a cow to slaughter and didn't care if I came back or not."

"That's not true," my father protested, the strength returning to his voice. "That should have been clear by sending Isabelle to rescue you after the failed assassination attempt. We weren't going to throw you to the wolves."

"What if I'd killed you?"

"That wouldn't have happened. Based upon your intel, we took additional precautions to ensure I had sufficient protection against any projectile or energy weapon."

"You turned a trap for you into a trap for them, is that it? Did you at least catch them?"

My father nodded. "We did. Bridgette herself captured Captain Wilson before returning to me and, based upon intercepted radio communication and hidden surveillance equipment, we were able to take the remainder into custody. Octavius' ship was surrounded in orbit and boarded."

"Should have killed them," I muttered.

"They will face justice."

I snorted. "That's all that matters to you, isn't it, Father? Justice. You don't care that your own daughter was put into harm's way, only that you went about things the 'right' way." I sneered. "You disgust me."

"Rachel!" Bridgette snapped, her face for the first time since I'd entered the room showing an emotion - surprise. "You don't talk to your father like that!"

I glared at my aunt. "A father wouldn't do this to his daughter. He's not my father." I turned to leave.

I felt a shift of energy and a cloud of dark mist materialized in front of me. It coalesced into Bridgette. Her arms were crossed and she glared at me. "No, you will apologize now. Your father made a tough choice but it was the right choice."

"Get out of my way," I said through gritted teeth, my anger barely under control. A part of me wanted to rip her arms from her sockets, though I knew fighting the Mistress of Shadows would be a mistake.

"Not until you apologize."

Instead of answering, I held my head high and advanced toward my aunt and the door beyond.

My aunt put her hand on my wrist and squeezed hard. "You aren't leaving this room until you apologize," she said, anger in her voice.

Something snapped in that moment. I gathered my power and unleashed it toward her chest. Her grip loosened as a massive force slammed her toward the wall and held her there with the force of five Tar Ebon gravities.

She hung splayed against the wall, arms and legs unable to move, head pinned to the wall. Her eyes closed briefly before opening and focusing on me. She tried to speak but could barely get out a breath.

"Rachel! Stop this at once!" my father shouted. I didn't spare a glance for him. I didn't hear a gun being drawn, so I was guessing he wouldn't kill me.

"I. Am. Leaving," I said, emphasizing each word. "Don't try to stop me." I released the pressure on my aunt.

"You little bitch," she wheezed after landing and straightening. "Did you think a little pressure could kill me?"

"If I wanted to kill you, you'd be dead," I stated, looking her in the eyes. "This was just a friendly warning."

My aunt snorted and rubbed her chest. "Next time..."

"There won't be a next time," I cut in. "I'm leaving. Forever."

"Rachel," my father's voice cracked. "Please don't. You're all I have!"

"You should have thought of that before you made me your unwitting spy," I declared. "Don't try to stop me again - I don't want to kill anyone today." Without another word I slapped the controls to open the blast doors and walked through. I ignored my father's continued pleading.

The guards in the hall re-entered and took their places again, barely paying me any mind. I supposed my father hadn't told them to apprehend me...for their safety.

Isabelle leaned against the wall in the hallway, watching as I emerged. "I heard a thud. Did everything go alright?" She quirked a small smile.

"Did you know?" I asked without preamble.

My cousin stared at me for several moments without blinking. "About the Dread Legion?"

"Are there any other secrets my father and aunt are keeping from me?" I asked sarcastically. "Yes, that one."

She maintained eye contact. "I had no knowledge of it until a few days ago, I swear."

"We were both lied to," I muttered.

"Rachel, you have to understand that it was for the good of the Federation. The Dread Legion posed a dire threat."

"So I was told. But since when does the good of the Federation trump my personal liberties?"

"Since its inception," Isabelle replied. "Our parents...they have sacrificed *everything* for the Federation, from the beginning. The Krai'kesh *are* coming, Rachel, and the Federation must stand united or it will fall."

I snorted. "Yeah, the boogey man is coming, so let's risk our children's lives and destroy any opposition to us in the name of survival. I don't even believe in the Krai'kesh."

"You should," Isabelle said softly. "They're real and they will come."

I shook my head. "Well, say hello to them for me when they come. I won't be around to see them." I strode past my cousin.

"Where will you go?" Isabelle asked to my back.

"Anywhere that isn't this cursed Federation."

"You'll break your father's heart. You're all he has left."

I whirled on her. "Everyone keeps saying that. I am *not* all he has left. He has you, and your mother, and your father and everyone else. He has people who love him. I don't...not any more. And besides..." I trailed off.

"What?" she prompted.

"My mother would still be alive if not for my father and the 'good of the Federation.'"

Isabelle stared at me, mouth open. "You still think that your father knowingly sacrificed your mother to the Empire? Even after everything I told you?"

I shrugged. "He sure didn't try to save her."

Isabelle shook her head, cheeks bright red. "If you still believe that then you deserve to leave. Your father sacrificed *everything* for your mother. When he learned her station was under attack he moved heaven and earth to reinforce her. He arrived minutes too late, but he went on to *avenge* her. An entire war was fought in her honor and he strode into the Imperial Palace and placed his sword at the throat of the emperor to accept their surrender. So don't you *dare* say he didn't care or that he didn't fight for your mother."

"Whatever," I said, not knowing what else to say. I turned to go again.

"You're still going to leave?" my cousin asked. "When will I see you again? We need you for the fight that will come."

"If I have anything to say about it, never. Or maybe in Hell, after we die. And well, if the Krai'kesh ever come," I stopped at the corner of the hall, "good luck."

"You're a coward," Isabelle spat as I turned the corner.

I passed through the halls of Clevis Base, lost in thought. I had a vague destination in mind and a few short minutes later emerged into the hangar bay.

The quartermaster saw me and approached. "Miss, we have a ship ready to take you anywhere you wish."

"Who ordered that?" I asked.

"The Supreme Commander," he said.

I spit on the floor, causing the man's eyes to go wide. "I'll make my own way." Without preamble, I bound myself to the space outside the hangar. I shot through the bay and out into the fresh air of Galywix II. Manipulating gravity and anti-gravity, I shot skyward faster than any starfighter, the G-forces ineffective against my power.

I would find my own way in the galaxy now, I decided. Space was vast and people outside of the Federation needed my help too. "Goodbye, Father," I whispered as the air raced past me and vacuum neared.

The End

Don't miss out!

Visit the website below and you can sign up to receive emails whenever Dayne Edmondson publishes a new book. There's no charge and no obligation.

https://books2read.com/r/B-A-ZEND-MTLX

BOOKS 2 READ

Connecting independent readers to independent writers.

Did you love *Ghost Ranger*? Then you should read *Emergence* by
Dayne Edmondson!

Aliens have invaded the Milky Way.

Captain Martin and his fleet at the opposite end of our galaxy
is all that stands between the emerging ancient aliens and certain
destruction of humanity. Even with the help of powerful magic, the
alien menace may be too much to overcome.

Elsewhere, Agent Hague chases down rumors of a secret cult
after an assassination attempt on the president of the Federation's
life.

With the emergence of the long-foretold aliens, the Federation
stands on the brink of destruction. Can Captain Martin and his
allies hold the line? Can Agent Hague uncover a plot within the
Federation?

A tribute to Star Wars books of old, and the first book in a new trilogy in the existing Seven Stars Universe, "Emergence" is set nearly two thousand years after "Shadows Fall" and features cameos from many of the longer-lived heroes of ages past.

Click now and jump into the adventure today.

Read more at https://www.darkstarpublishing.com.

Also by Dayne Edmondson

The Dark Tide Trilogy
Emergence
Eclipse
Ruin

The Mageborn Saga
Mageborn
The Cursed Tower
Halls of Light

The Seven Stars Universe
Ghost Ranger
Space Commando

The Shadow Trilogy
Blood and Shadows
Time of Shadows
Shadows Fall

Standalone
The Complete Dark Tide Trilogy
The Complete Shadow Trilogy

Watch for more at https://www.darkstarpublishing.com.

About the Author

Dayne Edmondson lives in southeastern Michigan with his wife and two young children, a boy and a girl. He writes part time and works a day job.

His books can be read in this order:

The Shadow Trilogy:
1. Blood and Shadows
2. Time of Shadows
3. Shadows Fall

Mageborn Saga:
1. Mageborn
2. The Cursed Tower
3. Halls of Light (coming 2019)

The Seven Stars Universe:
1. Ghost Ranger (coming 2019)

The Dark Tide Trilogy:
1. Emergence
2. Eclipse
3. Ruin

Dayne enjoys reading, writing, the occasional video game, watching TV with his wife, walking and spending time with his children indoors or out.

He writes and reads science fiction and fantasy. Some of his favorite authors/books include Robert Jordan, Brandon Sanderson, (almost) all the Star Wars EU books, Elizabeth Haydon, Christopher Nuttall and more.

Read more at https://www.darkstarpublishing.com.

About the Publisher

Dark Star Publishing is a small-press publisher of science fiction and fantasy novels. They place particular emphasis on books written **in** the Seven Stars Universe (the universe created by author and owner Dayne Edmondson).

For more information, visit https://www.darkstarpublishing.com

www.ingramcontent.com/pod-product-compliance
Lightning Source LLC
Chambersburg PA
CBHW020733250626
47155CB00003B/742

* 9 780998 426358 *